THE PUNT MURDER

PART AUTHOR OF

MOTIVE FOR MURDER

AUTHOR OF

PEARL AND PLAIN

AMBER AND JADE

GENESTA

CONSCEINCE

DELIA'S DILEMMA

COMMANDMENTS SIX & EIGHT

SWEETS AND SINNERS

WHERE THERE IS A WILL

ACEITUNA GRIFFIN

THE PUNT MURDER

Ostara Publishing

First Published Sampson Low Marston & Co Ltd 1936

Every reasonable effort has been made by the Publisher to establish whether any person or institution holds the copyright for this work. The Publisher invites any persons or institutions that believe themselves to be in possession of any such copyright to contact them at the address below.

ISBN 978 190628801-3

A CIP reference is available from the British Library

Printed and bound in United Kingdom

Published by······Ostara Publishing
13 King Coel Road
Lexden
Colchester
CO3 9AG

To
My Friend
MINNIE PORTER

"Tho' many minds there are which wish the deed
By only one fierce soul is death decreed."

THE PUNT MURDER

CHAPTER I

"IF I ever marry," reflected Martin Denham, "that's the sort of girl I want."

The time was an afternoon in June, the place was the small railway station of Wissingham. Martin had just got out of the train that had borne him with many stops from work and London to his mother's house on the river. The carriage had been hot, and he had been looking forward to a quick change into flannels, and tea and a book in his canoe. The sight of the girl drove these thoughts from his head. She had come down in the same train. Not a week-ender evidently, for she had a trunk as well as a suitcase, also a long package that looked like an easel. She had given up her ticket, and stood at the entrance to the station consulting the porter, who had stacked his trolley with her luggage. Outside was neither car nor cart, but a long empty road bordered with chestnut trees in bloom.

Martin seized the excuse of asking about a case of wine that his mother expected, and while the station-master consulted his book he watched the girl. It was the first time he ever remembered being so attracted by a stranger, for as a rule he was not susceptible. Certainly she was pleasant to look at, and had all the things that he admired. She was tall with narrow hands and feet, and the slenderness that comes from small bones and is not in the least angular. She had hazel eyes and a clear skin, but above all her face had character, and the voice was not only soft but decided. She consulted her watch. Martin heard her say she had expected to be met. Could she telephone for a taxi? The station-master overheard and joined in to explain that the telephone was only connected with other stations and not extended to the village. It gave Martin his opportunity.

"I shall be passing the Crown where they have a garage. Shall I send one?"

She turned to smile on him.

"Thank you so much—if it isn't out of your way."

Martin longed to know where she was going.

"The man may ask if you want him to take you far—in case he has another order."

"To Wissingham Abbey."

"That's Mrs. Holroyd's car now," said the porter.

A speck that had appeared at the end of the straight road resolved itself into a pale green car, driven at racing speed. As it tore up to the station the brakes were violently applied, and the one occupant put a blonde, hatless head out of the window exclaiming——

"Darling, I'm too frightfully sorry! The damned thing had a puncture—but I came along at seventy-five."

She got out as she spoke and enveloped the other girl in a warm embrace. Then catching sight of Martin she blew him a kiss—said—"Hullo, Martin dear!" and gave her friend another hug. As usual, thought Martin as he smiled back, Merle Holroyd looked as incongruous as a humming bird in the quiet English scene. She was tiny, quick in her movements, her hair was bright gold, she was dressed entirely in white, wore high-heeled sandals and no stockings, and her mouth and nails were crimson. She was extra-ordinarily pretty, but a contrast to her tall friend who did not use make up. The porter and station-master gaped with reluctant admiration.

"Are you down for the week-end? What about coming in to have a spot of dinner to-night? Do, my sweet. We want cheering, and it's Daria's first evening. Oh, by the way, I haven't introduced you. This is my very best friend, Daria Lane. Daria, this is Martin Denham. As she is going to stay with me for months and months you may as well know one another. Well, what about it? Can you come?"

Martin did not know if his mother had made any arrangements but chanced this.

"I'll love to," he said and meant it.

"That's all right. Eight o'clock. Well, how about the luggage?"

The porter had been strapping it on the grid.

"The suitcase will go inside. Hop in beside me, Daria," and the Hispano shot away down the road.

"I'd rather not do seventy-five now if you're not in a special hurry," said Daria, as they fled round the corner and Merle sounded her Klaxon through the narrow street of Wissingham, causing the vicar's and doctor's wives to jump to the pavement for safety. She avoided two dogs, a bicycle and a lorry, and settled down to negotiate the turnings of a country road. Some way ahead was a lodge and finely wrought iron gates. A prolonged shriek of the Klaxon, and a woman hurried out to open them. The car glided through and along a magnificent avenue. After nearly a mile Merle turned the car up a side road that led to the farm, and stopped on the top of a rise.

"Let's have a cigarette. I brought you here because this is one of our spot views."

Daria looked about with appreciation. The park was undulating, and studded with trees that were justly famous. The Tudor house which was now visible had been well placed against a background of beechwoods. Mellow and ancient, it rested in the June sunshine surrounded by terraced gardens, and below it to the right there was the gleam of water between the trees that edged the lake. It was one of those really beautiful country houses that belonged to an age of leisure and privilege, one of the departing and irreplaceable glories of our land. On this summer afternoon it was seen at its best.

"It is perfect," said Daria, sitting down on the grass by Merle's side. "You never gave me any idea it was like this."

"One gets used to a thing after a time, but I'll admit it is rather breathtaking when you first see it. Even now I understand what people mean."

"It's gorgeous," said Daria. "How old is it?"

"Incredibly ancient. Henry the Eighth gave it to a Holroyd ancestor, but it goes back beyond that. The main part is later,—James the First."

"They must be very proud of it."

Merle gave a curious laugh.

"Proud! It's their god. Why they even put up with me on account of it."

Daria looked up quickly.

"Is anything wrong, dear? I've never seen you since your wedding day, and your letters tell me nothing at all."

"No. They are not my strong point. What was that rude thing you used to call me? Illiterate. It's true. I hate writing. I thought I'd wait to see you. Daria, I'm *so* glad you have come."

Daria turned to study her friend. The two years had changed her. Merle was just as pretty, but of the type one associates with the screen rather than with county families. She was as lovable as ever, thought Daria with her quality of steady friendship, but in repose her face was sad, and a trifle hard. It struck her that this very rich girl was just as lonely as she had been when they had first met at St. Edmund's School, and just as much in need of her.

"Tell me what's been happening."

"I hardly know where to begin," said Merle. "It must be nearly three years since we had a real talk."

"Just about that," said Daria, "and that time I came over from Italy for your wedding I never got an opportunity to see you alone. I don't even know how your marriage came about. Where did you meet him?"

"Oh, that was old Lady Betchworth. Dad engaged her to present me, and to take me about. She had a wonderful connection and a vast derelict house. Dad paid up uncomplainingly, and I must say she did her utmost for three months. I couldn't stand her, nor she me, but she wasn't going to lose a good thing for the family. So she had Leonard up and ran him for all she was worth. Then Dad died, and I married him."

"But surely you were in love with one another."

Merle hesitated.

"It is difficult to answer that after two years of married life, but I thought so. And undoubtedly it pleased everyone at the time. They made a terrific fuss of me. You see the Holroyds hadn't a bean, and the house was falling to pieces. Whatever else they have against me they can't deny my money has been useful."

Daria was distressed by the bitterness of her expression.

"My dear, why do you speak like that? What have they done to you?"

Merle moved impatiently.

"It isn't a thing you can explain. According to their lights they've done their best, and it has been pretty heavy going for them as well as for me. I'm not easy, and just lately I think they have come to realize that nothing under Heaven will make me a lady."

Daria laughed.

"Darling, who do you mean by 'they'?"

"Mrs. Holroyd for one."

"Your mother-in-law! But surely you and Leonard are alone?"

"Good Lord, no! She lives with us. She always has, and always will."

Daria was surprised.

"But isn't that unusual. I thought in places like this there was a Dower House, to which the mother of the heir retired when he married."

"There *is* a Dower House, but it is let to an old cousin, who threatens to die if anyone moves her. Not that it would make all that difference. It is less than a mile away, and she'd be in and out all day long to see in what new way I was letting down the family."

"It must be a bore for you," said Daria thoughtfully.

Merle laughed.

"It's hell," she said briefly.

"And she interferes?"

"You'll see," said Merle, and added,— "I wonder what you'll make of Ida."

"Who's Ida?"

"Ida Pelham-Reeve. She is Mrs. Holroyd's niece. She is good at games, likes sport, runs the Girl Guides, and is a V.A.D. Oh, I can't tell you what a happy mixture she is of all the county works and pleasures!"

"But surely she doesn't live with you, too?"

"Not altogether, though she was brought up in the house. But she stays for months. She has always helped Mrs. Holroyd with her good works and county jobs. She is a sort of unpaid secretary."

"Does Leonard like this arrangement?"

"Leonard likes whatever he has been used to. His father died when he was a baby, and his mother ran everything, so it is a habit, and tradition is all they think of." She got up. "Well, come along, otherwise they'll think I've upset the car."

Daria felt worried. It was not only the words, for Merle had always expressed herself extravagantly, but her whole attitude showed discontent. Whether it was entirely due to the presence of Leonard's relation Daria could not tell.

They were now back in the main drive, and were sweeping towards the house. An expanse of beautifully kept lawn lay in front. It had been the old bowling green. A butler and two footmen came on to the steps at the sound of the Klaxon, and Merle took her guest into a huge stone-flagged hall that felt cold after the sunshine. It contained a collection of armour that was well known to connoisseurs.

"Where's tea, Burton?"

"In the Long Gallery, ma'am."

Merle put her arm in Daria's and led her up the shallow steps of the beautiful staircase. They came through an ante-room into the gallery in which hung pictures of varying merit of Holroyd ancestors. At the far end two women were sitting. Daria could feel their eyes on her as she walked down the narrow room.

Mrs. Holroyd, who gave the impression that she considered herself the mistress of the house, shook hands, and introduced Daria to her niece.

"I am glad you are safe," she said. "We sometimes think Merle is a little rash in her driving."

What tall women they were, thought Daria. Mrs. Holroyd could not be short of six foot, and held herself as if her spine was made of steel. She had clear cut features, and grey hair parted down the middle. She was certainly formidable, and was clothed with extreme simplicity and even shabbiness, as if she disdained to spend money on dress. Daria's eyes wandered to Ida Pelham-Reeve, the catalogue of whose accomplishments she had just listened to. She saw a handsome young woman of about six and twenty, with thick heavy brown hair worn in a coil at the back. She moved with the ease of an athletic person, but without grace for she was squarely built. She was dressed severely in a coat and skirt, shirt and tie. Beside these tall women Merle looked tiny. Daria continued to study them. Both had well-bred voices, and the assurance of their birth and surroundings, both fitted into this great house of old associations, whereas Merle did not. Daria had to admit her incongruity.

Mrs. Holroyd poured out the tea. Merle took hers and lit a cigarette. Mrs. Holroyd coughed.

"Merle, dear, if you wouldn't mind. Please not till after tea."

Merle's response was to remove herself and her cup to a distant window seat half-way down the gallery where she curled herself up with her legs tucked under her. From there she took no part in the conversation which flowed on easily. Mrs. Holroyd asked if Miss Lane had been recently to Rome. It was much changed she understood, and greatly improved under Mussolini. She herself had not been there for thirty years. Daria made appropriate replies. Ida got up at intervals to hand cakes, but did not say much. Presently a young man came in, followed by a spaniel.

"Hullo, Merle," he said as he came down the gallery. "Why so far from the tea table?"

"Your mother dislikes my cigarette."

Leonard was shaking hands with Daria who had only seen him once and that was on his wedding day. Her impression then had been of a nice-looking but not very interesting man. He had if pleasant manners, but looked as if he might be weak and obstinate, and have a difficult temper. She noticed that he kept on glancing uneasily at Merle who seemed to dissociate herself from the group. It was not a comfortable atmosphere, and it was a relief when Merle got up, and asked if Daria would like to see her room. She turned casually to the others.

"By the way, Martin was at the station, and I asked him to dinner."

"I'm glad, I always like old Martin," said Leonard.

Ida looked up at Merle.

"And Gideon Franklin?" she asked. "Surely he's coming."

"Yes. I asked him, too."

"I thought you might have," said Ida in smooth tones.

"Have you any objection?" flashed Merle.

"Why, no." Ida lifted her eyebrows. "What a funny question! What right have I to object to your friends, Merle dear?"

The undercurrent of hostility was strong. It puzzled Daria who had no clue to it. She had. never heard of Gideon Franklin, but she noticed. an air of constraint about Mrs. Holroyd and Leonard.

"Don't forget the Delahayes are coming too, and Major Wrey," said Mrs. Holroyd smoothly. "That makes us nine. I'll tell Burton."

Merle took Daria up to her bedroom. Like most of the house it was panelled and filled with fine Jacobean furniture. From the wide window there was a lovely view of flowers and clipped yews, and an expanse of ground laid out like the sunk garden at Hampton Court. The housemaid, who had been unpacking Daria's things, went out of the room.

"Heavenly," said Daria leaning out of the window and sniffing. "You have a wonderful home."

"Leonard has."

"My dear, isn't it yours, too?"

"Oh, no."

Daria looked at the harmony of colour, the smooth lawns and big cedars. It ought to be restful, and not full of jarring vibrations. She turned to Merle.

"Who is Gideon Franklin?" she asked.

"He is the man I'm in love with," said Merle simply.

CHAPTER II

DARIA was observant as people who have lived very quietly often are, and as she sat down to dinner she was interested in taking stock of her neighbours. This was a world from which she had been excluded for some years, for during her sojourn abroad her acquaintance had lain among the small colony of artists who lived cheaply on the Ligurian coast.

Everything at Wissingham Abbey was luxurious. The dining-room was finely proportioned, and the famous Van Dyck hung over the fireplace and gave her great pleasure as they ate food that shewed that the Holroyds employed an artist for a cook. Colonel and Mrs. Delahaye were quickly summed up, pleasant, ordinary people, who did not make much impression on the mind. Then Major Wrey, who was the Chief Constable, an old friend, and a remote connection of the Holroyds. He was talking to Ida as if she interested him. Ida, Daria noticed, was better looking than she had thought at first. Her classical profile and fine shoulders gave her a distinguished air. She was smiling and this gave her a pleasant expression.

Although Merle had her place at the head of the table Mrs. Holroyd was unquestionably hostess. She it was who attended to the older guests and directed the conversation. She was wearing an evening dress that had evidently done duty for several years. Her only ornament was a small diamond clasp, worn on a piece of black velvet round her throat. There was almost an insolence, thought Daria, in her complete contempt for clothes. Everyone knew who she was, therefore it could not matter what she wore.

Daria was aware that Leonard's eyes were constantly fixed on his wife. Merle, as usual, was the most noticeable person in the room. She had made her entrance after all the guests had arrived, and got herself up like a stage vamp. She had a wonderful white satin dress which left a large portion of her anatomy uncovered. She wore a gorgeous rope of pearls, and a huge ornament of flashing diamonds on one shoulder, and numbers of diamond bracelets on her left arm. Indeed her small person seemed to sparkle with every movement. At this moment she had turned her shoulder on Colonel Delahaye, and was talking in a very low voice to Gideon Franklin. Daria looked at him with a curiosity that was natural after Merle's dramatic announcement. She saw a man of thirty-five with a hard, clever face that she did not like. He would grow heavy in a few more years, and certainly had a Jewish ancestor. He talked brilliantly, but had an over familiar manner as he leant nearer to Merle to say something that could not be overheard. Daria had not attached much importance to the statement, but she thought her friend was making herself conspicuous. She decided to have it out with Merle who would always bear criticism from her that she would not stand from anyone else.

"You are very thoughtful," said Martin who was sitting next to her.

"I'm sorry. I have been such a long time away from civilization that I've forgotten how to behave."

"Tell me about it. Where were you?"

"In Italy. My mother was an invalid, and she had to winter out of England. We had very little money so we stopped there all the year. It was very cheap. I suppose lots of people would have found it quiet, but I liked it."

Her words recalled a vision of the lovely coast, the lights on the sea, the red sails of the fishing boats, the cypresses standing straight and black against the silvery olives, the simplicity of the white houses, the occasional visits to Pisa or Rapallo, also of the beloved mother she had lost.

"And then?" said Martin, who had a craving to know all about this girl who attracted him more and more.

"And then my mother died so I have come back. I think I shall stop in England and go on with my painting. We lived in a colony of artists and I studied under a good master. And now let us talk about you. Tell me what you do."

Martin was only too pleased. He told her he was a barrister and was in London all the week in Chambers, but came down most week-ends to his mother's house, which was on the river.

"It is lovely in the summer though of course it is getting built over. So long as you stay in the grounds here you can imagine yourself hundreds of miles from London. The Holroyds own such a lot of land that they keep their own atmosphere."

"It is a marvellous place," said Daria. "I am longing to explore it."

"Are you going to be here long?"

"Merle says so."

Daria gave a fleeting smile in her friend's direction.

"You are great friends."

"The greatest," said Daria warmly. "We were at school together, and she is one of those people to whom absence makes no difference. I suppose we were lonely when we met for we were both only children, and we got on from the first."

But extraordinarily different, reflected Martin. It was difficult to imagine Merle enduring the discipline of school.

"Did she like the life?" he asked.

"She hated it. She was always in hot water. She went through it like a tornado."

She shook her head at the recollection. Merle had not only been miserable and rebellious but unpopular because of certain qualities which were the result of being the motherless child of a millionaire who was too absorbed in business to look after her, and who supplied her with far too much money. She had not mixed well either with girls or mistresses, had set herself against games and lessons, and had been a small female Ishmael with one devotion, and that was for Daria who championed her and helped her, and realized the good that lay behind her difficult temper.

Again Martin smiled at the contrast, this soft-voiced girl who had the effect on him of a still summer night, and his spoilt, indiscreet, rich little hostess.

"Devastating," he said, "but it must have broken the monotony."

"It did," laughed Daria, "but she was always amusing and a perfect dear, and the most generous person I have ever met."

"Yes," agreed Martin, "it is wonderful what she has done round here. It doesn't matter what's wanted, she is always ready to pay, and seems to enjoy giving."

"I'm very glad you realize that," said Daria seriously. "I want her to have lots of friends. She has always needed them."

"Surely she has them."

"I hope so, but rich people don't seem to have very good ones," mused Daria. "People make up to them for what they can get, and they find it out and grow cynical."

It was at this point that Mrs. Holroyd, who had been trying to make Merle give the signal for the women to leave the dining-room, at last succeeded. Mrs. Delahaye, a plump pleasant person with a taste for gossip chatted away to Mrs. Holroyd, and presently began to talk about Gideon Franklin.

"Though he is our Member I have seen very little of him. Of course, I'm on the Women's Committee and go to his meetings, but I mean personally."

"I understand he is a very clever young man," said Mrs. Holroyd.

"You know him well?"

Mrs. Holroyd hesitated.

"I can't say that, but he comes here frequently," she said, and her tone showed Daria that Mrs. Holroyd's feelings for Gideon were not those of liking.

"Everyone says he will go far," said Mrs. Delahaye thoughtfully. "At first we were all a little doubtful. Of course, after dear Sir Alfred Melville he was a bit of a change."

"Why was that bad?" said Merle.

She had ignored the conversation until Gideon became the subject, now she leant forward animated and interested.

"Not bad," said Mrs. Delahaye amiably, "only just very very different. The Melvilles were such an old family, and no one knew this young man. His origin was a bit obscure. I don't mean anything unkind, but it was."

"But does that matter?" said Merle truculently. "Don't brains count?"

"Naturally, and please don't think I don't appreciate him," said Mrs. Delahaye pacifically, for Merle looked like a small ruffled bird. "All the same there's no denying that he didn't go down at first. I'm right, aren't I, Mrs. Holroyd?"

"Certainly he did not," said Mrs. Holroyd.

"But all that was at the start," continued Mrs. Delahaye. "For one thing he was hampered for money, but lately I think he must have come into some for he has given the most generous subscriptions to the hospital and the new buildings in Ridgenorth, and everyone is pleased. And he is a fine speaker. I think he is a very ambitious man, and from what I heard the other day he is likely to go far."

"What have you heard?" asked Merle, whose eyes were shining.

"We were told, and on very good authority, that there is going to be a general shuffle round in the Government this autumn, and that Mr. Franklin was being considered as one of the Undersecretaries. It is very creditable when you think that he has not been in Parliament for long."

"Yes—wonderful!" said Merle softly.

Mrs. Holroyd who seemed to find Mr. Franklin's possible advancement no reason for rejoicing now gave a little cough and changed the subject.

"Dear Mrs. Delahaye, tell me all about Isabel and her children. I haven't seen her since January," and with that the talk switched on to Mrs. Delahaye's married daughter, and Merle took no more part in it, but leant back, her eyes almost closed, and her thoughts evidently straying from her companions.

Daria tried to talk to Ida. She found her polite but aloof, and wondered if the girl had some reason for disliking her visit, yet surely Merle had a right to invite her own friends. There seemed a great many cross-currents in this odd household.

When the men came in Gideon came straight up to Merle, who rose without a word, and they walked out of the open window. Major Wrey went towards Ida who ceased to be apathetic, and brightened in a way that Daria did not consider flattering to herself. Mrs. Holroyd, Leonard and the Delahayes settled down to bridge, and Martin asked Daria to come and look at the moonlight on the lake.

The garden looked like fairyland as they went down the steps of the terraces between beds of stocks that scented the air.

"One forgets how lovely an English garden can be," said Daria.

She found his eyes fixed on her and looked at him enquiringly.

"I want to see you often," said Martin. "You and I have got to be friends."

"That's very kind of you, Mr. Denham."

"I felt it the moment I saw you at the station. I shall try to meet you whenever I can get down. Don't smile. I'm serious."

"But I shall smile if I like. You seem a very impulsive kind of person."

"I'm not as a rule. I have never been in a great hurry before, but now I feel I have been wasting time in not knowing you sooner."

"I don't think you've wasted much," said Daria demurely, moving down the steps.

"I want to know lots more about you. Where are you going to live?"

"I haven't any definite plans. When I leave here I may take a cottage in the country, with a room I can use for a studio."

"I hope it will be near here," said Martin. "I don't want to waste half the day getting to you."

Really a persistent young man! Nice looking, decided Daria, giving him a sideways glance, and she liked his voice, also the shape of his hands. But she was not swift in her friendship, though once her mind was made up her likings were permanent.

When they got back to the house Major Wrey who had to be up early was saying good night, and the bridge people were adding up their score, but Merle and Gideon had not returned. Leonard kept glancing towards the window, and it was evident that he was annoyed by his wife's long absence. The Delahayes were leaving when Merle came back. Her cheeks were flushed, her eyes were bright. Daria felt the tension in the atmosphere as the door closed on the guests, and thought Mrs. Holroyd's feeling of displeasure extended to herself. She wondered if Merle would come to her room to talk, but she kissed her at the top of the stairs and went off, and there was the unmistakable sound of a key turning in the lock. It was evident that if Leonard meant to lecture his wife he would have to wait till next day to do so.

CHAPTER III

SEVERAL days had passed. Daria had finished a sketch of the garden and had put away her things. She felt comfortably tired for she had been painting all day in the heat, and was glad to sit and admire the green of the turf, the gay border, and the dark group of cedars. There was a sound of voices, and Leonard and Ida came across the lawn in their tennis things. In spite of the hot sun they had played several setts. Leonard asked if she had had a satisfactory afternoon, and politely admired the painting. Daria watched the white figures as they went towards the house. Games made people good companions. She wished Merle would rouse herself to take an interest in country things, for it might draw her nearer to her husband.

On the whole she was enjoying her stay. Merle had made it clear that she expected her to remain a long time, so the Holroyds had ceased to treat her as a guest who needed attention, and left her free to do what she liked, so Daria who had not seen the English country for so long spent her days sketching when Merle did not demand her company.

Daria had had time to get her bearings. The household was divided into two camps, herself and Merle on one side, and the Holroyds on the other. Since her outburst on the day of Daria's arrival Merle had said very little about her husband and his relations, but they did not need explaining. Daria believed that their disapproval hardly stopped short of disgust. Mrs. Holroyd was the slave of order, she was a busy woman, and a born organiser. She was head of the Women's Institute, and President of the County Nursing Association, and she ran the League of Mercy. At Wissingham Abbey she was a despot. She was dignified, austere and a stickler for conventions, and Ida, who had been in her care from a child, had the same outlook. In religion Church of England, in politics Conservative they were rigid about their duties both to their neighbours and dependents. They lived in a small world that could still be self-sufficing. All this had been in danger of crashing when Leonard married Merle. The Holroyd securities had ceased, to pay, and they were faced with the almost unbelievable misfortune of having to part with the Abbey. Now thanks to Merle's fortune the house was repaired, the gardens in order, servants ministered to their comfort, and the old state of the Abbey was restored. But here the advantages stopped. Merle would not give Leonard an heir, nor would she live their life. Every morning the Holroyds breakfasted together at nine o'clock, and she remained in bed till she felt like appearing. She was bored by sport and county society, and said so. She might pay for the upkeep of the Abbey but its history and beauty meant nothing to her.

What did her husband feel about her, Daria wondered. At times undoubtedly her ways aroused in him a cold fury. Daria had seen him look at her. He had married an ignorant child, and had expected that he and his mother would train her They knew their mistake now. Not only did Merle recoil from their teaching, but she seemed to set out deliberately to flout it. Only the day before the Lord Lieutenant and his wife had been asked to a formal lunch, and Merle had come in twenty minutes late wearing for once an untidy crumpled cotton dress. Later Daria had heard angry voices as Leonard remonstrated. Why must Merle do things like that, and take pleasure in showing at her worst? Was it the revolt of a spoilt nature against an atmosphere of disapproval or was it due to some deeper cause? Merle was clearly dissatisfied, yet she had so much, looks, youth, great riches, and she had married well according to the world's ideas. Leonard was not easy to know, yet when Merle was not stinging him like a mosquito he seemed pleasant and courteous. She was too young and far too beloved by Daria to be allowed to trample on other people and provoke their hatred. Daria determined to get to the bottom of it.

She heard the sound of a car coming up the avenue and went in just as Merle arrived. The others had begun tea. Merle greeted them with a wave of her hand.

"How are you all ? It was grilling in town. Daria, darling, I hope you got a shady place to sketch, otherwise I'll be nursing you with sunstroke."

"We expected you back by the earlier train," said Leonard. "We sent to meet it."

"I didn't come by train. I lunched with Gideon and he drove me down."

The information was received in frigid silence. Daria knew that the Holroyds were beginning to resent Gideon. Merle drank her tea and passed her cup to be refilled. She did not seem at her ease, and when she spoke it was in a would-be airy manner that showed that she was about to say something that would prove unpopular.

"By the way, I'm going up next Thursday for the night. Gideon's speaking in the House."

"Thursday?" Mrs. Holroyd looked up. "Oh, no, Merle, you've forgotten. That's the day of the bazaar."

"Well, what about it?"

"You are to open it."

"Blast, so I am! Well, I can't. That's all about it."

"It isn't all," said Leonard. " You have promised, and your name is on the bills."

"Someone else must do it. What can it matter who opens the damned thing?"

"It matters considerably."

"Oh, Leonard, don't be tiresome. What's the thing for—the District Nurse? I'll send the Vicar a cheque. Then if they don't want they needn't have the bazaar at all."

"Really, my dear," said Mrs. Holroyd, exasperation in her voice. "You have very little imagination. Don't you realize that not only is the hall taken, but all the stall-holders have been working for months? Naturally they hope and expect that you'll buy freely, but they won't want all their work to go for nothing."

"I should have thought anyone would have been thankful not to have to sell at a bazaar."

"Then you know very little about village life," said Mrs. Holroyd drily.

"In that case if they are set on it someone else must do the opening. Why don't you do it yourself, Mrs. Holroyd."

"There are several reasons. For one I have not been asked."

"I'd hand you over as large a cheque as you want," said Merle with a tactlessness that made Daria wince.

Mrs. Holroyd's face was a study. She took up her embroidery in silence.

"Look here, Merle, you can't shove your engagements on to mother," said Leonard.

"And why not? Mrs. Holroyd has opened bazaars here for umpteen years. She could do it in her sleep."

"You are Leonard's wife, and in that position it is the recognised thing for you to do," said Mrs. Holroyd. "I had my share of it before Leonard married."

Merle picked up her bag and gloves and got up.

"Well, if you won't let's get someone else. How about Lady Fenwick?"

"Lady Fenwick is away."

"Then Mrs. Bedford."

"She would be entirely unsuitable."

Merle shrugged her shoulders.

"Then settle it yourselves. Only do please realize that I shan't be here. I am going to telephone and tell the vicar so now."

She went out, Leonard following. As Daria went out into the garden she could hear them arguing by the telephone. She saw nothing of Merle till dinner time when the barometer still pointed to stormy. Leonard sulked, Mrs. Holroyd kept up a bright conversation with Ida about a treat for the Mother's Union that was to be held in the grounds, and Merle talked across the table to Daria about a play she had been to in town.

As they were having coffee Merle suddenly addressed Leonard.

"I'm going to that sale to-morrow. Jasmine Cottage. Gideon and I had a look at it on the way here."

Leonard lifted his eyebrows.

"Indeed, and why should Jasmine Cottage interest you?"

"Merely because I think of buying it."

Apparently this announcement had the effect of breaking the ice. Mrs. Holroyd, Leonard, and Ida stared at her.

"Isn't the Abbey big enough? I should have thought you had enough space here," said Leonard.

"Space," said Merle leaning both elbows on the table and surveying him through the smoke of her cigarette, "but nothing of my own to keep or to give away. And whatever I choose to do is surely my affair."

"Entirely," said Leonard with deep displeasure.

"Dull as we may appear we have realized your wish to keep the management of your money," said Mrs. Holroyd. "You need not be perpetually reminding us of it."

It was the first time that Mrs. Holroyd had given expression to her feelings in front of Daria. The bitterness of her tone was almost startling, and it silenced Merle. She got up after a minute and put her arm in Daria's, saying—"Let's go into the air," and they went into the garden.

They seated themselves on the terrace. The night was clear and moonlit. It was a relief to get out of the tense atmosphere of the dining room.

"Merle, I'm unhappy about you," said Daria after a moment.

"Why, darling?"

Merle's tone was flippant, but the hand that held her cigarette trembled.

"Because everything seems going wrong. I can't keep on pretending not to notice."

"It not only seems, it is wrong," said Merle soberly.

"Is it Mrs. Holroyd?"

"Partly, not altogether, though she's the most powerful member of the clan."

"She ought to go."

"If old Cornelia Holroyd turned out of the Dower House she'd have another stroke. She's lived there for thirty years."

"Still there are other houses."

"I know. Of course," said Merle thoughtfully, "at first we didn't mean to have this arrangement permanently. Leonard thought it a good thing to have his mother there to teach me what's what. I didn't much care. Running a house bored me, and afterwards I thought she might as well go on doing it."

"I'm sure it is a mistake."

"Of course, she hates me, but no one could say she hadn't tried to get me into the right shape."

"Can't you have a talk to your husband?"

"Tell him to get her to turn out? I don't know that I want to now. I did at first, but now it is too late."

"Why is it too late?"

Merle did not answer. Her head drooped. Daria thought she was going to cry.

"When you wrote to tell me you were engaged you said you were both very much in love," said Daria.

"*I* was," said Merle.

"But he—I'm sure—"

"No. Never for a moment." Merle straightened herself, her voice grew hard. "I have never said this to a soul, but I'll tell you. When I went out that season in London I didn't like it and I didn't make friends. I had no manners and I hated Lady Betchworth and the formal parties. I meant to go back to dad at the end of the summer. Then he died and Leonard was sweet to me. When he said he loved me I thought it was true. So I married him."

She paused. Her cigarette was thrown away. Her hands were clenched.

"And then?" said Daria softly.

"And then I found out. He was kind and polite on our honeymoon, but I could see he was bored. I thought being so very British he hated a place like Maggiore, and then we got back and I found out."

"How?"

"By accident. A letter came addressed to Mrs. Holroyd. I thought it was for me and opened it. I remember the words—'I feel sure that your tact and patience will do wonders with her. Poor Leonard, I hope he is more reconciled. He has made a great sacrifice, but often a *marriage de convenance* turns out well in the end. And anyhow the honeymoon is over, and that I always think is the worst.' And then I knew the truth."

"Darling, I expect it was only some gossiping old woman."

"No. It was written by Mrs. Holroyd's sister who had been in the know since the start, and is deep in their confidence. I put it back in the envelope. That was easy because it had hardly been stuck down, and wasn't torn, and then I went and sat in the woods and thought it out. I'd been such a child, and I think I grew up then. I was only nineteen, but I'd been gullible and stupid. I saw then that people like the Holroyds were not likely to want a vulgar little creature like me. I was like a mongrel puppy in a prize kennel. They wanted money, and they had to have me to get it. I expect it would have been better if I hadn't loved Leonard at first. This place and the history seemed wonderful. And then I woke up and hated this mouldering place and its traditions, and I vowed that if they had the money they were going to pay for it. And I wasn't going to have the child of a man who only wanted me for that. So that's the situation."

Daria put her arm round her holding her close.

"It's vile," she said.

"It was for the first year. Now I don't care much."

Daria reflected.

"Sometimes things get better. That woman may have been mistaken. Leonard may love you more than you think."

Merle laughed.

"Oh no, my dear!"

"Anyhow, it is no use bearing malice. It makes it so difficult for yourself. Couldn't you be more conciliatory? After all it is your life and your home. You can't go on scrapping with them day after day."

"I agree," said Merle. "I'm fed up. I don't mean to go on."

"Then what will you do?"

"I'm not sure, but I can't spend my life with people who hate me."

"You jar, but they can't hate you."

"You're wrong. They do, and pretty badly. Since I read that letter I've been a disappointment and a shock. They wanted to persuade me to make a big settlement on Leonard and let him have the management of my money. And that I wouldn't do. I'll tell you why, Daria. One of the last things dad said to me was—'You'll be rich, and God knows if you'll be married for your money so keep it in your own hands.' So when

Mrs. Holroyd and Lady Betchworth and the family lawyer tried to make me I just stuck in my toes, and wouldn't budge. All I'd do was to make a will in Leonard s favour, and that one can always alter."

"And meanwhile," said Daria, "there's one thing that you need not do, and that's to remind them constantly that the money's yours."

"Very ill-bred of me," said Merle coolly, "but then I am rather common, darling. But except for that I can't see what they've to complain of. I have spent £20,000 on bolstering up the place so they have got something out of their bargain, which is more than I have."

Daria sighed.

"Wouldn't it make things easier if you gave way about things like the bazaar?"

"I'd have done it a year ago, but not now. I wouldn't miss Gideon's speech for the world. It is his great opportunity, he has been working on this slum clearance business for three years, and he will be magnificent."

"You see a lot of him?"

"As much as ever I can. This last six months since I've known him it has made all the difference. You have probably thought I've been neglecting you, but you must understand Gideon's the only one I'd have done it for. I just can't miss a single hour with him."

Her face was ecstatic. Daria recognised the strength of her emotion and did not know how to deal with it.

"What does Leonard think of this friendship?"

"It isn't friendship," said Merle. "I love Gideon."

"That's unlucky."

"It isn't. It has changed life."

"Don't be a fool, Merle. It is unlucky when a married woman falls in love."

"I haven't any of those inhibitions," said Merle shortly.

"Hasn't Mr. Franklin?" said Daria shrewdly.

It struck her that Gideon was not an "all for love and the world well lost" man, and Merle's hesitation confirmed this impression.

"I am sure he cares," she said at last. "He says lovely things. But of course he has to be careful. He is in such a public position."

"I am glad he is careful," said Daria with fervour.

She thought of Gideon whom she had now seen several times. There was something ruthless and grasping in his expression, not the face of a man who would let passion stand in the way of his career.

"I think he's the sort of man who would put his work first," she said in warning.

"But I can help him in that. I have," said Merle eagerly.

"How?" said Daria,—then as it dawned on her —"Oh, Merle, you haven't been giving him money!"

"You put it pretty horridly," said Merle flushing.

"Then you have."

"Not for himself, of course. How could you imagine that? But for the cause."

"I didn't know you took such an interest in politics," said Daria drily.

Merle blazed round on her.

"You are intolerable. If you admired someone and liked him, wouldn't you want to help? Anyhow it is not your business."

"No," said Daria gently, "only so far as it concerns your happiness."

Merle softened immediately.

"I know, and you and Gideon are the only people in the world that I care a hang about."

"Have you no feeling left for Leonard?"

"None, I think. We haven't a taste in common. I detest the people and the life and Wissingham seems to me like a prison."

"A lovely one you must allow," said Daria smiling.

"Yes, but still a prison. Every moment I stub my toe on a tradition. Why, if I want to move a bit of furniture there's an outcry. It has always stood there! No, my dear, I want a fuller life than that. In the world, not in a backwater."

"Merle, you were always too impatient. Give it another chance."

"And you were always an old Puritan. You are shocked because of Gideon."

"Apart from my inhibitions, as you call them, I don't think he is the man to make you happy."

"He is the only man I'll ever love," said Merle, and Daria smiled and wondered how many women had said that since the world began.

CHAPTER IV

MERLE came down to breakfast,—an unusual event, and Daria when she saw Mrs. Holroyd's face, decided that though Merle's mother-in-law might disapprove of her lazy habits, she preferred them to her company.

"As you are here perhaps you would like to pour out, my dear."

"I should hate it. I am sure I should give everyone the wrong things. I'm hardly awake."

"What has brought you out of bed so soon?" asked Ida.

"I'm going to have another look at the cottage before the sale."

This time the disapproval was felt rather than expressed. The Holroyds had probably discussed it, and decided that no good end could be served by refusing Merle her toy. She and Daria set forth as soon as they had finished breakfast.

Jasmine Cottage was about three-quarters of a mile from the village. It had been inhabited for several years by a young couple who had bought it in its original state and made alterations, building on a large living room. It was approached by a paved path bordered by flowers, and had a fair sized garden and an orchard that joined on to a wood. Merle got the key from an old woman who lived near, and told her they would go over it alone.

"What do you think of it?"

"It is charming," said Daria truly.

"It will be fun furnishing."

"Then you really mean to have it?"

"I do. It will want alterations. The bathroom is a cupboard at present, and I am sure there's an old fireplace in this room."

"When's the sale?"

"This morning at twelve. That's why I brought you in to have a look."

Merle's mind was made up. She and Daria drove into Ridgenorth where the property was being auctioned. There was some competition as several people wanted the house for a week-end cottage, but she secured it. She was to have immediate possession, and telephoned to the builder to meet her there that afternoon. She made him promise to put every available man to work on it at once. This was characteristic as Merle could never wait.

She was in good spirits when they started home, for buying and arranging had amused her. Daria thought it a good thing for the cottage would give her occupation and take her mind off Gideon and the difficulties with the Holroyds. She thought it the right moment to broach the subject of her departure. She wanted to get settled, and she was aware that the Holroyds thought her visit unduly prolonged. They were perfectly polite, but they counted her in the opposite camp and wished she would go.

Merle received the suggestion ill.

"You must be terribly bored to talk of it."

"I have loved being with you, and you have been an angel to me, but I must settle down and get a studio. You forget I have to earn my living."

"Now listen, Daria. You will find it much cheaper to live here for a bit, and save board and lodging. Later I'll help you to find a place. But you won't go now if you love me—while my life is in such a mess. Anyhow, promise not to make a single arrangement till we've talked it over again."

"It depends how long it is before we talk it over," said Daria, smiling.

But as she spoke she knew she would not go as long as Merle needed her. She had a premonition that the distrust and dislike that underlay her friend's life was likely to develop into something definite and dangerous.

• • • • •

Merle sat in the Ladies' Gallery of the House of Commons listening intently to Gideon's speech. She could see him very well, and thought for a thousandth time what a fine figure he made. He had the power of expressing himself clearly, and his voice was greatly in his favour. Every word was distinct, and seemed the best he could have used. The House was full, it listened with complete attention. Merle could see that her prejudice in his favour was not misleading her. That morning she had telephoned to wish him good luck, and to tell him she would be there.

"That is what I need. You are my inspiration," he had said.

"Inspiration!" It sounded wonderful. The words had given her a warm glow. Her heart was beating faster as she listened. Did he really love her, this man who was going to have a great future? It was amazing that he should care about someone like herself, thought poor Merle humbly, and a childish regret that she had not worked harder at school and knew so little overcame her. Gideon was ending. He knew he had succeeded, and this gave his words an added eloquence.

Merle sighed. Her hands were tightly clasped in her lap. She glanced at a stolid lady sitting next to her. How could she look so unmoved? And then her mind went back to the important question. Did Gideon really love her? She could not tell. Compliments, sometimes a touch of his hand, a caressing note in his voice, a look that told her that she attracted him. But so far he had not actually made love except by implication. The few letters she had from him and treasured were in the same strain. Devoted friendship, admiration, but nothing as Daria would have said that couldn't be read aloud in court.

Gideon sat down. A member of the Opposition was answering, but she hardly heard. The debate, as the wireless has it, continues.

Later, she went down to wait for Gideon. She was to dine with him, and met him with shining eyes. She had dressed very carefully and looked her best. Gideon, she had discovered, liked pretty clothes, and did not feel about them in the same way as the Holroyds who preferred dowdiness.

Gideon was appreciating his success to the full. People kept on coming up to congratulate him. He smiled into Merle's eyes, and enjoyed her beauty and her stammered words of praise. He had been anxious about the speech on which so much depended, and now the effort was over he felt almost light-headed. As he sat with Merle over dinner he poured out his plans and ambitions, conscious of the comfort of her presence.

They got up to go. Gideon had his car which he drove himself. It was nearly eleven o'clock, for they had dined late. Suddenly it seemed impossible to take Merle back to her club where she had a room for the night and go tamely to bed.

Gideon had a small flat off St. James's Street. He asked if she would come up for a few minutes. There was no hall porter on duty, but Gideon worked the lift that took them up. The flat consisted of a bedroom, bathroom and sitting room, and Gideon took his meals at his club. As the door closed Merle realized how entirely cut off they were from the rest of the world. The hum of the cars in the street sounded far away. Gideon helped her off with her cloak, and as he touched her bare arm he found she was trembling. Her agitation fired him, and in a moment he was raining kisses on her neck, her face, her hair. Merle made no protest. Her eyes were closed in ecstasy as she gave herself to his arms.

· · · · ·

All the Wissingham Abbey party, with the exception of Mrs. Holroyd had been having tea at Mrs. Denham's, and were sitting on the lawn by the river. Wissingham Regatta, which was the biggest local event, was to take place in a fortnight. There were numbers of entries, and a good many people were practising. Leonard and Ida went by. They were down for double punting.

"A good pair," said Martin as they went by, "they always carry off cups. They are partners in most of the local shows,—tennis and golf, too."

Daria watched them, admiring the precision with which they moved. Ida was a fine specimen of the outdoor girl, and Daria wished she would grow friendly. But the slightest advance brought about the sensation of coming up against a hard, polished surface. Ida would not unbend to anyone who was fond of Merle.

Daria's eyes wandered towards Merle, who was walking up and down the lawn with Gideon. As usual he was doing most of the talking, and she decided that the subject was himself. She had never heard him talk of anything else. He wanted an audience and at that moment he had an absorbed listener.

"You haven't attended to a word I've been saying," said Martin reproachfully.

"I'm sorry. I was watching the others. Martin, I wish you'd tell me what you think of Gideon Franklin."

"He is very able, and I think he'll go far."

"Yes,—that isn't what I mean. How much do you know him—the real him?"

"Very little," Martin paused. "I should think he is pretty well out for Number One," he went on slowly. "You know he is practically self-made. He was the son of a poor country doctor. An old lady in the village was fascinated by him and left him all she had. But it wasn't much. He got into Parliament, and worked tremendously hard, and now he's getting on I should think he means to take everything he can."

This opinion coincided with Daria's own, and it made her uneasy about her friend.

"I want you to promise me something. When I go away, be very nice to Merle. People round here don't realize what a dear she is."

"Of course I'll be nice if she'll let me. But you aren't going away yet, are you?"

"Merle insists on my staying till after the Regatta."

"So I should hope. The fireworks are very good. My mother always has a great do, and we illuminate the lawn and have an evening party. It would spoil everything for me if you weren't here. But you know that already."

Martin for once spoke discontentedly. He was definitely in love. In the past weeks he had seen a lot of Daria, and every week-end that he spent at Wissingham it had become an understood thing that she should keep her afternoons free for him. Usually they took tea on the river, and drew up in the shadow of the trees, and discussed everything that interested them in Heaven and earth. But that was as far as Daria would go at present. She liked him, liked him immensely, quivered on the verge of something more, but did not go over. And being truthful she would not pretend to more than she felt, and with that Martin had to be content.

It was nearly a fortnight later. For the past weeks, when she was not running up to London to meet Gideon, Merle had spent her time scouring the country to find old furniture for the cottage. Curiosity shops and sales amused her, and she developed a flair for appropriate and charming things. Old oak, lovely rugs, suitable china, were acquired, and the newest bathroom fittings and beds came from London. She had never furnished anything before and was like a child with a doll's house. Daria had been taken on most of these expeditions, but for the last few days, while the furniture was being assembled she had been excluded from the cottage. Merle was going to arrange it herself, and display the result as a surprise. The builder, galvanized into activity, had put on lots of men. The last picture had been hung, everything was swept and garnished, and Merle who had gone to put flowers in the vases expected Daria who had been formally asked to tea. She heard the click of the gate and came to the door, wearing a blue overall in which she looked like a schoolgirl.

"Come in," she said. "Tea is waiting and I've got a present for you."

Daria could never forget what she looked like as she stood there gay and triumphant. Merle's moods had been variable lately. Sometimes she was on the stretch, waiting for the telephone to ring, or watching for the postman. At other times she moved like a person in a dream, and fell into long silences and seemed as if the Holroyds and their concerns hardly affected her. She was always like this after her nights in town, and Daria could not understand why neither Leonard nor his mother seemed to notice. But they understood her so little that they took any difference of manner as part of her usual impossible ways. Mrs. Holroyd drove to her tea parties and meetings, and Leonard and Ida went to tennis tournaments on days when he was not occupied by his duties on the Bench and the estate. None of them seemed to know that trouble was brewing.

Since the night of Gideon's speech in the house Merle had been reticent. She had ceased to discuss the Holroyds, and was dumb when Gideon was mentioned, and Daria, who knew she would talk if she wished to, had not questioned her. Obviously Merle felt she would disapprove if she knew everything, and this accounted for her restraint. But that afternoon the cloud had lifted. She pushed Daria into the room where tea had been laid on the refectory table, on which the Spode china looked delightful and a bunch of roses were arranged in an old bowl in the centre. On Daria's plate was a long envelope addressed to herself.

"Open it," said Merle impatiently.

Daria obeyed and gave an exclamation. In her hand was the title deed of the property made out in her name.

"It is my present to you," said Merle, "and that will put an end to all this nonsense about looking for a home. Oh, darling, I do hope you're going to like it!"

CHAPTER V

"DARLING, I must go now."

"So soon," said Merle. "You seem only just to have come."

Merle and Gideon were sitting in Jasmine Cottage. Though it was now Daria's Merle had insisted that this fact was not to curtail her friend's visit to the Abbey. She must stay there till after the Regatta, though the date for her departure was now fixed for the following Monday. In the meantime, Merle was using the cottage for herself, and had made Gideon meet her there.

"We have been here nearly two hours," said Gideon, and added uneasily,—"Don't they ever wonder about us, Merle?"

She shook her head.

"Not that I know of. They just aren't interested. Leonard never cares about anything but the place, and possibly Ida. She is the only person who makes him human! Yesterday she went to a meeting at Heygate by train, and when he came in he found out that she wouldn't get back till late, as it's a foul cross country journey. He actually motored the whole way to fetch her and fished her out at the junction, though it made him late for dinner! He would never have done that for me." She laughed up at him. "Perhaps I ought to be jealous!"

Gideon did not respond. He was frowning.

"He might do that for Ida, and yet dislike the idea of his wife going about so much with me."

"Would you mind if he did? " asked Merle coolly.

The question seemed to startle Gideon.

"Mind! That's hardly the word! It would be damned awkward."

"Would it?" Merle leant back on the sofa, her head against his shoulder. "I don't think I should care."

Love fulfilled is a wonderful beautifier, and Merle was in great good looks. No one could deny that she was a lovely little thing, thought Gideon, but nevertheless he wished he had never let himself in for this. Every day she grew less manageable, she was rash, also obstinate, both awkward traits, also he was discovering the spoilt child element and did not like it.

"Of course you would care," he said sharply. "You don't know what you are saying."

"No, honestly, Gideon, I wouldn't mind the row. After all, what could happen. Leonard could only divorce me."

"Only!" Gideon's voice was strained. "But that would be fatal."

Merle stared at him.

"But if he did we could marry."

"Look here, darling," said Gideon, trying to keep the angry frightened tone out of his voice, "have you ever thought what being co-respondent in a divorce case would mean to me? Just blue ruin. Nothing less."

"But why? We'd have my money."

"Your money, yes,—but it would be the end of my career. A Member who has seduced the wife of his most important constituent! I'd have to give up my seat, and I don't suppose I'd ever get another. Don't you see it? You must."

"But how idiotic that seems," said Merle. "Lots of the nicest people are divorced nowadays."

"You'll never get the British public to take your view," said Gideon. "The morals of members have to be above suspicion. Only last year Reynolds had to clear out because of his divorce."

"How can your private life affect your public work?"

"It can't, but this isn't a matter of reason. The fact remains that you won't get votes if there's anything of the sort. So you see, darling, how *very* careful you must be."

"Would it be all right if Leonard let me bring the divorce?" said Merle.

"That would certainly be better, but would he do it?"

"I'll ask him," said Merle, simply.

Her calm filled Gideon with panic.

"For God's sake don't mention it at all, or even let him suspect."

He saw her frown and went on hastily.

"Can't we stay as we are?" He hesitated and the feeling of being caught in a trap came over him as he sought for some argument to convince her. "Don't you see, darling, that even if he consented to a divorce it would mean complete separation for ages. You and I could never meet before the case, and not for six months after. And how would you like that?"

But Merle sat very still. She was thoughtful.

"You *do* love me, don't you Gideon?"

"Of course I do."

His tone was impatient.

"Better than anybody,—better than anything."

"Haven't I said so?"

"But not as much as your career, I think."

"My dear, I have slaved for years to get where I am. I don't want to lose what I've worked for. And aren't we very happy meeting as we do?"

"We might be ever so much happier. We might be together all the time instead of snatching stolen meetings now and then. I hate having to hide it, Gideon. I can't even tell Daria."

"I should think not."

"But don't you hate secrecy? If our love is beautiful it is horrid to have to sneak about and tell lies."

"My darling, that is our misfortune. We should have met before you married Holroyd."

"Oh why didn't we?" said Merle with wet eyes.

Gideon was conscious of two things, one that he had outstayed the time he had allowed himself, the second that to leave her in this reckless mood was dangerous. The vague wish that he had never embarked on this intrigue changed into definite fear. Why had he been such a fool? On his part it had been started in a rush of emotion following the success of his speech. Merle stirred his senses, and he liked the flattery of her admiration. But against his career she counted no more than the suit of clothes he had discarded last year. But she was not going to be easily discarded. He put his arms round her and began to coax. Would she be very, very careful for his sake? It was all important. There were hints about an Under-secretaryship. The least breath of scandal and it would come to nothing. He knew how his darling wished to help him. He relied on her. All this was murmured between kisses until a sound from without made them start apart. It was the crunching noise of a footstep on the gravel path.

Ida had been playing tennis at a neighbour's, and on her way back had called in at the vicarage for two parcels for Mrs. Holroyd. As she walked slowly, for she was hot after her game, she caught sight of Merle's vividly painted car standing in the lane outside the cottage, and decided to ask her to take the parcels. Also Ida was curious about the cottage. She and Mrs. Holroyd had discussed it. The news that it was to be given to Daria had been received without comment, though it was clearly unpalatable, but there was a grievance because Merle had never suggested their seeing it. But this seemed a good excuse. So Ida opened the gate and went up the path. What she saw through the window was a blurred impression of two people in close proximity, and a sudden movement caused by their starting apart. Her first instinct was to go away, then deciding that she must have been seen she knocked at the door. Merle opened it. Her hair was very untidy.

"I was passing and saw the Hispano. I wonder if you will take these parcels for me, as they are heavy to carry."

Ida's face shewed nothing of the curiosity she was feeling.

"Of course. Will you put them in the back of the car," said Merle.

There was a hint of nervousness in her tone, and she did not suggest that Ida should come in.

"May I have a look round now I am here?" said Ida with unusual geniality. " I've never been inside."

She meant to find out who was that second person she had seen through the window, and before Merle could answer she walked past her.

"It looks very charming," she said. "What have you done in here?" and she opened the door into the sitting-room. "Oh! how do you do, Mr. Franklin?"

"I seem to attract visitors to-day," said Merle furious with herself because her cheeks were flaming. "Gideon caught sight of the car too, and called in, and I was shewing him round."

"Yes, I admire it enormously," said Gideon. " You have wonderful taste, both in colouring and furniture. Miss Lane is lucky, isn't she?" he said amiably to Ida.

"Extremely."

"I fear I must be off now," Gideon held out his hand to Merle.

"Shall we be seeing you to-morrow? We might have some tennis."

"Not to-morrow I am afraid. I shall be busy with my agent. Thanks very much all the same."

As he shook hands with Ida and went out he was uncomfortably aware of a keenness in her glance that he had never before remarked. What had she seen through the window? Surely not much. Yet he was not certain. It was the footsteps on the gravel that they had heard, and the pathway from the gate to the house came close to the window. Gideon would have liked to stop as he went out and get an idea of what could be seen of the interior of the room from the outside, but felt that Ida was watching. He drove off cursing.

Merle asked Ida if she would care to see the upstair rooms, and took her all over the cottage, listened to polite expressions of approval, and then the two girls drove back to the Abbey. Ida went into the morning room which was devoted entirely to Mrs. Holroyd's use, and having delivered the parcels and the Vicar's message, drew up a chair, and unburdened her mind. She and her aunt remained together until it was time to dress, and Mrs. Holroyd was noticeably thoughtful during dinner.

Leonard seemed in a good humour. Daria thought that he as well as the rest were relieved that her long visit was drawing to a close. Next Monday was to see the last of her. A nice girl, named Susan Harridge had been engaged to cook and do housework. She was the sister of Mrs. Holroyd's maid, and the family had always lived in the village.

"She has a tiresome old father," said Mrs. Holroyd, "but the daughters are superior and most respectable."

Merle, though reluctant to let Daria leave the Abbey, had given way. She announced that she would dine at the cottage on Monday night, a sort of inauguration meal.

"You can't spend the first evening alone. It would be too dreary. We'll have a bottle of champagne and drink each other's healths."

"You will find the village quiet after the Regatta is over," said Leonard. "So many people go away."

"I am looking forward to the Regatta. I have heard so much of it, and I've never seen one."

"It is a pretty sight if it's fine, but I hope we shan't have trouble this year with the people at the Fair."

"Do they have a Fair?" asked Daria.

"Quite a big one, roundabouts, and swings and fortune-tellers. Every kind of riff-raff. It brings gypsies and vagrants, and the whole village goes mad about it."

"I loved it," said Merle defiantly. "It is great fun doing coconut shies, and shooting at targets for incredible prizes, and it is picturesque,—all the flares and lights reflected in the river and the crowds. Wissingham becomes alive for one night in the year."

"Too much alive as you'd find if you were on the Bench," said Leonard.

It was another lovely evening and Daria and Merle went into the garden.

"I'll hate you to go," said Merle affectionately. "Still you'll be close by, and that's a comfort."

They began to talk about their schooldays, laughing and reminding one another of ridiculous incidents and Daria felt more peaceful than she had done since the beginning of her visit. It was had she known it, the last calm moments before the tempest.

They returned to the house about half-past ten. As they crossed the hall Mrs. Holroyd came out of Leonard's library and went upstairs without taking any notice of them. Daria and Merle were following when Leonard called out:

"Merle, will you come here. I want to speak to you."

Whatever he had to say took some time. As Daria undressed she could hear the murmur of voices below. Daria decided that Merle would not come in and say good night as it was so late so got into bed. She was asleep when a knock roused her, and the light was turned on. She sat up in bed blinking at Merle who looked very strange. Her cheeks were crimson, her eyes were bright with anger.

"Leonard has found out," were her first words.

"Found out what? " said Daria stupidly, and still half asleep.

"About Gideon and me."

This effectually roused Daria, who looked as disturbed as she felt.

"Sit down," she said. "I can't help till you tell me everything. What is there for Leonard to find, and how did he do it?"

"It was that spying cat, Ida! She saw us at the cottage and told Mrs. Holroyd."

"What did she say she saw?"

"Enough to make Leonard suspect. He said he wouldn't have Gideon meeting me, and then we both lost our tempers. He accused me of letting the family down and I said I didn't care. I told him I loved Gideon and wanted a divorce."

"Then Gideon *has* been making love to you?"

"Of course, but I didn't mean Leonard to know," said Merle naïvely. "Now the fat's in the fire, and I can't think what Gideon will say."

Daria thought this the least important of the difficulties ahead.

"What was Leonard's attitude when you asked him to divorce you?"

"I didn't. I asked him to let *me* divorce *him*. I told him I was sick of the life here, and had always loathed it."

"And what was his answer?"

"That it was I who made things unbearable. That his mother had tried to train me, but it was hopeless, that I dressed like a cocotte, and had neither tact nor sense of duty nor gratitude. I asked what I had to be grateful for, and he said for my rise in life and social opportunities. Then I saw red, and asked what they'd have done without my money to bolster up a broken down family living in a ruin."

"You shouldn't have said it," groaned Daria.

"Why not? It is about time they heard the truth, but I never could have believed that Leonard would be so angry. He went a curious colour, a sort of dirty white, and he said I thought that money was all that counted, and that up till now the Holroyd wives had given their husbands children, and had never had lovers. Then he began that endless business about wanting an heir to carry on the family, and I said some families had better die out."

Daria wondered if anything in this interview had been left unsaid.

"How did it end?" she asked wearily.

"By his saying that as long as I stayed under his roof I was not to see Gideon, and nothing would make him give me a divorce. And I called him a cad, and came up here."

Daria sat silent, and Merle began to cry.

"I can't think what Gideon will say. He told me no one was to suspect."

Daria gave her a little shake.

"Look here, Merle,—how much is there in this? Is Gideon actually your lover?"

Merle nodded speechlessly.

"Then I don't know what to say."

"I adore him," sobbed Merle.

"Then if Leonard won't have a divorce what are you going to do?"

"Leonard doesn't actually know how far it's gone," said Merle wiping her eyes. "He knows we love one another, but he thinks nothing's happened."

"I wouldn't be too sure of that," said Daria. "He is the sort of man who if he became suspicious would certainly think the worst."

"I'll have to see Gideon," whimpered Merle.

"Don't take any action till we've talked it over again," said Daria. " It is a nasty mess, and neither of us seems clear-headed enough to deal with it to-night."

She did not turn off the light when Merle went but sat up thinking. It was indeed a mess. She hated what had happened and was furious with Merle for muddling her life. It was difficult to see ahead or to prophesy what Leonard would do. Whatever his opinion he might adopt the tone that Merle's infatuation was a passing folly and merely try to prevent her meeting Gideon. Daria did not think the Holroyds would let the money go easily, and if Merle left she would take it. Merle would not submit to being kept apart from her lover, but in this Daria believed the decision would not rest with her. Gideon would be frightened and very ready to agree with the Holroyd's wishes if that would avoid scandal. Whether Merle would be manageable remained to be seen.

Daria worried till the dawn, then slept heavily for the next few hours, and was still drowsy when she was called. She was fully aroused by the sound of a motor. From one of her windows she could see the green car speeding down the drive. So Merle had not waited to talk it over. What fool's errand took her away?

Mrs. Holroyd and Ida were already at breakfast when she got down. Merle's mother-in-law assuredly knew of the scene of the night before but she looked serene as she remarked that it was another beautiful day. But Daria knew that she and Ida had been in the midst of an eager discussion which had ceased abruptly when she came in. Leonard arrived a moment later, said a general good morning, and rang the bell.

"Burton, send word that I want the car to take me to the 10.5."

"Going to London, dear?" said his mother. "When will you be back?"

"It depends. I can't say," growled Leonard.

He took his coffee cup and pulled the toast rack towards him. He drank half a cup, but left the toast untouched. Suddenly he looked up.

"Do you know where Merle has gone?" he asked Daria.

The question was so abrupt that Daria was startled.

"No. I haven't seen her this morning."

"She didn't say last night? I heard her go along to your room."

"I had no idea she was going anywhere," said Daria truthfully, and Leonard went out.

Ida who was looking after him cast reticence to the winds.

"She has gone to see that man, of course," she said, and her tone was so bitter that Daria stared, and Mrs. Holroyd gave her niece a glance of warning.

"Merle has never told us her movements, my dear Ida," she said smoothly. "Why should she begin now?" She rose from the table as she spoke. "You are very lucky to have these bright days," she went on conversationally to Daria. "I suppose you will do some more sketching."

She went over to the window and watched her son being driven away. Masterful though she might be Mrs. Holroyd evidently felt that events had got beyond her control. Daria took the hint and departed out of doors with her paint box, but made little progress with her sketch, for her mind was full of speculations about Merle. The foolish girl had undoubtedly rushed off to find her lover. Why Leonard had gone was less certain.

Was it to discover and confront them, or was he perhaps seeing his lawyer.

Fortunately Mrs. Denham and the two Miss Wiggins' had been asked to lunch. Miss Honoria and Miss Amelia Wiggins were ladies well on in the sixties, who were daughters of a former vicar of Wissingham. They had lived in the village all their lives. Miss Honoria was managing and efficient, with strong views and Miss Amelia her humble echo. Miss Amelia took pleasure in her neighbour's affairs, but her tendency to gossip was sternly repressed by her austere sister. Daria liked her much the better of the two. Mrs. Denham, as usual, was gay and good natured. She was full of the party she was giving on the evening of the Regatta, and the chances of the weather lasting.

"I won't listen to the Broadcasting. It always foretells depressions approaching from Iceland, and I really can't think what I'll do if it rains. I've asked double the number I had last year."

"I can't imagine how you know such a crowd, Ellinor," said Mrs. Holroyd. "I hardly ever call on new people."

"But I like new people," said Mrs. Denham cheerily, "and that reminds me there is such a nice young couple at Rock Lodge. The name's Aitken. They've got it for six months and may settle in the neighbourhood. You ought to call."

"What Aitkens are they?" said Mrs. Holroyd, a usual question with her.

"I haven't an idea. But she's pretty, and he does something in the City, and they use the house chiefly for week-ends."

"It doesn't sound as if they would be much use to me," said Mrs. Holroyd coldly to mark her disapproval of Mrs. Denham's habit of rushing at fresh people.

Before she left Mrs. Denham, who was always kind to Daria, expressed her pleasure that she was going to live in the village.

"The cottage is Merle's present to me," said Daria. "Isn't it a wonderful one?"

"Merle is the most generous girl I know," said Mrs. Denham warmly. "She's never tired of doing things for others. Is it true that she has promised to build us a village hall?"

"I believe so," said Mrs. Holroyd icily.

"Certainly we need it, the present one is a disgrace. But it's wonderful to be saved the tedium of bazaars and subscriptions, and to have one person shoulder the expense. She's a dear," finished Mrs. Denham with an enthusiasm that delighted Daria.

"And I'm very pleased that you are staying on, if I may say so, my dear," fluttered Miss Amelia. "It is so nice to see a young and pretty face."

Miss Honoria did not associate herself with these remarks. She thought her sister impulsive. What did they know of Miss Lane? Nothing but that she was Merle's friend, and an artist, and neither fact was a recommendation.

"Poor dear Ellinor," said Mrs. Holroyd as the guests drove away, " she is a bad judge of character. Anyone can take her in. And she always has some protegée on whom she wants me to call."

The day dragged on, and it was nearly dinner-time when the green car shot up the drive. Merle had returned but Leonard was still absent. She kept them waiting twenty minutes, and when she came down she had changed into an extravagant tea gown of orange chiffon and was more made up than usual, but Daria saw that her eyelids were pink.

"Return of the prodigal!" she said with a challenging glance at Mrs. Holroyd and Ida. "Why did you wait for me?" She put her arm through Daria's. "Well, darling, did you have a good day at your painting?"

Dinner was difficult. Mrs. Holroyd spoke occasionally, Ida not at all, and Merle chatted defiantly to Daria. Dessert was on the table before she said:

"By the way,—where's Leonard?"

"In town, I believe," said his mother.

"In town! What is he doing there?"

"He didn't tell us," said Mrs. Holroyd, her eye resting on her daughter-in-law with unmistakable dislike,—"no more than you did."

Yes, it was an unpleasant meal in spite of the efforts of a good cook, and soon after Merle said she was sleepy.

"Come up and help me undress," she said to Daria, and the two went out.

Merle shed her tea gown for a dressing gown, and curled herself up on the cushioned seat by the wide open window. They were in the sitting-room adjoining her bedroom, and they were almost in the dark as she had turned off all the lights except a small shaded lamp.

"I expect you want to know what I have been up to," said Merle defiantly.

"I do."

"After I left you I couldn't sleep a wink, and I knew I wouldn't rest till I'd seen Gideon."

"And did you see him."

"Yes, but it wasn't easy. He wasn't at his club, or at the House of Commons, and it was quite late when I got him at his flat."

"Do you mean you went there? As things are that was very foolish."

"I had to talk to him," said Merle sullenly, "and tell him what happened."

It seemed useless to debate the point.

"Well," said Daria shortly, "what did he say?"

There was a hesitation. Merle did not seem to find this an easy part of her narrative.

"Of course he is worried,—not knowing what Leonard intends to do."

"What does that mean? Doesn't he want to marry you?"

Again silence. It was prolonged, but the light was so dim that Daria repeated her question before she realized that Merle was crying. She came over and put her arms round her.

"Of course, he wants to. You know he does, don't you, Daria? "

"I wish you'd give him up," said Daria sighing.

Merle twisted herself out of her arms.

"That's the one thing I'll never *never* do. I love him so *fearfully.* If he left me I think I'd die."

"You wouldn't, darling. You'd feel awful for a bit, and then you'd be glad. He cares for no one but himself."

"How dare you say that!" Merle's voice rose, and Daria whispered "Hush!" but she went on furiously: "You don't know anything about it. You have never had a lover. How should you, just nursing your mother abroad. And he is different from other men. He is going to be great and mix up in all the big things. Not a country squire like Leonard, with a mind on nothing but rearing pheasants! Oh God! how sick I've been of it! Leonard has *got* to give me a divorce."

"And that's what Gideon wants?" demanded Daria inexorably.

"He does really. He wasn't himself to-day. He thought I hadn't been careful. But it will be all right if Leonard is reasonable because then we will be married, and if I am the injured party people won't be stuffy about it in the constituency, will they? Please say they won't Daria."

"I can't say it, Merle. I don't know."

"I'll make it worth Leonard's while. I will settle a big sum on him."

"Do you suppose Leonard will agree to that? I am sure he won't."

"He can either do it, or lose my money," said Merle with a hard ring in her voice. "Oh I know what you are thinking. Your taste is offended by my saying that! But what is this marriage but a money transaction? That's the only reason the Holroyds wanted me. If I died to-morrow do you think any of them would care? I believe it would be a relief for as things stand Leonard would get it all."

"I do loathe the way you talk. It isn't like you. It is just a nasty little hard streak. All the rest of your character is so generous. I can't bear to hear you."

"Money is my only weapon, and I'm going to use it," said Merle. " I am going to alter my will. If Leonard gives way he will be perfectly comfortable, otherwise he'll have to manage as he can."

"Darling, forget the money part. I want you to give Gideon up. He will never make you happy."

"If he doesn't no one can. If I want anything badly I must have it," said Merle.

Poor little spoilt child, thought Daria, brought up by a father who valued everyone according to their rent roll, and never loved by anyone but herself. Daria began to plead.

"Go back to your husband, and begin again. I'm sure he is fond of you, and you haven't given him a fair deal. If you had children——"

"No, no,—I couldn't. I'd hate a little Holroyd, and I'd be terrified," said Merle. "With Gideon now it might be different," she added dreamily.

Daria grew impatient.

"Did Gideon like you running after him all round London? " she asked.

Merle drew away angrily, and it was clear that the shot had gone home.

"And where was Leonard?" continued Daria. "Supposing he followed you and saw you together?"

"I don't know where he was, and I don't care," said Merle.

Nothing was to be gained by prolonging the argument. Merle went into her bedroom, and Daria lingered by the window. The stocks below in the garden smelt deliciously, and Daria put out her head to sniff and cool her flaming cheeks. It was a cloudy evening and the objects were dim, but she got an impression of movement. She peered out. There was a seat, and on it she thought she could make out a figure. Then someone got up, stepped on to the grass border and glided towards the side door. A woman's form, but whether it was Ida's or Mrs. Holroyd's she could not say. Both were tall and both had worn black. Whoever it was must have overheard a good deal of the conversation.

CHAPTER VI

THE day of the Regatta had started deceptively in brilliant sunshine. The Re-gatta itself was a popular event as many of the residents were taking part. For several days there had been a bustle of preparation, railing in the enclosure, constructing a judges' box, and putting booms on the course. Caravans had arrived the day before, and the swings, roundabouts and booths were put up in the fields opposite to Mrs. Denham's garden which was on the other side of the river.

Mrs. Denham was the possessor of about twenty acres of land, of which six acres were river frontage. She had a moderate-sized Georgian house, and a lovely garden which was her pride and her extravagance. The lawn where she had placed her seats was illuminated by hundreds of fairy lamps arranged in an elaborate pattern. Beyond this along the river's edge was the rock garden that was justly esteemed by other gardeners, and beyond again a wild garden with winding paths that ended in a thick shrubbery and a fine group of trees that overshadowed a large boat house.

The Regatta went well in spite of two showers that made everyone anxious about the fireworks and evoked pessimism in Mrs. Denham, who feared her party might be spoilt. But the sun came out again, and the thunder in the distance rolled away. Leonard and Ida won their cup, finishing in fine style amidst applause.

The tilting in canoes, and the greasy pole took longer than usual, and then the prizes were distributed by Lady Weatherby. She and Mrs. Holroyd had done this turn and turn about as long as anyone remembered. The secretary of the Regatta had spoken a word of thanks, cheers had been given, and everyone had scampered off to get some food before the fireworks. The river was now alive with punts. Mrs. Denham and Martin snatched a cold meal, and hurried to inspect the lighting of the lamps by the gardeners. Mrs. Denham looked anxiously at the sky. There were dark clouds and once there had been a heavy roll of thunder as in the morning.

"If only it will hold off," said Mrs. Denham, like every other British hostess. "If they have to come indoors, Martin, do you think the house will burst?"

Not only had she asked everyone as she had told Mrs. Holroyd, but her friends had written back to ask if they might bring two young cousins and an uncle who was an Old Blue, and the numbers had swelled to large proportions.

Apart from the bank of clouds on the horizon the sunset had been wonderful, the river had been on fire, and the fairy lights twinkled like little sparks on the lawn. Opposite the crowds of people who were being conveyed over by ferry, or their own boats were silhouetted against the flares of the booths. Mrs. Denham took up her position at the top of the lawn to receive the first guests, and Martin stationed himself at the bottom near the rows of chairs to greet the people who landed from their boats. Presently he saw the Holroyd party coming down the slope. They were characteristically grouped, Mrs. Holroyd in front, Ida and Leonard together with Daria following, and Merle some paces behind, rather as if she had nothing to do with them.

"We are rather early," said Mrs. Holroyd shaking hands, "but I enjoy your mother's garden so much by this light, and I am going to look at it before the fireworks begin." She turned to Merle who had now joined them. "Haven't you brought a coat. How foolish! You will certainly get a cold."

"Thanks but I'm not a chilly person, and I've got this."

Merle put a long scarf round her neck.

"That's not enough," said Daria, for Merle's frock was a thin silk. "Let me borrow a coat from Mrs. Denham. I am sure she has lots of spare ones."

"No, darling, I don't want it. See," and Merle wound the scarf round twice, and let the ends hang down behind.

"Merle thinks that a scarf and her pearls are as good as a fur coat," said Ida.

"And why shouldn't I wear my pearls if I choose?"

"Why not indeed," said Mrs. Holroyd, "except that they look a little unsuitable."

"I am sure dear Mrs. Denham's guests are beyond suspicion," drawled Merle.

Mrs. Holroyd's eyes flickered at the impertinence.

"Well, I hope you won't be so unwise as to go over to the Fair," she said, speaking with commendable self-control.

She was justified in her protest, thought Daria, for the great rope that had belonged to an exiled princess, and which Merle had secured for a fabulous sum was very noticeable against the simple Shantung frock.

"I enjoyed the Fair last year," said Merle, "so I haven't made up my mind."

"With twenty-five thousand pounds worth of jewellery! Well, it is your own affair."

"Exactly," said Merle.

Mrs. Holroyd's glance rested on her. How she did hate her daughter-in-law, thought Daria uncomfortably. She moved away very quietly followed by Ida, and went into the further part of the garden. Daria saw that Merle was watching the groups of people who were now arriving and felt sure she was waiting for Gideon. Presently she saw him coming down the lawn. He was close to them when he noticed Merle and swerved off to the left without speaking. The movement had been almost instinctive, but it left neither of them in doubt that he was deliberately avoiding Merle. Daria glanced at her friend, and saw her face flame into anger. Without a word she turned and followed, and Daria saw her hurry through the groups of neighbours and disappear into the garden beyond in the direction taken by Gideon.

"Don't you go wandering off with the others," said Martin coming back to her. "Sit down here and then I'll get a chance of speaking to you."

Daria did so. It was no use following Merle. A good many people had taken seats, and she liked to watch the effect of the crowd and the boats slipping past in the half light. She was very worried about the state of things at the Abbey. She did not know what time Leonard had returned the night before but he was in his place at breakfast. As far as she knew there had been no clash between Merle and the rest during the morning. People had come to lunch, and they had all gone to the enclosure for tea. But there there had been trouble. Gideon had kept away from Merle, and Daria had borne the brunt of a distressing scene of hysterics when they got back to the Abbey, and as a result she still felt mentally tired.

Martin was busy with his guests, and she was glad to be alone. She leant back and watched a patch of stars on the edge of the bank of clouds. It was very still and oppressive and her head ached. She supposed it was the thunder in the air, but she had a sense of foreboding and depression.

Martin came back to her with Mr. and Mrs. Aitken, the young couple Mrs. Denham had spoken of when she lunched at the Abbey. They were both pleasant, he an ordinary clean-shaven man with public school and games written all over him, and she fair, fluffy and confidential.

She told Daria all about herself. She had only been married a short time, they both liked country things, and they adored the river. She was very cross because they had to go away early next day to stop with a dull aunt and would not be back till Tuesday when the weather might have broken. Her voice murmured on till the first rocket screeched into the sky.

Wanderers from the garden beyond came hurrying back to secure seats, and there was a confused crowd of dark figures. Daria looked round to see if Merle or any of the Holroyds were near, but could not distinguish any of them. She watched the fireworks with the enjoyment of a child. Floating groups of coloured stars, lovely bushy streamers of glittering gold, rosy smoke behind the trees that stood out as if drawn in ink on a background of coloured parchment. Everyone was gay. Martin slipped into a chair on her other side. A triumphant burst of stars illuminated the watching crowds at the Fair. Martin's spaniel who was frightened by the constant poppings crawled for refuge to be near her master. Martin and Daria's hands met as they stroked her, and for a moment his fingers held hers.

The last set piece with "Good Night" was just lit when a growl of thunder and some heavy drops of rain brought everyone to their feet. It was only the edge of the storm, but it sent everybody scampering up the lawn to the house for shelter and refreshments.

"How tactful of it to wait till the end," said Daria as she ran indoors.

As Mrs. Denham had foreseen the house was filled almost to bursting point. Drinks and food were spread on tables in several rooms, and it was difficult to find one's own party. Daria did not come across any of the Holroyds till the rooms began to thin. A good many of the people who had been at the Regatta all day were tired, and began to say good-bye. Mrs. Holroyd came in talking to Colonel Delahaye.

"Have you seen the others?" she asked Daria. "I think we ought to be going."

"I'll look," said Daria and went off.

Ida was in the drawing room with Major Wrey, Leonard was having a whisky and soda in the dining-room, but Merle was nowhere to be seen. For the matter of that neither was Gideon, and Daria thought it only too probable that her indiscreet friend had remained with him in the other garden. It was stupid and terribly like Merle, but Daria thought it odd that Gideon should make himself conspicuous, the more so as he had so evidently tried to keep out of Merle's way. She went to the window, and found that the rain had stopped for a time, though the clouds were still heavy.

"I'll go and have a look in the garden," she told Mrs. Holroyd.

There were plenty of people about. The guests who had come by river and tied up their boats along the bank, were now getting into them. She came across the Aitkens who said they had left theirs in the distant boathouse. Daria walked with them through the rock garden and by the winding paths to where the boathouse lay at the extreme end of Mrs. Denham's river frontage. She called Merle's name but there was no answer.

"Your friend must have gone back to the house by another path," said Mr. Aitken as they paused on the top of the steps that led down to the boathouse.

"I should advise you to hurry back," said his wife with a glance at the sky. "It is pretty black, and I expect we'll get a soaking."

The Aitkens got into their punt, and paddled off quickly in the hopes of reaching home before the new storm began, and Daria walked back by the upper path. The garden by now was completely deserted, and Martin met her as she reached the house.

By this time most of the guests indoors had also left.

"You haven't found her?" said Mrs. Holroyd.

"No, I couldn't see her anywhere."

"Someone must have driven her home."

"Perhaps Gideon Franklin did," said Ida.

"He went off early," said Mrs. Denham, "before the fireworks ended, but I thought he was alone."

"It is no use waiting any longer," said Leonard impatiently. "If she is not in the garden it is clear that someone has given her a lift."

"I must apologize, Ellinor," said Mrs. Holroyd, "for staying so long."

"But I've loved the opportunity of getting a little talk with you," protested Mrs. Denham.

They said good-bye, and got into the big Daimler, which Leonard drove.

"Very inconsiderate of Merle," said Mrs. Holroyd irritably, "she might at least have told us that she was going early."

But when they reached the Abbey, Burton said Mrs. Leonard Holroyd had not come in.

"She is probably having a joy ride," said Ida. "Perhaps she has gone over to the Café de Vienne to dance."

Daria thought this unlikely. Gideon would not want to do such a thing, but it was possible that she had persuaded him to drive her and had made him draw up by the roadside, and had miscalculated the time Mrs. Denham's party would last. Daria lay awake for some time listening for the sound of a car, but fell asleep without hearing it.

Next morning Merle had not returned, and an icy reserve prevailed among the Holroyds. It was Sunday. At ten minutes to eleven Mrs. Holroyd, Ida and Leonard started for church across the park. The living was in Leonard's gift, and every Sunday the Holroyds made an impressive entry into the huge pew set in a side chapel among Holroyd monuments, where they could worship at the same time, but more exclusively than the rest of the congregation. Daria felt too worried about Merle to be able to adjust her mind to the Litany, but said she would walk a little way with them. Mrs. Holroyd said stiffly that that would be very pleasant, and Daria set out with her, Leonard and Ida following. Daria spoke nervously. She knew what she meant to say would not find favour.

"Mrs. Holroyd, I'm worried. I can't think where Merle is."

Mrs. Holroyd picked her way carefully. They had taken a short cut across the grass.

"If that is because you think that she has met with an accident, I shouldn't distress myself," she said. "I think that is most unlikely."

"I wondered if you had rung up anyone to find out if they'd seen her?"

"Certainly I have not," said Mrs. Holroyd. "As you have been in the house for some weeks you must have noticed that it is not the first time that Merle has gone off for the night."

"But I can't believe she'd go from a party and without a word to anyone. She would know that I—we would be anxious."

Though, thought Daria, if Mrs. Holroyd was anxious she disguised it admirably.

"I do not pretend to understand Merle. She will no doubt have some explanation when she returns."

"I should feel more comfortable if we made enquiries."

"What sort, and from whom?" said Mrs. Holroyd chillingly. "Please don't be precipitate, Miss Lane. Neither Merle nor Leonard are likely to be grateful for unnecessary fuss."

They had reached the churchyard. Mrs. Holroyd turned to wait for the others, her manner indicated that the subject was closed, and Daria walked away. Perhaps Merle would be at home when she got back. But Merle was not. Lunch came and passed, and so did a long afternoon, while Daria sat within reach of the telephone. After tea she set off across the park to the cottage. It had occurred to her that it was possible that

Merle would expect her to do this, and might have called and left a message. But again she was disappointed. Still she could use the telephone here without having to ask the Holroyd's permission. Merle had had it installed, and had paid a year's subscription. Strange, thought Daria how thoughtful she was in some things, how unimaginative in others. She had already settled every bill connected with the house. It was one of the principles instilled into her by a self-made father, who had suffered when he began his career from the unpardonable selfishness of people who keep a small tradesman waiting for his money.

Daria put through a call to Gideon Franklin's house. She was answered by his butler who said that Mr. Franklin was away on a visit, but he intended to go to his flat in town next morning. He was not expected to return to the country till the end of the week.

During dinner the Holroyds discussed the news in the Sunday papers and Mrs. Denham's party, but Daria saw that in spite of their outward composure they had grown uneasy. She thought what a curious family they were, and how little she knew them after all these weeks. What lay under Mrs. Holroyd's iron self-control? An autocratic nature that loved to rule, and a passionate love of family and home for which she was prepared to sacrifice herself and anyone else. And what went on behind the mask Ida showed to the world? Did she care for nothing but Girl Guides and games and staying with her relations? Yes, thought Daria, she cared for Leonard. Her voice changed when she spoke to him. What a thousand pities that he had not married her instead of Merle.

Leonard was the hardest of all to read. When he was not actually driven beyond endurance by his wife he gave nothing away, but it struck Daria that all the time she had been in his house she had never seen him look happy except when he was taking active exercise. Merle's money had certainly not brought contentment for any of the people who enjoyed it.

Leonard had picked up a book after dinner, but for half-an-hour he had not turned a page. Mrs. Holroyd and Ida were knitting in silence. It was certain that they must all be wondering if Merle had gone to her lover, though family pride had kept them from asking. Once Leonard glanced from behind his book at Daria. She realized that it must be humiliating for him to have no idea where his wife had gone nor what she meant to do, and to know that she was aware of it. It did not surprise her when Mrs. Holroyd laid down her work and said in her even voice:—

"Leonard, dear, I think it might be a good thing if we telephoned to town to know if Merle is at her club, or that hotel she goes to. We should know what to do with any letters."

Leonard spoke indifferently.

"If you think so."

"I wonder Ida if you would mind——"

"Certainly, Aunt Octavia."

A quarter of an hour later Ida returned. Merle was not stopping at either place, nor did they expect her.

"I daresay we shall get a letter in the morning," said Mrs. Holroyd with apparent calm.

But the morning's post brought nothing from Merle, and Daria's anxiety grew. This was the day when she was to have moved to Jasmine Cottage, and when Merle and she were to dine together. There could be only one explanation. Merle had run away with Gideon and had persuaded him to take her straight from the party. Yet that did not seem to fit. Would he have taken her direct to his house for the night? The butler on the telephone had said that Gideon had gone off for his visit early on Sunday morning, and was then going to London. This might not be true, but the only way to be certain was to go up to town and see what she could learn at Gideon's flat. If she found Merle the situation would at least be clear, and this doubt and suspense ended. It meant that she could not go to her new home that day, so she had to ask Mrs. Holroyd if they would keep her till Merle returned as she did not like to take possession of the cottage in her absence. Mrs. Holroyd said she quite understood, and Daria started for the station, stopping at the cottage to explain matters to her new maid, Susan Harridge, who was to come in that day and might dislike sleeping there alone. Susan said she would get her father, who worked close by at Mr. Aitken's to come in for a night or two, and Daria caught the train to London.

The hall porter where Gideon had his flat said Mr. Franklin had returned that morning and gone out immediately. His secretary, Mr. Grainger, had been with him.

"You do not know where it would be possible for me to find him by telephone?" asked Daria. "It is important."

The porter said he thought Mr. Franklin usually lunched at St. Stephen's Club, but that was all he could tell her, and Daria went off to fill in the time shopping. It was in the Army and Navy Stores that she had the luck to run across a neighbour of the Holroyds, an old bachelor named Humphreys, who stopped to speak to her. She remembered that he was a member of the same club, and asked if he thought there was a chance of Gideon being there.

"Yes. I have just come from the club, and was talking to him a quarter of an hour ago. Rather pleased with himself I thought," chuckled Mr. Humphreys.

"I wonder why," said Daria quickly, her mind on Merle.

"He wouldn't tell me, but I could guess. He spent the night at Sir Edgar Somers', and people aren't asked there as a rule unless there's something brewing in the political world."

Mr. Humphreys had once been a member, and took an absorbed interest in everything connected with the House.

"Would women be asked?" said Daria.

"Good Lord, no! Sir Edgar hates them. His sister, Mrs. Burns, runs his house, but he turns even her out when he has his business interviews." Mr. Humphreys looked kindly on Daria, for he liked good-looking young women, and added: "I'm very glad that you are going to settle in our part of the world, Miss Lane."

They parted and Daria went straight to the telephone. She rang up St. Stephen's Club, heard that Gideon was still there, and asked if he would speak to her. After a little delay he came.

"What can I do for you, Miss Lane?"

His voice sounded strained, and when she asked if he could spare a few minutes and meet her outside Westminster Abbey he agreed. They met and walked through Dean's Yard into the Cloisters. Daria could see that he was nervous, and she lost no time.

"Mr. Franklin, can you tell me where Merle is?"

Whatever he had expected it was not this, and he was obviously surprised.

"Merle? No. Isn't she at home?"

"When did you see her last?" said Daria bluntly.

"On Saturday night at the fireworks."

"Did she give you any idea where she was going?"

"I had no idea she was going anywhere."

Though Gideon's astonishment appeared genuine he seemed uneasy.

"I wish you would explain. I don't understand," he said.

"She disappeared at the party. We all thought that someone had given her a lift home, but she has never been back, and she is not at her club. You are great friends, and I thought she might have told you her plans."

"I assure you, no. I parted with her in the garden and went home early. Next morning I drove to Warwickshire, stopped the night with Sir Edgar Somers, and came to town this morning. I have had no communication with anyone at Wissingham."

"It is very strange," said Daria flatly.

"Extraordinary. I can't account for it in any way."

Gideon seemed less distressed than Daria thought he ought to have been.

"Of course she'll turn up or write," he added more cheerfully.

"If nothing's happened to her," snapped Daria.

"But what could have happened? If someone had given her a lift and there had been an accident you would have heard from the police long ago."

Certainly Merle had a very reasonable lover. Daria was not comforted by his calmness.

"Then I needn't take up your time. I only wanted to know if you had seen her. If she *does* happen to ring up you'll tell her I'm worrying, won't you?"

"Of course, but I feel sure you'll hear soon."

More troubled than when she started Daria returned to the Abbey. She walked fast from the station. Perhaps when she reached the house Merle would be there laughing at her anxiety. If not surely a letter would have come by the second post. She hurried on to the terrace where the Holroyds were sitting. They told her there was no news.

Daria told them she had seen Gideon and what he had said, a delicate subject considering what they all knew of Merle's relations with Gideon. A bleak pause followed.

"That was very thoughtful of you," said Mrs. Holroyd icily.

Her tone conveyed that Daria had taken a liberty, and her eyes looked hard as flints.

"Of course," she went on, "Mr. Franklin did talk to Merle at the party and might have heard her plans, but as he did not I am beginning to feel a little uneasy. What do you think of ringing up the police, Leonard, and asking if there has been any report of an accident."

Leonard said he thought it might be a good thing, and again the obliging Ida went to the telephone.

"You don't think she might have slipped and fallen into the river?" said Daria.

"Why should she?" said Mrs. Holroyd in her reasonable voice, "and if she had Merle was a good swimmer, also there were lots of people about."

It was sane but unsatisfactory, and Daria fidgeted away, and went into the room where Ida had been telephoning. Ida put down the receiver and looked an enquiry.

"What did you hear?"

"Nothing. There is no report of an accident."

Her indifferent glance took in Daria's distress. It seemed to surprise her. "I shouldn't worry," she added.

"But I do," snapped Daria, her nerves in a jangle that was not soothed by the other's calmness. "So would anyone who cared about her."

Ida raised her eyebrows, but passed this politely.

"I don't see what more we can do. Merle will roll up in a day or two as if nothing had happened. She always follows her impulses."

"She would never have gone without leaving a message. She intended to be at home when I moved."

"She may have given a message to someone who forgot to deliver it."

So calm, so sensible, and Daria would have liked to slap her face. It is easy to be philosophical when you don't care two hoots, she reflected, and went out of the room.

CHAPTER VII

ALBERT HARRIDGE, the gardener at Rock Lodge, enjoyed little except grievances. These he cherished for many years, even after the people who were responsible for them had forgotten the incidents. He had lived in the village since he was born, and was something of a character. He was a widower with three daughters, one married, one employed as maid by Mrs. Holroyd, and the third Susan, who had been engaged by Daria. He disliked all police because he had once been had up for drunkenness, and he abhorred the Holroyd family because they had discouraged his habit of dropping in to see his daughter. He had been handed on to the Aitkens when they took the house, and added them and their cook Edith to the list of his dislikes. He did not hold with young people who made all sorts of demands on a gardener's time outside what he considered his own job. So when Edith told him that her mistress had left word just as she was getting into the car to drive off on Sunday morning that Harridge was to clean out the punt directly he arrived on Monday, he said it would have to wait till next day. Edith, his sworn enemy, who was always making complaints about the vegetables, persisted, and increased his obstinacy. Irritatingly she pointed out that there had been showers on the day of the Regatta and this would do the punt no good, also that she wanted the tea basket which the Aitkens had omitted to bring in when they came back from the fireworks. So muttering that if he wasted his time on boats the path would remain unweeded he walked off ignoring her parting shot that it might have given him something to do in his spare time.

To prove his independence Harridge did not go near the boathouse till Tuesday. It was late in the morning because the cook had had the effrontery to ask if he had done the job, but it could no longer be postponed because Mrs. Aitken was due to return that afternoon. Filled with distaste, and brooding over his dislike for the pert Edith, he walked down to the boathouse.

The punt had been hired for the summer. The Aitkens had got one with a frame work on which a cover could be fitted in case of rain. The tarpaulin had been removed from the main part of the boat, and lay in a heap in the stern.

"Probably covering tea-baskets, and cushions, and umbrellas and what not," muttered Harridge crossly, "and I'm expected to carry it all up to the house, though what those idle hussies of maids are doing I don't know."

He began to heave at the tarpaulin, which was heavy. As he had supposed there was plenty underneath, but it was a queer shape that did not suggest tea-baskets. He took hold of something and gave a pull, then stopped. Sticking out from beneath the heavy folds was a human foot. For a startled second Harridge thought somebody had crept into the boat, and had gone to sleep, then the rigidity of this foot and its position undeceived him. He dragged back the cover, and gave a cry of horror at what he saw. A small woman lay crumpled up, as if the body had been compressed into that unnatural position while it was still warm. Around the neck was a yellow scarf. She had been dead for some time and her face was horribly distorted from strangulation. Harridge let out a shout, and still shouting he stumbled up the lawn to the house.

"Have you seen a ghost? Whatever's the matter?" said the cook, who was at the sink and saw him pass the window, then catching sight of his ashen face she caught his arm, and pushed him into a chair.

"Drink some of this. You've had a nasty turn," she said, holding a glass of water to his lips.

Harridge explained.

"A dead woman in the boathouse! But I'll come down."

The news might be terrifying, but Edith was not going to miss the thrill. But when she had looked at the dreadful figure she too felt sick.

"Poor soul, I wonder who it is. She's dressed like a lady."

She was a stranger and knew very few of the inhabitants by sight.

"She looks like young Mrs. Holroyd," said Harridge, "though I don't see how it could be her."

He might dislike the Holxoyds but somehow the idea of anything so terrible did not fit with Harridge's conception of what should happen to people in "the big house."

"Well, whoever she is," said Edith briskly for Harridge still seemed too dazed to take action, "the best thing is to telephone to the police. Also we must see if we can get on to Mr. Aitken at his office."

"You do it," said Harridge. "I can't manage these new-fangled things."

"Best cover her up," said the cook, and went running back to the house, leaving Harridge in the boathouse.

Robinson, the village policeman arrived half-an-hour later, with Doctor Edwardes. Robinson telephoned the news to his superiors, and a fast car brought Major Wrey and Inspector Travers to the spot. The question of identity was solved at a glance by Major Wrey, who presently drove to the Abbey to break the news to the family.

* * * * *

When Daria looked at the disfigured face of the friend she had loved it was not only grief but furious anger that filled her mind. At that moment she vowed never to rest till she knew who had done this thing. She saw Merle as she had been only three days ago, young, gay, beautiful and only twenty-one, a mixture of follies, generosity, and kindness, the person of all others in Daria's world who would leave a blank that nothing could fill. She decided to leave the Abbey immediately, for she was in a mood when she could not endure the sight of the Holroyds.

They had behaved with dignity when the dreadful news was brought, but it was clear that sorrow had little place in their feelings. Horror perhaps, but on whose account? Publicity awaited them, the sordid details of an inquest, press photographers. Worst of all, possible questions about the terms Leonard and his mother were on with the deceased, probings into their private affairs the thought of which filled them with disgust. In death as in life Merle was an irritation and an embarrassment. Apart from this it was not improbable that her removal was a relief. Both Leonard and Mrs. Holroyd knew with Merle alive scandal was inevitable. After the events of the past week she would never have gone back to the old existence at the Abbey. Daria wondered if she was wrong in attributing these feelings to the Holroyds, but she was too miserable and bitter to be just.

She went to find Mrs. Holroyd to tell her of her intention to move, and was told by Burton that she was in the library. Daria opened the door. The room was a long narrow one with deep window embrasures. As she advanced over the thick carpet she saw Mrs. Holroyd and Leonard standing in one of them with their backs to her, talking earnestly.

"I am sure Gideon Franklin will be discreet," said Mrs. Holroyd. "I telephoned to him directly Major Wrey left. Besides it is just as much to his advantage as to ours."

They heard Daria and turned.

"Oh, is that you, Miss Lane?" Mrs. Holroyd looked less composed than usual.

"Mrs. Holroyd, I think I'll go to the cottage this evening. It is very kind of you to have put up with me for so long, but I am sure you would prefer to be by yourselves."

"It is considerate of you to say that. Of course, we don't want you to hurry," said Mrs. Holroyd politely.

"I think it would be better."

"Just as you like. The car can run you down when you are ready."

A few more civilities, and Daria returned to her packing, but she was thinking over the sentence she had heard. She supposed it referred to the quarrel and suggested divorce. The Holroyds wouldn't want the story of Merle's infatuation for Gideon broadcast. It must go against the grain to approach him on the subject but even that was better than publicity.

There was no possible doubt that suicide or accident were out of the question. It was a case of murder, and later in the day Inspector Travers presented himself at the Abbey. Enquiries had to be made by the police, but before despatching the Inspector, Major Wrey impressed on him the necessity of using tact with the bereaved family. Not only had the Holroyds been established in the county for centuries, but they were universally respected. It seemed hard that they should be involved in a case of any kind. Inspector Travers thought of this as he drove slowly up the avenue. The Holroyds seemed to merit the regard in which they were held. They were true to their traditions, they had been good landlords, supporters of the Church and Throne, the men were fine shots, and rode well to hounds, and their women were virtuous and charitable. Then when the fortunes of the family declined Mr. Holroyd had married the very rich lady who had been murdered. The main thing was to find the murderer without delay.

Over this the Chief Constable had been optimistic, and the Inspector agreed that the case seemed simple. Although there had been a regrettable delay in finding the body owing to Harridge's dilatoriness it had not mattered as much as it might. The Fair, which as Leonard Holroyd told Daria, attracted shady characters, had brought a man who was well known to the police. A certain Bill Shadwell who had already served two sentences had been seen during the afternoon. The loss of two notecases and a watch had been reported by people who had visited the roundabouts, and later Shadwell had crossed the river in the ferry, and had been seen in the lane that joined Mrs. Denham's garden. Some time after one of the gardeners had found him actually in the garden by the boathouse, and had warned him off, and locked the gate. But the wall was not high and it would have been easy for anyone who wished to return to climb it. The body of the murdered woman had been found in the punt which the Aitkens had stored in the boat-house near which Shadwell had been seen, and when it was found the valuable pearl rope

THE PUNT MURDER

had vanished from her neck. Since then Shadwell had disappeared. The Inspector had already got into touch with the man at the booth where he had been working, for the inhabitants of the Fair had gone no further than the next town. This man swore that he had not seen him again and the surrounding people said the same. A description of Shadwell was now being circulated.

Major Wrey and the Inspector had spent some time in Mrs. Denham's garden, though there was little to learn. Owing to the three days that had elapsed and several heavy showers it had not been easy to discover anything from the footprints. Also the gardeners had rolled the path, and cleaned up the boathouse. It seemed probable, however, that there had been a struggle, for some of the branches of a flowering shrub had been broken, and there was a long slurred mark as if someone had slipped, also there was a smear of blood on the dead woman's dress. It was easy to imagine the crime. The man lurking in the bushes, and catching sight of the pearls. The experience he had had in other jewel robberies would tell him that they were real, or he might have heard of them beforehand. A stealthy approach, the throttling to prevent a cry, and possibly done without intention to kill, then the feeling of panic as the limp body went sagging to the ground,—the search for a hiding place, and the small figure shoved out of sight under the awning. After this the murderer would have pocketed the pearls and made off. The loss of a motor bicycle that had been left in the lane had already been reported.

One unfortunate thing had happened. When Harridge had been left by the punt while the cook went to ring up the police he had occupied his time with a mop and cloth, and had obliterated finger-prints and any evidence that remained. When rebuked he had been surly, and did not seem to realize the extent of his offence though the Chief Constable expressed himself with freedom. It was infuriating, thought Travers, for whoever had pushed the dead body under the awning would have had to handle the sides of the punt, and would have made his get away quickly probably forgetting to remove evidence.

Inspector Travers was shown into the library. He was impressed by the room, with its panelling and tall bookcases, and the fine view out of the mullioned windows. A banksia rose tapped against the panes. It seemed to give a touch of lightness to the austerity.

Mrs. Holroyd sat straight as a post in an upright chair. She was in black with a large onyx brooch fastening her dress, and a jet necklace and earrings as her other ornaments. She was knitting a grey woollen shawl for a guild to which she supplied three garments every spring. The Inspector had brought a note from Major Wrey. Mrs. Holroyd read it.

"I understand that you wish to question us all about my poor daughter-in-law. I am afraid we can help you very little."

"It is just a formality. I hope you understand that, Mrs. Holroyd."

"Perfectly. Please ask anything you like."

But she had a tight look about her mouth, reflected the Inspector. She'd never tell what she didn't want.

"I understand that Mrs. Holroyd had been over to the Regatta Enclosure during the afternoon, and had gone round the Fair. Can you tell me if she was wearing her pearls?"

"She was."

"And she still had them on when she went to the party?"

"Certainly. I remember because both then and later in the evening I begged her to leave them at home. But she was self-willed like many young people."

"Will you please tell me exactly what happened in the evening."

"We returned here for dinner, and afterwards we went to Mrs. Denham's party."

"All together?"

"Yes. My son drove us. There was his wife, Miss Pelham-Reeve, Miss Lane, who was staying with us, and myself."

"What occurred when you arrived?"

"After we had spoken to Mrs. Denham we went into the other part of the garden. We had been asked for nine-thirty, and the fireworks did not begin till ten."

"Did you stop together?"

"No. My daughter-in-law saw Mr. Franklin, and had something she wished to say to him, and caught him up. Miss Lane, I believe went straight to the seats by the river. I talked to some neighbours, then my son and I went towards the rock garden."

"Did you remain in that part of the garden till the fireworks began?"

"Yes. Then we went back immediately."

"While you were there did you see your daughter-in-law again."

Mrs. Holroyd hesitated.

"Just for a moment."

"Did you speak to her?"

"Yes. My son and I both did. Then we left her. It was growing dark, and we went back to the lawn."

"Where was Mr. Franklin?"

Mrs. Holroyd's eyes flickered.

"He was with her when we came up, and then he went away."

"Why didn't Mrs. Leonard Holroyd accompany you when you went back to the party ? "

"She had a bad headache, and said she would stop there quietly and watch the boats and the lights of the Fair, and not talk to people."

"When you left her did you notice any other people about?"

"There may have been a few, but it was very dark by then."

"When did you miss your daughter-in-law?"

"Not till we wanted to go. When we went indoors Mrs. Denham's house was very full, and I concluded she was in one of the other rooms. When we didn't find her we thought she might have taken shelter from the shower in the garden, and Miss Lane went to look. Then we supposed she had had a lift home and come back earlier."

"Were you worried when you discovered she was not here?"

"Not really. My daughter-in-law was independent and unconventional. Sometimes she would go off quite unexpectedly. Miss Pelham-Reeve suggested that she might have gone somewhere to dance."

"With such a bad headache?"

"Her headaches were very much a matter of moods."

"But next day?" persisted the Inspector.

"We thought she had gone to her London Club, and telephoned there to ask."

"And on the Monday?"

"Miss Lane went to town, and made enquiries, and afterwards we rang up to ask if any accident had been reported."

The Inspector thanked her and asked if he could see Mr. Holroyd. Mrs. Holroyd went out and Leonard arrived in a few minutes. He looked pale, grave, but quite composed. His story was the same as Mrs. Holroyd's. They had joined Merle who was talking to Mr. Franklin, and afterwards they had left her alone.

"I wondered if you could help us to throw any light on the tragedy," said the Inspector. "Do you happen to know if your wife had any enemies?"

"None that I know of."

"I think the Chief Constable told you that a man called Shadwell had been seen hanging about. I suppose you did not catch sight of him?"

"No. But there are a lot of bushes round the boathouse, and it was getting dark. It would have been very easy to remain concealed. My wife was not wearing a coat, and her pearls were very noticeable. That supplies a motive for what would otherwise be incomprehensible."

The next person to be questioned was Ida. Her answers threw no light on the matter. She had seen Merle walk off with Gideon, but she had not spoken to them. There were a lot of winding paths in the garden and she did not know if she had returned to the lawn before or after Mrs. Holroyd and Leonard. . . . No, she had not noticed any of the Abbey party while the fireworks were going on. She had sat down next to some strangers, and then they had all run into the house out of the rain.

"As far as you know Mrs. Leonard Holroyd was not the sort of person to make enemies?" said the Inspector.

There was a distinct hesitation before Ida answered.

"She was not popular with everyone, but I know of no one who would have wished to hurt her."

There seemed to be no more to be learnt from the Holroyds, a self-controlled family, thought Travers, who gave no impression of inordinate grief, though their clothes and manner were correct. In the course of the next day or two enquiries in other places showed him that young Mrs. Holroyd was not their sort, and hardly fitted with county traditions, made up, lots of jewellery, a law to herself. He could quite believe that the formidable mother-in-law would detest her, and the husband did not seem bowed down. And that Miss Pelham-Reeve, she would probably side with the others. All very natural, yet the Inspector, who had experience, got the impression that all three had something that they guarded. If it had not been for the Chief Constable's attitude he would have liked to probe further. He decided that there had probably been some scandal to which the Holroyds would be sensitive, and village eyes which little escapes might help him to discover what it was. In the meantime he went off to interview Mr Franklin, who had been walking with the lady not long before she was murdered. Gideon received the Inspector civilly.

"As you were among the last to see Mrs. Holroyd, I thought you might be able to help us."

"I would be only too thankful if I could," said Gideon. "The Holroyds have been kind neighbours, and the whole thing has been a most horrible shock."

"That I can imagine," said the Inspector sympathetically, and there was a suitable pause before he added—

"I suppose that when you were walking together Mrs. Holroyd did not give you the impression that she was worried about anything?"

Gideon looked up sharply.

"What exactly do you mean?"

"You did not think she was afraid."

Gideon's face cleared.

"Oh no." He paused and added,—"What is in your mind, Inspector?"

"Nothing very definite, Mr. Franklin. I just wanted to find out if Mrs. Holroyd seemed just as usual."

"Quite, I think."

"Do you remember what you talked about?"

"Nothing in particular. The neighbours, and an exhibition we had been to in town. She somtimes lunched with me when she came up. No, it was very ordinary."

"You walked in the direction of the boathouse?"

"We did."

"Then when did you leave her?"

"Her husband and Mrs. Holroyd joined us. I heard the first rocket go up, and left them. I wanted to show myself at the party as I had decided to leave early."

"You did not come across the others later when they found she was missing?"

"No, I knew nothing about it. You see I never went into the house and said good-bye before the fireworks ended. I had some work to do when I got home, and was making an early start next day. The first time I heard that there was anything wrong was when Miss Lane saw me on Monday, and said that Mrs. Holroyd had not returned. I am afraid I am not much help, Inspector."

The Inspector drove off to see Daria. It struck him at once that Miss Lane was not in the catagory of people who were bearing the loss of Merle with resignation. She had evidently been crying bitterly. But she was able to give little information about the evening of the Regatta for she had never left the lawn.

"You were a great friend of Mrs. Holroyd's?"

"She was my greatest. I have been staying with her for weeks."

The Inspector paused, then asked the question he had put to the others.

"Should you think she had any enemies?"

This time the answer was different.

"She had the Holroyds," said Daria.

CHAPTER VIII

THE inquest was held in a big room built over a barn, which was let to the village by the farmer to whom it belonged. It was an isolated building that stood in the middle of a field, and was inconveniently placed, but was all that Wissingham possessed when it wanted to hold whist drives or meetings. Merle had promised to build them a new hall in the centre of the village that coming autumn. Now it was improbable that they would ever get it.

Albert Harridge was giving a description of how he found the body. He was in a truculent mood and had already managed to offend the Coroner. Since the moment of the discovery Harridge had had much to try his temper. Everyone had blamed him. Robinson, the village constable, who was his sworn enemy, had proceeded to question him in a manner that had thoroughly put his back up, and shortly after he had received a sharp rebuke from the Chief Constable who blamed him because while the cook went to the house to telephone he had taken a cloth and done what he could to clean the sides of the punt, and make things look tidier. It seemed pretty difficult for a man to know what to do when first he was told to clean and then not to. That had been followed by the return of the Aitkens. Mrs. Aitken, who was naturally scared and suffering from the shock, gave vent to her nerves by storming at Harridge. Why had he not obeyed her orders, and attended to the punt on Monday? Hadn't he understood his instructions? Whereupon his own work to see to, and anyhow he didn't take orders from a young woman like Edith Small, a girl who didn't know her place, and if anyone was accused of idling all he could say—

It had ended in the Aitkens paying him a week's wages and discharging him, and jobs were not easy to come by in these days and at his age. Now the coroner was at him about it too.

"And when you cleaned it up are you sure you did not remove anything?" he asked.

"If you mean did I take anything what didn't belong to me I've lived in this place nigh on sixty years and no man can say——"

"We how that, Mr. Harridge. But we want to find out if you left everything as you found it."

"Of course not. I took the umbrellas and cushions to the house, as was my duty," growled Harridge.

"It was *not* your duty. Your duty was to leave everything untouched till the doctor and police arrived. Now, please pay attention to what I am asking you. Did you notice anything lying about? "

Harridge said there had been a programme and one of the flags that were sold to augment the Regatta funds.

"And that is all? You are sure?"

"I've said so," said Harridge with a glare of resentment.

Doctor Edwardes came next. In his opinion Mrs. Holroyd had been strangled with her own scarf. It was a long one, and had been wound twice round her neck and the ends hung down her back. It looked as if she had been attacked from behind. It was unlikely that a stifled cry would be heard in the clamour that went on both sides of the river, with the music from the roundabouts and swings, and the clamour of the children. Mrs. Holroyd was exceptionally small, and had little physical strength. From its position it was clear that the body had been pushed under the tarpaulin while it was still warm. Details followed to prove that death had taken place as long ago as the night of the regatta.

Daria had been given a seat near the Holroyds, and her mind wandered from the gruesome recital of medical evidence and fixed itself on the family. Mrs. Holroyd in correct black sat with her suede-gloved hands folded in her lap. Leonard was by her side, and next to him was Ida, whose black coat and skirt made her look older. All three were so controlled that it seemed as if all expression had been wiped off their faces. Daria knew that they were feeling the strain of the publicity. Yes, that was what they minded, thought Daria savagely. The poor little life cut short was less of a tragedy to them than the fact that the name of Holroyd should appear in every paper in large headlines. People of their class weren't murdered. That was what Mrs. Holroyd thought.

And the publicity had been worse than even she anticipated. All England had rung with the "Punt Murder." Merle's beauty, her fortune, the antiquity of the Abbey had been exploited. The illustrated papers were full of it. Journalists had arrived like a cloud of locusts. The outer gates were locked, and the lodge-keepers had orders to admit no one without Mrs. Holroyd's permission. Even so, stray people were found in the park photographing the house, and men with cameras stood outside the church on Sunday to take snap shots of the bereaved family. And there had been a regular army of photo-graphers as they came into the inquest. It was all odious.

The Aitkens were now called. Both were nervous. Mrs. Aitken, looking like a pretty china doll, was inclined to be peevish and tearful. Their accounts tallied. They had spent the afternoon at the Regatta, and after tea, which they had on the river, they had put the mackintosh cover over their things at the end of the punt in case there was a shower. Rock Lodge was up the river, and they had to pass Mrs. Denham's boathouse to get to her lawn. They saw it was nearly empty, and decided to leave their punt inside and walk through the garden. After they had been to the house for refreshments they met Miss Lane, who said she was looking for Mrs. Holroyd. The three of them walked to the boathouse. The Aitkens went off, and Miss Lane returned. The river was very dark, and it was impossible to see what was in the boat. They had paddled quickly for fear of another shower. Some drops of rain were already falling when they reached their boathouse, and this made them decide to leave the cushions and tea basket till next day. In the morning they overslept, and went off in a great hurry as they had a long way to drive and Mrs. Aitken's aunt expected them in time for lunch. It was just as she was going out of the gate that Mrs. Aitken ran back to tell the cook to ask Harridge to give the punt a good clean out on Monday morning.

Then followed Blake, Mrs. Denham's gardener. He told how he had been to light the fairy lamps round the house and on the lawn before the guests arrived, and had then gone across the garden so as to let himself out into the lane. He had taken a short cut across the grass, and surprised a man who was on the steps of the boathouse, and was peering inside. He was small and had a slight limp, which did not however prevent him from moving with agility, and Blake remembered seeing him at the Fair that afternoon. This answered to the description of Shadwell. Blake supposed he was looking for boats deserted by their owners who had landed, in which things were very often left. He called out to know what the man was doing.

Shadwell looked scared, and muttered a lame excuse. He said the door from the lane had been open, and he had just stepped in to get a good view of the river, and meant no harm. He had been shepherded out, and Blake had locked the gate.

Mrs. Holroyd, Leonard, Ida and Gideon Franklin gave their evidence. Their stories were the same as those told to Inspector Travers. All had walked in the garden, and all with the exception of Ida had seen Merle at some time during the last quarter of an hour before the fireworks began.

But no one could throw any light on the murder. They agreed that Merle had remained by the boathouse alone.

Though unfamiliar with inquests, it struck Daria that the questions were perfunctory. The police had their own ideas, and did not want too much publicity at the moment. The Coroner gave a formal expression of sympathy with the family, and a verdict of Wilful Murder by person or persons unknown was pronounced. The Chief Constable walked with the Holroyds to their car, and Inspector Travers went off to continue investigations that led him to London.

• • • • •

Bill Shadwell was sitting in a mean lodging in Battersea kept by a certain Alf Hart. On the table before him was a newspaper brought in to him by his friend a few minutes ago. It contained a clear description of himself reinforced by a police photograph, and it said he was wanted. Bill, as he read it looked stricken. Alf Hart, who was not naturally nervous, had emphasized the fact that his hospitality could no longer continue. He had brushed aside Bill's passionate assurance that he had had nothing to do with the punt murder. He said that after he had been caught in the garden he had pinched a motor bicycle and made straight for London. Alf agreed that this might be true, but that his daughter when going round to the Rose and Thorn had seen an undoubted busy lurking in the street. That being so it seemed to Bill as to Alf that it was a question of going quickly, and not using the front door.

Bill put on a pair of goggles, slipped into a ragged overcoat lent to him by his friend in consideration for a one pound note, one of the several that had been gathered in on the day of the Wissingham Regatta, and then went cautiously to the back. Alf Hart's house had a door into a yard where stood several brewer's drays. Like a shadow he moved behind them, and looked into the street. A man's figure stood in a doorway halfway down. Bill hesitated. It might be better to wait. But while he paused his mind was made up. There was a loud insistent knocking on the door of the house he had just left. Undoubtedly the police had arrived, and there was not a moment to waste. Alf could be trusted to do his part to delay, but he must risk the figure in the street. It was on the right. He emerged and turned to the left. A shout hailed him, but he quickened his footsteps. The man behind began to run, blowing on a police whistle. Bill darted down a side street, through an alley, and across a road. If only he could board a tram! But there was no tram passing. He turned, twisted, but could not throw off the pursuer, and the whistle shrilled in his ears.

There was a policeman ahead moving towards him. He dashed down a narrow winding street, and shot into a main thoroughfare. He thought he was gaining, when he heard a shout ahead. Another policeman had become aware of the chase. He was so close that Shadwell was almost in his grasp. It was at the corner of a cross road. He jumped clear, heard a warning shout, and tried vainly to avoid the heavy lorry that had come up behind. A grinding of brakes, shouts, a gathering crowd, police elbowing their way, a white-faced driver, and beneath the front wheel of the lorry the crushed body of the man who had been known as Bill Shadwell.

CHAPTER IX

DARIA soon realized that she was fortunate in having secured Susan Harridge as her maid. Susan was a complete contrast to her father, a cheerful soul, who made the best of people and things, and was obviously content with her surroundings and her new mistress. The tragedy that so deeply affected Daria had had its effect on her own life, for her father's loss of a job was a misfortune to his family. He lodged with his married daughter Anne and her husband, George Green, but though this was a possible arrangement when he was employed all day it did not answer when he was continually in the house.

"He's that difficult, Miss," Susan confided to Daria, "and he can't help interfering. He loves his gardening, so he sets to work and digs up George's, and there's words about it. He'll only do things in his own way, and won't remember that the place is theirs. And it's the same with the children. He gives them orders, and tells Anne she don't know how to bring them up."

Susan was worried, and Daria reflected.

"Do you think he would come and do some work for me?" she asked. "I couldn't afford to have him more than three times a week, but I'd be glad if he'd do that, and if he finds a whole time job he could always leave."

"That *is* good of you, Miss," said Susan gratefully.

This had happened immediately after the inquest, and four days later the news of Bill Shadwell's death reached the village. It was first telephoned to the Holroyds by Major Wrey, who was full of sympathy with his old friends.

"There is little doubt now that the wretched man committed the murder. His flight was practically a confession, backed up by the pains he took to conceal himself. It was running from the police that brought about his death. I called in at Scotland Yard and laid the facts before them."

"And they agreed?"

"They quite realize that there is no evidence to connect anyone else with it. We imagine that he took the pearls, and during the following two days succeeded in passing them to a confederate, and they got frightened when he found the police were looking for him."

"I think that is the only sane view," said Mrs. Holroyd with a sigh of relief.

"I am very glad for all your sakes that we have found the solution."

"Thank you. It has been very trying,—a most terrible and shattering experience. Do you think it will put an end to this horrible publicity."

"I do indeed. Things are so quickly forgotten nowadays. As soon as the papers have finished describing Shadwell's death they will forget the affair, and boom some other sensation."

"I hope you are right," said Mrs. Holroyd fervently.

Events proved that he was. At first the papers were busy with descriptions of Shadwell's hiding place and the chase, but in three days the sequel to the Punt Murder ceased to be news. It was considered that the case had been solved. Very satisfactory, said Major Wrey and the Holroyds. Inspector Travers assented, but not as heartily as his chief. Mrs. Denham and Martin expressed thankfulness that the thing was settled, for Martin could not bear to see the strained expression in Daria's eyes, and his mother, who had been deeply distressed at the horrors that had happened at her party, felt relieved to think the dreadful subject that absorbed the village might be allowed to drop.

But Daria was not content. The news had been told her by Susan, and after the maid had gone she sat still. The book she had been reading tumbled to the ground, and she did not trouble to pick it up. She was intent on an idea. The doubt which had come to her from the moment Shadwell had been suggested as the murderer grew. She considered the evidence of the Holroyds and Gideon at the inquest. It was slick and convenient, but it rang false, for it did not fit facts as she knew them.

She got up, for she felt a nervous desire for movement. Walking always helped her to think, and she started off across the fields. She had just got over a stile when she saw Major Wrey coming towards her.

Major Wrey, having sent his telephone message, thought he would go over to the Abbey as he had so often done before the murder. While everything was in abeyance it had seemed better to keep away, but now there was no longer any reason why his pleasant relations with the Holroyds should not be resumed. Of course it had been terrible about Merle, poor girl, but he had been chiefly concerned about the effect on his friends. For he saw Merle from the Holroyd angle,—a little vulgarian who had been a trial, and from what he heard not too steady. A sordid story ending in a tragedy, and particularly distressing for people like the Holroyds who had the distaste of the well-bred for notoriety.

The solution, he thought, had come in the best way, for it would have been painful for his friends if Shadwell had been brought to trial, and would have prolonged a thing better forgotten. Now Leonard would inherit the poor girl's money, and in time he would get a second wife,—a suitable one this time, and have a family. After this Major Wrey's thoughts drifted to Ida in connection with himself. A charming girl, good looking, accustomed to country life. They knew the same people. It was true that he was forty-eight, but she must be quite twenty-six. When everything had blown over he would see a good deal more of her.

Major Wrey had driven to Wissingham, but as he came near the village he found his engine was missing, and decided to leave the car with the mechanic at the local garage, and walk to the Abbey. The sight of Daria advancing towards him gave him no pleasure. He saw her, too, with Holroyd eyes, also she was not the type that appealed to him, brainy, he thought, and artistic, a thing he distrusted. It must be a bore for the Holroyds to have her planted in the village. But he was naturally polite, so stopped to say a few friendly words, adding that he supposed she had heard by now that Merle's death was solved and Shadwell was killed.

"It is a relief to know the truth. At first I feared we might have to call in Scotland Yard, but it turned out to be a simple matter,—not that that mitigates its sadness," he added hastily.

"Is it simple, and is it the truth?" said Daria following her thoughts.

"Undoubtedly." Major Wrey spoke with surprise and displeasure.

"I wish I could feel as sure as you do," said Daria.

Major Wrey thought this verged on impertinence. Expert police opinion had declared itself satisfied. The criminal had been found and the motive supplied. It was hardly Daria's business to express doubts when the Holroyd family had accepted the solution. Still he made an effort to speak with moderation.

"Absolute proof is difficult when a man is dead, but Shadwell gave himself away by bolting, and then remaining in hiding."

"I can't see that that is at all conclusive. He had been in prison twice for theft, and may have thought the police were after him for the things he took at the Fair. Later he would have seen the account of the murder, and knew he had been seen close to the boathouse. Afterwards his description was posted everywhere. Surely he had every reason to hide. But that doesn't prove that he killed Merle."

"There is not a shadow of proof that anyone else did," said Major Wrey, trying to be patient. "And Shadwell's record was bad. He had had a long stretch for robbery with violence. Your poor friend had a fortune round her neck. Honestly, Miss Lane, I can't see why you can't accept the theory like everyone else."

"I wish I could," said Daria, "but something tells me that it isn't the explanation. Major Wrey, couldn't the police go on investigating?"

She spoke pleadingly, but saw that he was offended.

"If I did not understand your feeling for your friend I should resent that," he said, frowning. "It implies carelessness and indifference on our part, which I deny. You can't produce a single bit of evidence that points to anyone else. There were other doubtful characters in the neighbourhood, but we believe they did not cross the river during the evening as that was the time when everything was active at the Fair."

Daria considered him. A stupid man, she decided, but honest. Undoubtedly he believes what he is saying, and he doesn't know that his wish to get the matter tidied up quickly for his friends influences him. But it does.

"Did you believe the story the Holroyds told at the inquest?" she asked.

"What do you mean?" asked Major Wrey, considerably startled.

"You knew them well so you must have realized that a serious quarrel was going on between Leonard and Merle."

"I think you exaggerate. I know she did not get on well with her in-laws but——"

"It wasn't a case of not getting on well. They had had terrific scenes. Two days before the Regatta she had threatened to leave Leonard, and also intended to alter her will. Did you know that?"

"Merle Holroyd was rather unbalanced in some ways, if you'll forgive my saying so, and very emotional. I do not think threats of that kind mean much."

"I am sure she meant these and he knew it. I hate to tell you this, Major Wrey, but I want justice. She and Leonard had been quarrelling over Gideon Franklin."

"I do not know what you want to imply, Miss Lane, or whom you are accusing."

"I am accusing no one, but I do ask myself whether they could have had the sort of interview they describe on the night of the fireworks. Merle had reasons to be furious with Gideon, and Leonard with both of them. Not vexed or irritated or anything mild, but simply at white heat. Yet according to themselves they met in the garden, had a friendly chat and parted. It isn't possible. A lot more happened than they said."

THE PUNT MURDER

"I don't agree with you. The Holroyds are well mannered people. They were at a party at a friend's house. Even if their quarrel was serious they would behave decently. I must speak plainly, Miss Lane. You have been their guest for a long time, and it seems to me peculiar that you should insinuate things against them."

"I was Merle's guest."

"That is an absurd distinction. It was her husband's house, and you were in it for many weeks, and because of that you had the opportunity to see all the little disagreements that are usually kept from outsiders. There are quarrels in most families, especially when people have such a different outlook as Mrs. Holroyd and Merle. But that doesn't imply anything sinister. You give the impression of being very ungrateful."

Daria was unmoved.

"But Merle was my friend, and she was murdered, and gratitude and conventions don't seem to me to matter very much. That is why I still beg you not to pigeon-hole the case."

"And I tell you that it is closed unless new and real proof is produced. By this attitude you only stir up mud, and hurt the memory of your friend."

"I know all that," said Daria.

"And it doesn't weigh with you."

"I want justice."

"Good Lord, woman!" said Major Wrey, beside himself. "You are really impossible! I suppose nothing anyone can say will stop you from causing real distress to the Holroyds, and inflicting needless injury, but I give you one warning. There is a law of libel!"

"Even that doesn't move me," said Daria, "but I'm sorry I've annoyed you. I have been stupid in the way I worded it, and I hope you'll forgive me. All I feel is that I can't accept the matter as solved. I don't believe anyone knows who murdered Merle."

"It is no good arguing, so I'll say good day, Miss Lane."

Major Wrey took off his hat and stumped away across the fields, the attitude of his shoulders expressing his extreme displeasure at what he felt was wicked obstinacy.

Daria returned to the cottage. A long envelope was lying on the table, and on opening it she found a copy of Merle's will with a letter from Messrs. Harding and Willis, her London lawyers. In this she learnt that she would, in due course, receive the sum of £15,000. Tears rolled down her cheeks. At the moment this proof of Merle's affection was almost unbearable. It intensified her loss, and the. horror of the manner in which it had come about.

She turned the letter over, thinking deeply. When Merle decided to make a new will she had given instructions to Mr. Ryman, the lawyer in Ridgenorth. It was to have been her weapon to compel Leonard to give her a divorce, but of course there had not been time to sign it. Daria now remembered that Merle had told her that she had an appointment with Mr. William Ryman for Monday morning. She reflected on the difference it would have made to the Holroyds if it had gone through.

It soon became clear that Major Wrey had not kept silence about Daria's attitude, for the following afternoon Mrs. Holroyd came to pay a formal call, an honour that Daria doubted that she would otherwise have received.

Susan, who was awed and flustered by her arrival, showed her into the sitting-room and went in search of Daria who was gardening at the back of the house. This gave Mrs. Holroyd time to make a thorough examination of the old furniture and the charming fittings that were the result of Merle's activities. It added to the annoyance she had felt on hearing of the legacy. Merle's fortune was large, but her mother-in-law grudged any money that had been diverted from Wissingham Abbey. But when Daria came in her manner was irreproachable. She complimented her on the house, and they talked of this and that, but Daria knew they would presently come to the purpose of the visit.

"I hear that you have seen Major Wrey, and he told you what the police think."

"Yes," returned Daria, "but I didn't agree with them."

Mrs. Holroyd sat up a little straighter than before. The decks were cleared for action.

"That seems to me an unhappy and unjustifiable point of view. The police are conscientious and clever. One must accept the decision of experts."

Daria was silent.

"We as a family have done so," continued her visitor, "and I think that ought to weigh with you."

"Mrs. Holroyd," said Daria, "I don't want to be impertinent, but I must ask you one question. If this had happened to anyone you loved would you rest when you weren't satisfied by a theory everyone wanted you to believe? You, too, are a partizan, and I know you wouldn't."

THE PUNT MURDER

For a moment Mrs. Holroyd's eyes looked at her with a flash of understanding, then the shutter fell.

"I can see you are sincere," said Mrs. Holroyd, "but none the less mistaken. You were in poor little Merle's confidence and you know that she and Leonard did not always agree. Please don't think I am apportioning blame. The thing is over. Now what end can be gained by making their quarrels public? Nothing is easier than to start vulgar gossip, but it would surely be kinder to Merle's memory to be quiet."

"You mean even if I think she was murdered by someone else?"

At this abrupt question Mrs. Holroyd frowned.

"There could have been no one else," she said impatiently. "The motive was obvious. The poor child's pearls."

"They have not yet been found, have they?"

"No. Major Wrey says it is still possible, but one must remember that Shadwell had plenty of time to get them taken out of the country." She rose. "Well, Miss Lane, as a favour to us all I must beg you not to express your doubts to other people. And one other thing. I telephoned to the lawyer and he says he imagines there will not be a very long delay about getting the will proved. I know he was writing to tell you of your legacy."

"Yes. Merle was always wonderfully good to me."

"She left money to an old nurse in Australia, also to a clerk who was in her father's employment. The rest of the estate naturally goes to my son."

Though Mrs. Holroyd spoke composedly there was a challenge in her eye. She knew that Daria was aware that this had been no longer Merle's intention.

"There was some idea of a different will," she continued. "Or so I believe, but it was never signed. I do not know what it contained, and I shall not enquire."

CHAPTER X

"YOU don't eat enough to keep a bird alive, Miss," said Susan. "Isn't there anything you'd fancy?"

Her round, pleasant face showed so much concern that Daria felt compunctious but helpless. Susan thought comfort to the mind could be supplied in the shape of big meals, and since the tragedy Daria had no appetite.

"I shall be hungry soon," she said. "And Susan, I really like your cooking very much. Don't think it is that."

"You worry all the time, Miss, that's what it is," said Susan.

She was clearing away, and Daria stood looking out of the window. She felt miserable, and in need of someone who would give her moral support, for her attitude about the question of Shadwell had not only brought her the hostility of the Holroyds, but it had vexed kind Mrs. Denham. Mrs. Holroyd had enlisted Martin's mother on her side. The two ladies might not have much in common but they were on good terms as neighbours, and Mrs. Denham hated anyone to be upset. It seemed to her that to reopen this distressing subject could only give pain, and nothing could bring Merle back to life. She was troubled by Daria's apparent indifference to the Holroyds' feelings. She was fond of the girl, and knew that Martin's happiness was bound up in her. This made her anxious that Daria should not grow morbid over her sorrow, and very gently she urged her to take up ordinary life, and try to forget. But Daria was unexpectedly obstinate. She had set herself a task, and until She herself was convinced she was not going to abandon her search. Mrs. Denham was hurt, and showed it, and there the matter rested.

Daria turned round, for she had been seized with an idea. Susan knew everybody in the village, and was more likely to hear what was being said than any of the people Daria was likely to meet.

"It's true that I'm worried," she said, "and I think you could help me."

"Anything that I could do, Miss, I'm sure."

"Well, it's this. I don't believe we know all that we might about that evening when Mrs. Holroyd was killed. It seems as if someone on the river must have seen something. Boats were passing up and down. The river is like a high road."

THE PUNT MURDER 73

"That's so, Miss, but from what they say the poor lady was murdered behind the boathouse, and if that's true no one could see anything."

"Not of the actual murder, but perhaps somebody noticed an incident that didn't seem important at the time, and didn't think it worth mentioning. Do you think you could ferret about, and see if there is any kind of talk going on. It doesn't matter if it seems silly or wild. It might lead one in the right direction."

"I'll do my best, Miss," said Susan, who rather fancied herself in the role of sleuth.

She was a girl who combined intelligence with zeal, and she pursued her enquiries both on her afternoon out, and when she went into the village to shop. Each evening she made her report. It did not, however, amount to much. Naturally the village was engrossed with the subject, but when sifted the talk was nothing more than speculation. During the half-hour before the fireworks began the inhabitants of Wissingham had been occupied with getting across the river, and those who stayed in boats were intent on taking up a good position close to the fireworks, and the part by Mrs. Denham's boathouse was not near enough for them. Lots of people had noticed figures strolling about the garden, but there had been little to remark in this.

It was nearly a week after Susan had started her enquiries that she came in with an odd piece of information.

"Tommy Webb, Miss," she said. "He saw something rather strange."

"And who is Tommy Webb?"

"Webb's the cowman at Haine's farm, and Tommy's a sharp boy. He is about eleven. Mr. Webb had a boat lent him, and he took Mrs. Webb and her sister and Tommy. Webb was kept a bit late at the farm, and they were rowing down fast to get a good place, and came close to the bank. It seems that the others had their heads turned looking at the swings and lights of the Fair, but Tommy happened to look at Mrs. Denham's garden."

"And what did he see?" asked Daria breathlessly.

"He thinks he saw people fighting."

"Fighting! But that sounds really important. Tell me exactly what he said."

"That there were four or five people talking together, and suddenly one of the gentlemen hit the other hard, and knocked him down. It was this side of the shrubbery by the boathouse."

"Could he see who it was?"

"No, Miss. It was getting very dark."

"And he has never told anyone?"

"No. It seems he called out to his mother at the time, but Mrs. Webb is a very superior woman, and she scolded him, and said: 'That's Mrs. Denham's party, and gentlemen know how to behave themselves and don't fight,' and he must have been mistaken. But Tommy says that he did see it, and that one of the ladies ran over to the gentleman on the ground, and tried to push the other away. Mrs. Webb did turn to look, but she said the gentleman must have slipped of himself, and of course the other hadn't hit him, and Tommy wasn't to talk about it, and she spoke very sharp. Then they got to the fireworks, and he forgot all about it."

"How long was this before the fireworks began?"

"He couldn't say, but it must have been some minutes, for they had time to get right opposite the set pieces, and even then it didn't begin at once."

"I'd like to see Tommy Webb," said Daria.

Susan, who was full of resource, contrived it. Tommy, who had a craze for all things mechanical, was waylaid on his way to school, and told that the lady at Jasmine Cottage had a book she would give him if he called. Susan provided cake and jam and a well fed Tommy was ushered in to Daria who displayed the coveted book. They talked of this and that, and he was led to confide his ambition to become a mechanical engineer. Gradually the conversation passed from model engines to fireworks, and thence to the Regatta, and by degrees the story was extracted.

It was much the same as Susan had reported, but Daria pressed for a fuller description.

"Could you see what these people were like?"

But Tommy had not developed the power of observation to any marked extent, and he started drawing on the table with his finger.

"Did either of the ladies seem young?" persisted Daria.

After some hesitation Tommy decided that one was. She was small and had on a light dress. It looked white.

"And the others?"

Tommy had a vague impression that everyone else looked tall, but the real thrill had been watching the gentlemen fight.

"He gave him a proper swipe, so he did, Miss. Mother said it was nonsense, and they were only making play, but it wasn't like that."

"And he fell right down?"

"Yes, against a bush. Then they seemed to be talking angry and the little lady ran over."

"Did you see what happened then?"

"The gentleman got up and dusted himself, then we went round that bit where there's a bend in the river, and I didn't see no more."

There was nothing else to be learnt from Tommy, and Daria was left to ponder on the meaning of the incident. What did it amount to? Nothing much as it stood. A quarrel had taken place, and, though she suspected it involved the Holroyds, there was no proof. The description of a small woman in a light dress applied to many others at the party. The story of a small boy which would not be backed by his parents was hardly sufficient evidence to submit to the sceptical Major Wrey. But it was a pointer. Daria intended to find out if anyone else knew of a quarrel that had taken part at that time not far from the boathouse. She decided to have a look at the ground. The next day would give her an opportunity for it was Saturday, and she had arranged to go to the Grange, and let Martin take her on the river.

It turned out a fine afternoon and when she arrived Martin was waiting for her with the tea-basket. They walked to the bottom of the lawn.

"If you'll wait here I'll fetch the punt," said Martin.

"Mayn't I come with you?"

"Are you sure you won't hate it?"

"I'm sure I will, but I want to come all the same."

Daria had not seen that part of the grounds since the night of the Regatta as she shrunk from doing so. It looked very different in the sunshine. There were few boats on the river, and the scene was peaceful and beautiful. They came to the trees and shrubs that screened the boathouse, and Daria stood looking about her. Susan had been right. The boathouse itself lay parallel to the water, and the bushes grew close to it, and it would have been impossible for anyone on the river to see what happened behind it. It was a big place for it had been built for a launch, but was occupied only by a punt and a canoe.

"How many other people put their boats in here that night?" she asked.

"No one but the Aitkens'. It was too far from the house, and most people came from the other direction and tied up near the lawn."

Daria surprised Martin by walking on the outside of the shrubbery, and glancing from that to the river.

"At the inquest they said there were marks as if there had been a struggle. Do you happen to know the exact place?"

" I think so. I came round with Inspector Travers. Just about here." Martin showed a bush near where Daria stood. "Yes, this must be it. You can still see where the branches were broken."

"But this isn't behind the boathouse. It could be seen from the river."

"At a certain angle," said Martin.

Daria pondered. This might not be the place where Merle was strangled, but the broken branches might bear witness to the quarrel recorded by Tommy. She looked about, but the tidy gardeners had left everything in order, and there was nothing more to recall the tragedy. She gave a little shiver, and said she was ready to go out when Martin liked.

They put the cushions in the punt and Martin paddled up stream. She sat opposite him, and he watched her face. She was so deeply engrossed in her thoughts that he saw she had forgotten his existence.

"I wish I could stop you looking so sad," he said impulsively as he noticed the dark lines under her eyes.

" I can't help it. I know you think I'm tiresome."

" I don't. I only want to help you, but you don't give me a chance. You treat me like an outsider."

"That's unfair. You and your mother are my only friends here, but she is angry with me. She thinks I'm obstinate and cruel. Oh, Martin, I don't mean to be! But I have simply got to know the truth. Merle relied on me, and I can't let her down because she is dead. Won't you try to understand?"

"My dear,—I want to, but don't be furious when I say I can't see what you suspect."

"I can't say definitely myself. But every night when I try to go to sleep doubts seem to hammer in my brain." She hesitated. "Would you mind if I told you them? I think it would ease my mind if I said them out loud."

"Go ahead. You know what I feel about anything that worries you, so talk just as much as you want."

Daria sat forward, her hands clasped. She spoke haltingly at first, then the words came out like a flood as if speech was a necessity.

"How can I put it clearly? You knew Merle, but not intimately. You saw she'd been spoilt and was tactless and impatient. You couldn't know how loving and generous she was underneath. But when she found she'd been married for her money she turned bitter. She'd no feeling for tradition or conventions, and she was a hopeless wife for Leonard. But the Holroyds hated her far more than she hated them.

THE PUNT MURDER 77

Of that I'm sure. It was a dreadful atmosphere, Martin. A sort of suppressed, well-bred hatred, just as if a lot of evil gases were being bottled up. Everything she did jarred. How she spoke, what she wore, and she knew it. And the feeling grew stronger because it had no outlet. And then she fell in love with Gideon and wanted Leonard to divorce her."

"And how did that appeal to Gideon?"

"It didn't, and she had begun to find that out. There was a flare up at the Abbey, Merle rushed up to town to see Gideon and Leonard followed. I still wonder what he found out."

She paused.

"I think Gideon was badly frightened. And now I'm going to tell you something that no one else knows. On the afternoon of the Regatta when we were in the enclosure he avoided her. She tried to talk to him, and he—he almost ran away. I think it was a terrible shock, and it had a tremendous effect on her. When we got back to the house she came to my room. She was almost beside herself. She walked up and down and raved. She said she didn't care what happened to Gideon or herself, but she'd never give him up. Also she meant to leave the Abbey whether Leonard gave her a divorce or not. If Gideon wouldn't marry her she'd expose him. She would tell everyone the whole truth, and then Leonard would have to divorce her. And she was not going to let Gideon haver. It should be settled at once,—that night."

"What happened then?"

"She went to the telephone and spoke to the Ridgenorth lawyer about her new will. She had already given him her instructions. She said she was not sure about its provisions but she wished him to have it ready for her to sign immediately."

"I don't quite understand."

"I think she intended to leave everything to Gideon, and had had the will drawn out that way, but if he failed her she would have changed it again. The lawyer made an appointment for Monday morning."

"Wait a moment, Daria. Do you think anyone could have overheard this conversation?"

"If they wanted to. There are telephone extensions in several rooms at the Abbey, and you could listen in by lifting the receiver."

"I see," said Martin thoughtfully, "and after that did she calm down?"

"Sufficiently to come down to dinner. Then when we got to the party I saw her following Gideon, and I knew there'd be a scene, but I couldn't do anything, for I'd said all I could, and I might as well have tried to stop a stone from a catapult."

There was a pause. Daria lay back, her eyebrows drawn together in a frown.

"I can't help thinking what a lot of people had something to gain by removing Merle," she said presently.

"My dear, that's not very reasonable. You might say that every time anyone inherits a considerable fortune."

"There's Gideon. Merle threatened his career."

"Still M.P.'s with important futures don't usually commit murder."

"I know all that, but I'm going through the lot, probable or improbable. I even considered the Aitkens, but that's not possible. They were close to me on the lawn, I saw them in the house, and afterwards I walked with them to the boathouse."

"Yes, I think that lets them out," said Martin.

"Then there's Mrs. Holroyd. She's strong-minded. She must have known that if Merle did what she threatened all that she'd worked for would go overboard. It was her money that kept the Abbey. Second, Leonard. He had the same motive, and both he and his mother would feel the shame of a family scandal like divorce. Also he was probably jealous. Third Ida, though I can't see what she would gain. Sometimes I thought she might care for Leonard, but even so she would know there was talk of a divorce, and would wait."

"It seems," said Martin, "that you've fixed on the three most respectable people in the county for your suspicions. You mayn't like them, but you can't deny that they are that. It would be unthinkable."

"To you because you have lived close to them all your life as a neighbour, and found them polite and ordinary. But not to me. You don't know what goes on in their minds. They are strong-natured people, and everything they value most was being outraged."

"Though I see your point I still incline to the Shadwell theory. When he got into the garden he probably meant to burgle the house while everyone was busy with the party. When Blake was safely out of sight he came back over the fence, and saw Merle standing where the others had left her with the pearl rope round her neck. And by the way, did you know that the necklace was broken? Major Wrey mentioned it to me when I met him a few days ago at the club. That showed there had been some sort of a struggle."

"How did they know that as they never found it?"

"Apparently a pearl was found in the folds of the scarf," said Martin.

"Well, I feel better for having talked it out," said Daria, "though I can hardly flatter myself that I've won you to my point of view."

"No, but I'm always on your side, whether I agree with you or not."

"That's very sweet of you, Martin, dear."

"I can't bear to see you brooding. I have to be in London all the week, but I want you to promise to come in and see my mother whenever you are lonely."

"I don't think Mrs. Denham would want me constantly in and out."

"Mother likes you enormously."

"And I think she's the kindest woman I ever met. But I'm not as lonely as you think. I am getting to know all the best people. Miss Honoria and Miss Amelia Wiggins called yesterday and asked me to sing at a Woman's Institute party."

"Do you sing?"

"In a humble way," said Daria, who had a charming voice. "Anyhow I like to oblige those old ladies. They are like people in Cranford or Jane Austen. Miss Honoria is rather petrifying, but the younger one is a dear."

"Poor Miss Amelia has been snubbed and bullied for nearly sixty years. The only time she brightens is when her sister goes away."

"Then she'll have the opportunity to brighten on Monday. Miss Honoria is off to Eastbourne, and Miss Amelia is coming to tea with me to celebrate her freedom."

They had been drifting downstream, and were close to the bank by Mrs. Denham's garden. Neither of them wanted to go in. It was pleasant to lie back against the cushions and talk. Daria took the boathook and held on perfunctorily, for the river close to the edge was shallow, and there was so little stream that they hardly moved.

Martin, who was opposite to her, and had watched every change in her expression, leant forward suddenly.

"Darling," he said, "I love you and I want to marry you."

This speech, delivered without preamble and accompanied by the seizure of her hand made Daria drop the boathook.

"Martin, my dear, don't startle me like that! Now see what you've made me do!"

She had pulled up her sleeve and her arm had gone into the water.

"Damn the boathook! Didn't you hear what I said?"

Daria saw the anxiety in his eyes, and smiled at him deprecatingly and with affection. In his presence she lost something of the frozen horror that had descended on her since Merle was murdered, but the shock she had undergone made it impossible to respond as he wanted. It was as if a peaceful stream had had its progress checked by a landslide. For the moment she could not drift towards love and safety.

"Martin, don't make me answer. I'm fond of you, and grateful, but just now I can think of only one thing—that somebody who was awfully, awfully good to me died in that way. Do say you understand."

"Perhaps I do, and I'll wait,—only don't let it be too long, darling."

"No longer than I can help," she said and gave his hand a reassuring squeeze, then leant over once more to recover the boathook. She did not want to have to argue and explain, or to listen to pleadings, and Martin seemed to realize this for he did not press her further.

The boathook had got securely wedged.

"What a lot of weeds," said Daria, pulling.

"They usually cut them when they do the Regatta course, but the blighters forgot to come this side this year, and I was not here to jog their memories."

"It's coming now!" Daria gave a jerk and brought away a patch of ribbon-like weeds, and then exclaimed—

"Martin, there's something besides! Look! I think— no, I'm sure—those are Merle's pearls!"

CHAPTER XI

"SUSAN," said Daria, "you have been a great help, but I feel we are only beginning. Don't you think somebody besides Tommy might have noticed something useful?"

Susan nodded.

"I keep on asking, Miss, you may be sure. There's a lot of talk going about, but it is difficult to make sense of most of it. I often wonder——" she paused.

"What?"

"Whether any of the gentry know more than they say. Folks don't want to be brought into a thing like this."

Daria felt she was right. People talk loosely enough in a general way, but in a case that may come into court the fear of having to give evidence imposes caution, but she was hampered by being a newcomer with no intimate friends but the Denhams, and if there were whispers behind closed doors she was unlikely to hear them. Besides this, her position as Merle's friend might be a handicap, and prevent people from telling her their suspicions if there was anyone who shared her discontent with the verdict of the police.

She reviewed her strategy up to date, and was not pleased. She had allowed her feelings to get the better of her judgment, and had made the mistake of rousing Major Wrey's antagonism. Though honest he was obstinate, and would be more difficult to persuade than he would have been if she had approached him tactfully. In any case it was unlikely that Tommy's story would impress him.

Still, thought Daria, she had neglected one person who might help and that was Mrs. Denham. Not that Martin's mother would conceal anything intentionally. She had been already questioned, and being a truthful woman would have answered to the best of her ability, but this was at a time when everyone had decided on Shadwell as the murderer. It was possible she might not have been asked certain things that Daria wished to know.

To tackle her was a job that Daria disliked. Mrs. Denham was not only Martin's mother, but she had been exceedingly kind and very sympathetic about Merle. But she had been hurt when her advice was not followed and since then they had avoided the subject, and this made it more difficult to talk to her. But Daria had determined never to let her own inclinations stand in the way of her quest, and as she had decided that it must be done there was no point in putting it off. She had a standing invitation to go to the Grange whenever she pleased, and she set off directly she had finished her tea. Mrs. Denham was upstairs when she arrived and sent word that she would be down in a moment. Daria sat down to wait.

On ordinary occasions Daria felt soothed by the atmosphere that Mrs. Denham contrived to impart to her surroundings. The old-fashioned room expressed the character of the lady to whom it belonged, with its gay chintzes, big bowls of roses, and the groups of Dresden china figures on the mantlepiece. The lawn sloped to the river, and was shaded by big trees and fringed by flower-beds. Opposite were meadows and distant woods. It was so peaceful that it was impossible to believe that a tragedy had taken place within its grounds.

Mrs. Denham came in, full of welcome. Daria thought what a pleasant person she was. She radiated content, and made the most of the good things she enjoyed. She was comfortably off without being rich, and she loved her home and liked to stay in it. She was always willing to do a kindness and was really beloved. If she had a defect it was that she took an exaggeratedly charitable view of her neighbours, but this, as Daria had to own, was not only a fault on the right side, but a most unusual one.

"I hope you won't mind my coming again so soon."

"My dear, I'm only too pleased. I hate to think of you being so much alone. It isn't good for you. Now are you sure you wouldn't like some more tea?"

Daria refused, and let Mrs. Denham do the talking for the first few minutes before she introduced the reason of her coming.

"I suppose Martin told you about how we came to find the pearls?" she began.

Mrs. Denham moved uneasily.

"Yes, it was very curious."

"I wonder what the Holroyds think of it. It seems to dispose of the theory of Shadwell having done it."

"I don't think it has altered their view," said Mrs. Denham with distaste, for she was a person who never wished to think of things that were disagreeable. "I saw Mrs. Holroyd, and she told me that they suppose the man was tempted by the sight of the necklace, but did not actually mean to kill poor Merle. When he found he had used more violence than he intended he threw them away in a panic." She shuddered. "But it is a very horrible subject. Do try not to dwell on it, dear."

Daria leant forward.

"Dear Mrs. Denham, I'm so sorry, but do you mind if I talk about it just this once. I do so want to ask you more about that evening. Just things you may have noticed."

"What is the good of stirring it up? It is bad for you and all of us."

"It is no worse to speak than to think and worry about it. It might even set my mind at rest."

"Well, if it will do that——" Mrs. Denham paused. "What do you want to know? I told everything I could to the police, and that was little enough. I stayed on this lawn all the time until we came back to the house."

"You may have noticed something out of the ordinary."

"No my dear, I didn't."

"Well, let me ask you one or two questions. Let us take the Holroyds to begin with. Did you see them after the fireworks began?"

Mrs. Denham pondered.

"I didn't see Leonard till we got back to the house, nor Ida. I had stopped at the top of the lawn receiving people, and some of them came late. After the first rockets had gone up I came down to where everyone was sitting. By that time it was too dark to distinguish anyone but the people who were next me. The only one of the Wissingham Abbey party that I saw was Mrs. Holroyd. I remember that because I was fussed to think she hadn't found a seat. I don't think we had provided enough. People brought friends that we didn't expect. I made her come to the front."

"Whereabouts was she when you caught sight of her? "

"Right at the back. I suppose she had stayed rather a long time in the other garden, and no one had noticed that she hadn't a chair."

"Did she seem the same as usual,—in manner I mean?"

"Certainly. Why should she not?"

"And what about Mr. Franklin? Didn't he go away before the others?"

"Yes, he came to me a little time before the fireworks ended to say good night. He said he had work to do, and was going away early next morning. It was to stay with Sir Edgar Somers. That impressed me because I'd heard that Sir Edgar isn't social and when he asked people it often meant promotion. I knew Gideon Franklin was ambitious, and we'd all read his speech in the House." Mr. Denham took up her knitting and added in a casual tone—"But I daresay it wasn't only the work. He had had that tumble in the garden."

"A tumble?" said Daria with quick interest.

"Yes. I told you it was getting very dark, and he had stumbled over a root and got himself in quite a mess. I wanted him to let my parlourmaid attend to him because he had cut his hand, and I saw he had a handkerchief round it. But he was very nice and considerate, and said the maids had plenty to do without bothering about him, and it was nothing but a scratch. So I told him to be sure to put iodine on it when he got home. That's always safe, and it isn't wise to neglect things. I knew a case——"

"Did he seem at all disturbed?" said Daria eagerly.

Mrs. Denham reflected.

"Perhaps he did. A fall is a nasty thing, and he's rather heavy. That is why I wanted him to go indoors and get a drink before driving home, but he wouldn't."

"Can you remember what time it was when he came up to say good night? Was it soon after the fireworks began?"

"Quite half-way through. Probably more. Perhaps ten minutes before the end. It was just as I was wondering whether the maids would realize when to bring in the coffee. It is always such a nuisance to calculate about that. Sometimes they bring it too soon and it gets cold, and if they don't get it before the fireworks end the people have to wait. But I don't see why you are asking all these questions, dear. You can't possibly think that Mr. Franklin had anything to do with that dreadful affair. Why, he was a great friend of Merle's,—in fact——" Mrs. Denham paused in confusion. One did not speak evil of the dead, and it was probably nothing but gossip, and if Merle and Gideon had been a lot together it was accounted for by her interest in politics. "He was a great friend of *all* the Holroyds," she said firmly.

"I am only trying to find out where everyone was that evening, so please don't be cross if I ask silly questions. When he left you, did he go straight up the lawn?"

"I believe he went back into the other garden. You know there is a gate at the top that opens into the garage yard. He had not brought a chauffeur, and I think he went that way to avoid being stopped by people and having to say good night."

"And that is all you remember?"

"Yes, for a very few minutes after there was that shower, and everyone rushed into the house. It was a real downpour, and though it is such a short way some of them got quite wet. It brought a lot of mud on to my carpets," said Mrs. Denham ruefully.

Daria could extract no more, but what she had learnt seemed to her of importance. In her own mind there was now no doubt that Gideon was the man who had been knocked down in the quarrel which had been witnessed by Tommy. The difficulty was to get proof that this involved the Holroyds. She remembered their evidence. According to them the meeting in the garden had been commonplace and friendly, and this account of it had been supported by Gideon. What they had sworn at the inquest they would maintain, and Gideon would stick to the story of his fall over the root of the tree. So this was only a beginning, but it was a step in the right direction.

Daria went over the scene as she imagined it. If it was true that Gideon and the Holroyds were the people engaged in this quarrel what would have happened next? According to Tommy there were several figures on the lawn. If these were Leonard, Mrs. Holroyd and Merle it was certain that the dispute would not have ended without a great deal more being said on all sides. If their story were to be believed Merle had refused to accompany them to the fireworks, and this sounded probable. Daria could conjure up a picture of the others moving away, and Merle standing alone. She might have had trouble apart from this clash between Gideon and the Holroyds. What had passed between her and her lover before the others came? It was impossible to be sure, yet Daria thought that the fact that he had not remained with her spoke for itself. Merle had said that she meant to know his exact intentions. Was it not possible that she had learnt them with a clearness that left no room for doubt? Then while she stood there in a tumult of distress someone had come behind and twisted that scarf. But which of them was it? Or was the whole idea and her inclination to fix the guilt on one of these three persons the distortion of a disordered mind? Mrs. Denham, had she been asked this question, would certainly have said so, and the Chief Constable would have agreed with her.

• • • • •

Miss Amelia Wiggins was having tea with Daria under a tree in the garden. She was eating scones with cherry jam and Devonshire cream, and thought guiltily of Miss Honoria, who discouraged gluttony as well as gossip. For some days she was to be free from Honoria's critical eye, a respite she appreciated. Not that she permitted herself to be disloyal to her dominating sister, for whom she had a humble admiration, but it was nice to be able to do and say what she liked without being called to account when she got home. Miss Honoria, she realized, was cleverer and far more discreet, but if one had been born with an inclination to babble it was agreeable to indulge it now and then. And when interests are confined to the narrow limits of a village it is not human to be indifferent to the doings of one's neighbours, and to want to talk about them.

"I am so glad to see you looking better," she said, looking at Daria admiringly.

She had conceived a romantic liking for her new friend, and was pleased because this charming girl paid more attention to her than to Honoria, which was as unusual as it was gratifying.

Daria smiled and thanked her, and said she was quite well.

"I felt worried about you. It must have been a terrible shock, and for dear Mrs. Denham too. It all happening at her party, you know."

Daria shrank. She forced herself to discuss Merle's death when she had something to learn, but so far she had not considered Miss Amelia as a source of information.

"We all had a shock," she said.

"Indeed, yes. Oh! it was dreadful! As long as I live I'll never forget that night," said Miss Amelia.

To Daria's surprise her voice shook. Looking up she saw that the old lady was really disturbed.

"Why do you say that?" she asked.

Miss Amelia was certainly in the grip of some emotion. She grew pink, opened her mouth as if to speak, then changed her mind.

"No one knew about it for several days," persisted Daria.

"Not what had actually happened," said Miss Amelia. "No one could guess that, but I did know that something was wrong,—not with poor Mrs. Leonard Holroyd, but with someone," she added, confusedly.

"What exactly do you mean?"

"Honoria won't let me talk about it, but it rather preys on my mind. I know you won't repeat what I tell you but——" she took a sudden gulp of tea, and blinked at Daria,—"there was a fearful quarrel," she said. "Most frightening."

"A quarrel?" said Daria, unable to conceal her eagerness.

It had the effect of making Miss Amelia cautious.

"Perhaps I ought not to have said anything about it. . . ."

"Why not? Please go on, dear Miss Amelia. Aren't we friends?"

"Honoria said the Holroyds would be furious if I did."

THE PUNT MURDER

"All the same you might tell me," urged Daria very gently. "I'd be so grateful if you would. It might explain things that are puzzling me."

"I don't see how it could do that," said Miss Amelia, then as Daria waited she went on—"Of course I ought not to have heard what I did. Only it wasn't my fault. It was just a misfortune, though Honoria says things like that never happen to her. And they don't. I suppose I was born careless."

"What did happen?" said the puzzled Daria.

"Something came down," said Miss Amelia in a rush, growing pinker. "It was most embarrassing. The string gave way, and I just had to go for shelter. I had been looking at the water garden, and as I got beyond the little pool I felt it happen. I heard people behind, so I just clutched my skirts and I went to those thick bushes near the boathouse. I thought I couldn't be seen from the river, and that no one would come as far as that. And it was then I heard it all."

She stopped, her eyes round at the recollection. There was no question that she had interested her listener.

"What was it that you heard?"

"First it was a woman sobbing. It was a dreadful sound, hopeless, yet angry. And then a man's voice said—'Don't, please don't, darling! I swear it will be all right. Nothing need change.' And she cried out—'How can you talk like that after what you've just said?' He seemed as if he wanted to comfort her, but she wouldn't listen. She called out quite loud 'I tell you I won't! I don't trust you. You have got to decide now . . .' and then after a moment—'Understand, whatever happens, and whatever it means, I'll never give you up!' You know, my dear, I suppose I oughtn't to say such things to you, being a young girl, but at first I thought it was one of the maids who might have got into trouble. Such things are very sad, but they occur even in a quiet village like ours. But whoever it was I didn't want to hear, but I simply couldn't find that string. I was so fussed that I suppose it made me clumsy. I didn't hear what they said next, but it sounded as if he was trying to coax her and just then there were footsteps, and some other people came up, and the big quarrel began."

"Do you know who they were?"

"No. It was all so confused. There was a man who seemed dreadfully angry. He said some words I hardly caught, and then spoke roughly and used a very nasty expression. 'You swine!' he said. After that there was a horrid scuffling sound as if people were struggling, and a fall, and a woman's voice said—'Don't—don't!'"

"Was it the same woman?"

"I think so, but it seemed as if several people spoke at once, and I was dreadfully frightened. It had got so dark behind the trees. Then all in a minute I found my string and tied it and crept away as quietly as I could. It would have been so awful if they had heard me and followed. I *was* thankful to be on the path once more and see where I was going. I felt quite faint when I got back to the lawn, and Mrs. Richardson kindly lent me her smelling salts."

"It was horrible for you," said Daria consolingly. "And are you positive that you can remember nothing else ?"

"No, I don't think so. I rather imagined I heard footsteps as if one of them had walked away, but the voices went on."

"You are sure you did not recognize any of them?"

"Not really. At the time I thought of nothing but getting away. It was only afterwards when I heard of the murder that I wondered if . . . well, I don't know. It mightn't have been young Mrs. Holroyd's voice after all, but I did get that impression even then. You know she had a funny way of speaking, not quite like us, being I think from Australia."

"You didn't think of telling all this to the police?"

"Yes I did, but Honoria wouldn't hear of it. I didn't tell her all, but I did say I had heard people quarrelling and wondered if it had anything to do with what happened after, but she said it was foolish to mix oneself in such things. And as it turned out she was right, for they found out that it had been done by that dreadful Shadwell, and Honoria said I must see how wise it was not to say anything. Why, I might have been called on to give evidence, and all about nothing, and if any of the guests had so far forgotten themselves as to fight at dear Mrs. Denham's party their names might have come out, and it would have been most disagreeable. But now that it is cleared up," added Miss Amelia blithely as she accepted another helping of Devonshire cream, "it doesn't so much matter having told you."

"I'm glad you did," said Daria.

CHAPTER XII

"WELL, what do you make of it?" said Major Wrey fretfully. He sat in his office facing Inspector Travers. On the table between them lay a letter that had cost Daria much thought before she had drafted it to her satisfaction. The Inspector read it through twice. He looked up at his chief, and gave an answer that he feared would be unpalatable.

"I think it worth while going into, sir."

Major Wrey put out his hand and drew the paper nearer, frowning at it distastefully.

"There's not much to go on, and it means stirring up a lot of mud. This young woman has had an obsession from the first."

He paused. Travers did not speak.

"All it proves is that there was a quarrel," continued Major Wrey crossly, "but how do we know it had anything to do with any of the Holroyds?"

"We don't, sir, but of course *if* it was them it——"

"Even so what does it amount to? It is I fear a matter of common knowledge that poor Mrs. Leonard Holroyd did not get on well with the others. A dispute would not have been unusual."

"No, sir, but at the inquest they gave a very different account of the events of the evening."

"True, but though I don't defend that, I do understand that they had a natural shrinking from letting the Press hear of it. Can't you imagine the headlines?"

Travers said he could, and paused respectfully.

"I was convinced that it was Shadwell," said Major Wrey truthfully. "Did I tell you that I met this Miss Lane, and she was really very objectionable, just after the man was run over? It seems that she got it into her head from the first that someone else did it."

He frowned. An odious girl, tiresome, meddling, settling herself to ferret out things behind the backs of the police, just as if they didn't want to find out who had murdered that poor creature. He wanted to prove her wrong, and still hoped to do so, but it seemed as if some further enquiry might have to be made. He must be on his guard not to allow friendship for the Holroyds and dislike for Daria to influence him.

"Those pearls," he said thinking aloud. "Odd finding them there, though Shadwell might have thrown them away."

"He might," said Travers, "but I don't think he would. Nor do I believe that Shadwell was a killer."

"But I thought you were convinced at the time ? "

"I can't say I was, sir. I've never felt quite comfortable about it, yet there didn't seem anything to go on. At that period we hadn't heard of Mr. Franklin's fall."

Major Wrey straightened himself.

"What it amounts to is that we shall have to make further enquiries. Mind you I don't expect much result, and I'm annoyed at the vexation it is going to cause. But if properly handled there is no need that the matter should become public. I suggest that you go and question Mrs. Holroyd and her son, and also speak to Mr. Franklin. You will probably find that none of them had any connection with the quarrel. According to this letter Miss Wiggins can't swear to any of the voices though she has a vague idea she recognised Mrs. Leonard Holroyd's, but it is easy to make a mistake like that. The fact that the poor girl was murdered would suggest the idea that she was one of the people concerned, but it may have been an entirely different group of people."

"Quite so, sir."

"Very well. Deal as tactfully with it as you can."

"Yes, sir, but before we begin I think it would be just as well to get an idea what was in that will."

" The will ? Surely we heard that."

"Not that one, sir. I see in Miss Lane's statement that she lays stress on the new one that was never signed. It might help to know what it actually contained."

"I see," said Major Wrey irritably, "that you are not disinclined to re-open the case. Very good. I leave it in your hands."

Major Wrey, who was a conscientious if rather stupid man, saw that there was no other alternative, but as he returned to his papers he wished that Daria had never come to the Abbey. It was the more annoying as he was particularly anxious to stand well with the Holroyds on account of Ida, and though she did not seem to come into the doings of that evening she always identified herself with anything that concerned her aunt and cousin, and would bitterly resent any action that brought more trouble upon them. Travers should bear the brunt of their displeasure, and he himself must soften everything as much as he could.

Inspector Travers did not share the anxieties of his chief about the Holroyds' feelings. He was socialistically inclined and did not like County families, also he had spoken the truth when he said he had never taken Shadwell's guilt as a certainty. He was madly keen on his work, and he shot back into the case like a ferret after a rabbit. He went off to interview Mr. Ryman, the lawyer in Ridgenorth who had been directed to draw up Merle's will. There was the possibility that it might have been destroyed, but this he found had not been done. Mr. Ryman demurred at first at having to produce it, but a telephone call to the Chief Constable convinced him. Travers read it through, and decided that it certainly provided food for thought. There were bequests to the same people in Australia, an extra £10,000 had been left to Daria, £20,000 had been divided between specified charities, and the residue was to go to Gideon Franklin.

"I see there is no mention of Mrs. Holroyd's husband or his family."

"None," said Mr. Ryman drily. "It was altogether so unusual that I ventured to remonstrate, and say that it would put Mr. Holroyd in a difficult position, but the lady was obstinate. She said the money was entirely her own, and she could throw it down the gutter if she liked."

"That is interesting. Did she say anything else?"

Mr. Ryman reflected.

"She made one or two curious remarks, or so they seemed to me. She said—' After all, this isn't likely to be the last I shall make. Things may happen to cause me to change it.' To which I replied most sincerely—'I very much hope so, Mrs. Holroyd,' for indeed I felt the whole thing to be unfortunate, and probably the result of some passing quarrel with her husband. She made rather a strange answer. She said—' I don't think I mean what you do, Mr. Ryman. I don't suppose the Holroyd family will benefit in any case.' "

"When did this conversation take place?"

"It was on the Thursday before her death."

"And when was the new will to be signed?"

"On the Monday morning after the Regatta. She had an appointment for twelve o'clock."

Inspector Travers thanked him and went away pondering over this conversation. It looked as if Merle even while she was making the will in his favour had strong doubts of her lover, and this coincided with Daria's account. The inspector was beginning to feel that this young woman, so abhorred by Major Wrey, was an asset. She had a clear brain, an eye for detail, and the fact that she meant to get at the truth at any cost would make her a valuable ally. It might of course be necessary to warn her against letting her zeal overpower her judgment.

He was undecided about his next step. Unless he could surprise some admission out of Franklin and the Holroyds it would be difficult to fix them with the quarrel. His task was not easy. It was wise to remember that Gideon Franklin was a rising man who would make a bad enemy, for he was not a person to forget a grievance. On the other hand his ambition might help. He would fear publicity, and would want to stand well with the police. Travers decided to put Gideon first on his list of interviews, and to prevent his sending a warning to the Holroyds before he had seen them. With this in his mind he called at the telephone exchange where his brother-in-law was in charge, and arranged that for the next three hours the line to Wissingham Abbey should be out of order, then rode off to Risborough where Gideon lived.

Gideon was dictating letters to his secretary. He received the inspector with an air of surprise.

"I am a busy man, Inspector, so I hope you won't keep me long."

"No longer than I can help, sir," said the Inspector, and glanced at the young woman whose head was bent over her notebook.

"That will do for the moment, Miss Symes," said Gideon.

"I am sorry to trouble you again," said Travers when Miss Symes had gone out, "but certain things have been reported to us in connection with the death of young Mrs. Holroyd, and the Chief Constable thought you might be able to throw some light on the matter."

Gideon's face shewed little, but the hand that lay on his knee was suddenly clenched.

"I thought that was cleared up," he said evenly.

"Not entirely," said Travers, who had decided on bold tactics. He looked straight at Gideon. "I want to ask you why you failed to tell us of the quarrel that took place between you and Mrs. Holroyd a short time before she died?"

At this Gideon changed colour, but he spoke calmly.

"What makes you think there was a quarrel?"

"It was overheard and reported to us."

The decision in his tone carried weight. Gideon hesitated, and the Inspector saw with relief that he was on the right tack, and gave him no time to reflect. He got out his notebook.

"You see, sir, your first statement was a bit misleading. Perhaps you would kindly give me your account of it now."

"I should like to know the name of your informant, and what you have been told."

"I am afraid that's impossible. The letter we received was confidential. All I can say is that a lady had some trouble with her dress and went behind the bushes to adjust it, and seems to have remained some time, so that she was able to give a description of what was said and done. This concerned two quarrels, at the end of which it seems there was a scuffle and a fall. I may say that Mrs. Denham bears out the fact that you mentioned that you had had a tumble when you said good night to her. You see, sir, I am being quite frank with you, though I don't think you have been the same with us." He consulted his notebook. "On the evening of the Regatta you said you had walked towards the boathouse with Mrs. Leonard Holroyd, and talked about nothing in particular, that the elder Mrs. Holroyd joined you later with her son, and that you left them when you heard the first rocket go up. This as you see hardly tallies with what we have since been told. I now wish to hear if you have anything to add to it."

Gideon hesitated, then smiled ingratiatingly.

"I confess that I did not tell you everything at the time; but I had a reason for not saying more than I was absolutely obliged."

"And that was?"

"It puts me in an awkward position for it is a delicate matter," said Gideon. "I hope you and the Chief Constable will understand this, and not let it go further. Mrs. Leonard Holroyd was a delightful enthusiastic woman, but something of a spoilt child. She had been very kind about my work, and we became friends. I was grateful, and perhaps I was indiscreet in the things I said. Anyhow she misunderstood me. This is rather difficult, Inspector."

"She was in love with you, and thought you were with her," said Travers bluntly.

Gideon bent his head.

"She imagined so at the moment. She was a creature of impulses and not very happy, also she had nothing on earth to occupy her time. It would soon have passed."

He paused, but Travers merely waited for him to continue.

"Well, that evening I was obliged to let her see the truth. It was a painful scene, and in the middle of it Leonard Holroyd came up with his mother. I gathered that she had let him suspect that there was more in it than there really was. Leonard was angry at finding us together, and he lost his temper."

"You quarrelled and he knocked you down," said Travers, who had begun to dislike Gideon.

"He struck at me, and I slipped and fell into the bush nearest me."

"And then?"

"The older Mrs. Holroyd asked me to go and I did so."

"You left the three together?"

"Yes."

"And you did not see Mrs. Leonard Holroyd again?"

"I did not. I went back to the lawn, and as you can understand I felt upset and not in a mood for meeting people. Beside that I was muddy and dishevelled. So I told Mrs. Denham that I had tripped over the root of a tree, and made my excuses."

"Did you go through the house?"

"No. I took the side path in the other part of the garden. It leads direct to the garage where I had left my car. I had not brought a chauffeur."

"You say you went back to the lawn and said good night to Mrs. Denham. Was that immediately after leaving the Holroyds?"

Gideon seemed to hesitate.

"N-no. I was feeling rather queer, and I waited a few minutes."

"Waited where?"

"At the back among the crowd."

"For how many minutes?"

"I can't say. It might have been five or ten. The fireworks made an infernal noise, and I meant to go off without saying good-bye, and then I happened to see Mrs. Denham."

"During that time did you catch sight of Mrs. Holroyd or her son?"

"Just before I left I saw Mrs. Holroyd. I did not see Leonard."

"And when we questioned you?"

"I decided that it was my duty to protect Merle Holroyd's name from scandal. Also I have a great respect for the others. They have been very good to me ever since I came to the neighbourhood, and if this had got into the papers they would have felt it terribly. Besides that it had no bearing on the murder, which would have been the only justification for making it public. One can imagine the sort of construction that would be put on an incident of that kind."

"Mr. Franklin, are you aware that there was a smear of blood on Mrs. Holroyd's sleeve?"

"I think it was mentioned at the inquest."

"And that when you said good-bye to her Mrs. Denham says you had a bandage round your hand."

"You think it was my blood? You may be right, Inspector. When I fell I scratched my wrist, and it bled rather freely. Mrs. Leonard Holroyd ran to me when I lay on the ground. She might easily have brushed against my hand."

"I did not notice your wrist when I saw you."

"Why should you? When I got back I put on New-skin, and it healed in a day or two."

"You say you left the three together. Have you any idea what passed between Mrs. Holroyd and the others after you left?"

"None."

"Can you describe what they were doing when you came away?"

"Merle Holroyd was crying. She was very hysterical by that time."

"Her husband had not threatened her?"

"Certainly not. You cannot possibly imagine, Inspector, that Leonard Holroyd had anything to do with the murder. I must say I cannot see where this is leading, and I think this probing into a purely private affair most unnecessary. Now I have told you everything as far as I know it, and I hope the Chief Constable will let the matter drop."

Gideon half rose as if to show that the interview had ended. The Inspector did not move.

"Did Mrs. Holroyd tell you that she intended drawing up a new will in your favour?" he asked.

"She may have, but I didn't pay any attention. Mrs. Holroyd made all sorts of wild statements. She was capable of making and changing her will a dozen times."

"Well, sir, thank you for seeing me. I hope I have not kept you too long," said the Inspector politely.

He went off elated by the result of his interview. It was now definitely established that the quarrel had been between Gideon and the Holroyds, and this knowledge would make the inmates of Wissingham Abbey easier to handle. It also opened a vista of possibilities into which he would have to go very fully before he returned to Major Wrey with his report.

His reception at the Abbey was hostile. Burton kept him waiting a few minutes, and then he was asked to come into the library where Leonard and Mrs. Holroyd were sitting. Travers made his explanation. The Chief Constable had sent him to ask certain questions on account of information they had received that morning.

"Major Wrey! I am extremely surprised at his doing so." Mrs. Holroyd laid down her embroidery, and looked at him with displeasure. "It seems unlike him to be inconsiderate. The affair has been a terrible shock to us all, and we were trying to put it out of our minds and resume our ordinary lives."

"The Chief Constable wouldn't trouble you unless he was obliged, but in a case like this he cannot let friendship interfere."

Mrs. Holroyd considered this impertinent. She gave the Inspector an intimidating stare.

"No one would expect or wish such a thing," she said icily. "But we were questioned fully at the time, and told all we knew."

"Not quite everything," said Travers. "No mention was made of the quarrel that occurred in Mrs. Denham's garden between Mr. Holroyd and Mr. Franklin."

There was a moment's silence. The Inspector who was watching Mrs. Holroyd closely saw her expression change, her eyes flickered, then her features grew impassive.

"Please go on, Inspector. What do you know of a quarrel?"

"We know that your son came upon Mrs. Leonard Holroyd and Mr. Franklin together, and as a result Mr. Franklin was knocked down."

Mrs. Holroyd bent her head.

"That is a fact, though I consider that you have expressed it offensively. But this unpleasant scene took place in my presence and as it could have had no connection with my daughter-in-law's death there was no reason to refer to it."

"I cannot agree with you. The police should have been told."

Leonard who had been leaning against the mantlepiece while this conversation went on now broke in, and though his voice was carefully controlled it was clear that he was angry.

"I am willing to admit the quarrel, Inspector, but I dislike your attitude. Whether she was alive or dead you could hardly expect me to drag my wife's name into the papers. I wished to protect it, and the incident was private."

"Well, sir, let us leave it at that, but since it has come to light I should be grateful if you would give me your account of what happened. I may say I have already heard Mr. Franklin's."

Leonard hesitated.

"This is very disagreeable," he said after a moment, "but I suppose I cannot refuse. To put it briefly my wife had asked if I would let her divorce me, and I refused. At Mrs. Denham's party my mother and I came on her and Mr. Franklin in the midst of an emotional scene, and I lost my temper, and knocked him down."

"And then?"

"Mr. Franklin got up and went off."

"What did you do next?"

"After a few minutes my mother and I left."

"And Mrs. Leonard Holroyd remained behind?"

"Exactly."

"What passed between you and your wife before you came away?"

"I told her that I could not have her meeting Mr. Franklin any more."

"And what was her answer?"

"Is this really necessary?" said Leonard who looked very white.

"I am afraid so."

"She said she would meet whom she chose."

"And then?"

"I do not remember all I said in reply, but as I have just told you we then left her."

"Where?"

"Just at the back of the boathouse."

"She was all right then?"

"Quite, Inspector. I assure you I had not murdered her."

"If," said Mrs. Holroyd, "I had been told that I should have to listen to my son being insulted in his own house I could not have believed it."

"Mrs. Holroyd," said Travers, "a murder has been committed. You seem to forget it."

"That would be difficult, but I should have thought the fact entitled us to consideration. The Coroner and jury certainly thought so."

"They did not know that the police had been misled. It would have saved us all trouble if you had chosen to be frank with us from the start."

"Is that all you wish to know?" asked Leonard.

"Not quite. I have to ask you Mrs. Holroyd, what part you took in this quarrel?"

"Very little. I asked Mr. Franklin to leave us, and a little later I begged my son to come away. I was afraid that our voices might be overheard from the river. My daughter-in-law was crying and very uncontrolled."

"Did she speak to you?"

"She did," said Mrs. Holroyd with bitter emphasis. "As far as I remember her exact words were—'I don't care a damn about anything to do with your mouldy family. I'm going to leave, whatever Gideon does, and I'll take my money with me.' My daughter-in-law had not an even temper, Inspector."

"And it was then that you and your son came away?"

"That is so. I thought solitude would give her an opportunity to calm down. We were, after all, at a party."

"You saw no one else near?"

"I did not, though from what you have said some eavesdropper must have been there, or so I imagine since Mr. Franklin is hardly likely to have volunteered this information."

"You are quite right. Someone overheard a good deal that was said." Travers got up, adding—"And now Mrs. Holroyd may I speak to Miss Pelham-Reeve ? "

"She will not be able to tell you any more than she did last time," said Mrs. Holroyd quickly.

"All the same I should like to see her."

Mrs. Holroyd rang the bell. She marked her displeasure by remaining silent till Burton came.

"Burton, take the Inspector to the morning room, and ask Miss Ida to go to him there."

Travers, very much in disgrace, received chilly bows, and went out. The interview had not been pleasant but this did not trouble him. He believed he had heard most of the truth, but could not help wondering what had been kept back. Beneath her apparent indignation Mrs. Holroyd seemed anxious. But though he puzzled over the origin of this impression he could not pin it down to anything that had been said.

A few moments passed and a maid came in. She was a tall girl with a long face, thin lipped, and looked incredibly respectable. Travers remembered that she was Ellen Harridge, Mrs. Holroyd's maid.

"Miss Ida says she is sorry but she will have to keep you waiting for a few minutes. She is getting ready to go out."

"That's quite all right. I am not in any hurry," said the Inspector, and smiled ingratiatingly for he had an idea that this young woman might be got to talk. "I am afraid you've had a lot of trouble at the Abbey in the last month," he added sympathetically.

Ellen looked at him doubtfully as if uncertain how to take this remark.

"Losing your poor young mistress in such a fashion," explained Travers.

"Mrs. Leonard Holroyd was never my mistress. I attend to Mrs. Holroyd and Miss Ida."

He took note of the tone of dislike and went on conversationally—

"She was very pretty. I should think it would have been nice to be her maid."

"That's a matter of taste. Cecilia, the head-housemaid, looked after her. Myself," said Ellen with a sniff, "I like to serve real ladies."

The Inspector showed surprise.

"Wouldn't you have called her one?"

"I should not," said Ellen emphatically. "Plenty of money to burn, of course, and heaps of frocks, but stagey things. Not the sort people, wear in a house like ours. And all that make-up. I wonder how her husband could stand it."

"Perhaps he was like many another and had to," said the Inspector jovially.

Ellen made no comment and he went on.

"I expect she must have given a lot of trouble."

"I should say she did." Ellen's lips tightened. "I don't know how they stood her ways."

"They don't look as if they took things lying down. Perhaps there wasn't much to stand."

"But there was!"

"Do you mean she was rude to them?"

Travers' inward comment was that he had got her fairly going. It was clear that Merle had done something to arouse the woman's spite.

"I should say she was. Resented their knowing anything about her. When she bought the cottage and furnished it for that Miss Lane she wouldn't even ask them in to have a look at it."

"Perhaps she wanted to keep it as a surprise till it was ready."

"Not from everyone," said Ellen with a twisted smile. "Mr. Franklin knew pretty well what it was like."

"Why do you think that?"

"Because I have a friend who worked there. He had forgotten his tools and went back to fetch them."

"And what did he see?"

"That he didn't say exactly being most particular," said Ellen primly. "But it's my belief she bought it for a meeting place and gave it to Miss Lane as an afterthought. My friend said on several occasions he'd found two ashtrays full of cigarette ends."

"Perhaps Miss Lane——"

"No, it couldn't have been her, because Mrs. Leonard didn't let her go there till it was all ready. That I do know. Not that she wouldn't have connived I don't doubt if she'd been asked, and her dear friend had made it worth her while."

"Did the older Mrs. Holroyd know about this?"

"I hinted it to her when she was changing her dress the night of the Regatta, which was my duty."

"How did she take it?"

"She was very aloof as she often is, and pretended not to understand, but I think she knew already."

"Then you believe that Mrs. Leonard and Mr. Franklin——" began the Inspector in a shocked voice.

"Of course I do. She was always writing to him—almost every day. The letters lay on the hall table waiting to be posted."

"Then she didn't do it secretly?"

"No. She didn't care who knew."

"I wonder if Mr. Franklin wrote to her as often," mused the Inspector.

"No. Burton and I used to sort all the letters before I took up the early morning tea to my lady and Miss Ida. It wasn't often that I saw one in Mr. Franklin's handwriting."

Her voice trailed away as the door opened and Ida came in. She wore a short skirt and jumper and sensible shoes. She greeted Travers breezily as Ellen faded from the room.

"Well Inspector, I hope you won't keep me long. I am due for a round of golf and I am already late."

"No longer than I can help. I had your statement but I want to ask if you knew there had been a row between Mr. Holroyd and Mr. Franklin on the evening of the Regatta in Mrs. Denham's garden?"

Ida looked at him with frank eyes.

"My aunt mentioned it to me later."

"But you heard nothing of it at the time."

"Nothing whatever."

"You, too, walked in the garden before the fireworks began."

"Certainly, but not in the part near the boat-house."

"Then you were not with your aunt and cousin."

"For a short time, then we separated."

"What did you do after that?"

"I looked at the boats on the river, and spoke to some friends in a punt, then I went back to the party."

"Did you get there before Mrs. Holroyd or her son?"

Ida hesitated.

"I don't quite know when that was. I didn't meet them."

"Did you see anything of Mr. Franklin?"

"I thought I saw him in the distance, but I couldn't be sure. The light was poor, and I wasn't interested."

"Did you join any friends?"

"No, the chairs seemed full, and as I was wearing a thick coat I sat on the bank."

"When Mrs. Leonard Holroyd did not return that night didn't it seem strange that no enquiries were made as to the cause of her absence?"

"That was asked at the inquest," said Ida composedly, "but it didn't. My aunt told me of the row, and we agreed that Merle had gone off in a tantrum. She might have wanted to make us feel anxious."

"I gather that you did not care very much for your cousin's wife?" said the Inspector.

For a moment Ida's impassive face changed.

"No," she said, and that one word conveyed volumes.

A moment later her expression was as serene as ever.

"Is that all you want to ask me? "

"Yes, thank you. I won't keep you from your golf any longer."

The Inspector rode down the long avenue with a sensation that even the windows of Wissingham Abbey frowned on his receding back. He knew that he had not used the tact enjoined on him by his chief, but he had at least got further than he might have done had he followed Major Wrey's directions. When he had passed beyond sight of the lodge gates he halted and sat down under a tree on the common to think about what he had learnt in these various interviews. It was easier for him to take an unbiased view than for the Chief Constable, who could not believe that people like the Holroyds could be mixed up in a crime. Unlikely perhaps, thought Travers, as he considered their blameless record, but human nature has some queer corners, and one must face the fact that both mother and son had much to gain by the removal of Merle.

He took them in order. First Gideon. That quarrel must have been bitter. Now that it comes out that it was overheard they all admit it, reflected the Inspector as he lit his pipe, but it is difficult to check their movements for the next half-hour. Soon after half-past ten everyone went into the house. Gideon Franklin and the Holroyds agree about the time he left them with Merle. Probably it was about a quarter of an hour later that he said good night to Mrs. Denham, after which he returned to the garden and took the path to the stables. Or so he said. But did he go straight there? It wouldn't have been difficult to slip along the other path and rejoin Merle, and not unnatural if he had happened to see Leonard and his mother return to the fireworks party. Obviously he and Merle were lovers. It was likely that Gideon would want to know what had passed between her and the Holroyds after he left them together. The Inspector had formed a clear impression of Gideon's sentiments. Whatever he may have felt in the past his ardour had cooled. A broken hearted lover does not speak in that tone. It was possible that he feared discovery and might welcome the removal of what threatened his career. That will had been a queer one. Gideon's casual reply when it was mentioned had not deceived Travers. He was not the sort of man to be indifferent to money, and according to Miss Wiggins' statement he knew Merle was offended by something he had done, or more probably had omitted to do.

Then came Leonard. Was it a fact that he and Mrs. Holroyd returned together? Might he not have stayed behind to continue the quarrel? His alibi was his mother's story, and Travers judged that she would support her son in any circumstances. It seemed that no one had noticed Leonard at the fireworks, and even if he had accompanied Mrs. Holroyd he would have had time to slip back later, taking cover behind the shrubs.

Mrs. Holroyd herself could not be ruled out. Physically she was a big, strong woman and it was certain that she hated her daughter-in-law. They all had the opportunity to murder the poor girl, even Ida and Miss Wiggins, thought Travers, smiling a little as he remembered the fluttering little spinster. He decided that it was time he was getting on. By now the formidable Miss Lane might have acquired more disquieting details.

On the way through the village he stopped at the telephone office. There he heard that within a few minutes of his leaving Mr. Franklin that gentleman had tried to get through to Wissingham Abbey. Unfortunately, said the operator with a wink, the line was temporarily out of order.

"It might be put right now," said Travers grinning back as he got on to his motor bicycle.

He found Daria doing a sketch of her flower border. He studied her with attention as they walked back to the house. A good-looking young woman, but not the soft type that undertakes a thing and gives it up unfinished. She had a firm jaw and steady eyes. Brains, too. He remembered her lucid statement. She might be stirring up a lot of dust, and it might all come to nothing but there was no question as to her sincerity. Travers realized that neither the quarrel nor the motive provided actual proof, but he had a hunch that there was a lot more to learn.

"I have read your letter Miss Lane."

"I expect you think I am a meddlesome woman," said Daria.

"No, I don't. I feel much obliged to you. You have helped in two ways. First in finding the pearls and then getting to know about the quarrel."

"Then you *are* going to look into it," said Daria with a sigh of relief.

"Certainly, though you must be prepared for the difficulty in proving that the crime was done by anyone but Shadwell. If somebody else committed it he or she was lucky to have him at hand and seen close to the boathouse."

"I must just go on till we get the truth," said Daria simply. "If I hear anything that seems important may I come to you?"

"Please do." Travers smiled at her. "I find you very valuable. To begin with you live in the village and hear all the gossip."

"I don't myself, but my maid, Susan Harridge, has been helping. It was she who found Tommy Webb."

"Susan Harridge! I have just been having a talk with her sister."

"Ellen! She's a detestable woman, and totally different. She always hated Merle."

"So I gathered. Do you know why?"

"Yes. Merle caught her ferreting among her private papers, gave her a piece of her mind, and wanted her dismissed. But Leonard wouldn't back her as the girl was Mrs. Holroyd's personal maid. Ellen's story was that she had come to Merle's sitting-room with a message and found it empty. The window was open and some letters blew on to the floor and she was putting them back on the writing table. Mrs. Holroyd supported her. But Merle said there were no loose papers, and the letter she was reading should have been inside the drawer. There was an awful row. Merle always said she spied on her, and I think it was true. She detests me because I was Merle's friend, and she was furious when Susan came to me."

"Then the sisters don't get on?"

"No. She has always lorded it over her father and the rest of the family and tried to manage them. Susan says she gives herself airs on account of her position at the big house. She is a good servant, and Mrs. Holroyd and Ida find her invaluable."

"Everything you say gives the impression of perpetual discord between Mrs. Leonard Holroyd and her in-laws. You were there some weeks. Did you notice it all the time."

Daria told him this was so, and gave a full account of different incidents during her visit.

"Thanks, that's given me a clear picture," he said. "Not a pleasant one. Now I wonder if you can help me to find anyone who saw these people between the time of the quarrel and the finish of the fireworks. How about Mr. Franklin? Was anyone about when he fetched his car?"

"Yes," said Daria. "Susan told me so to-day. Mrs. Denham's chauffeur was in the yard when he came in."

The Inspector gave a nod of approval.

"Did you hear which way he came?"

"By the side gate through the garden. The chauffeur had been taking a peep at the fireworks through the trees and hurried back. He remembered the incident as he was surprised that anyone should leave so early."

"What about the time?"

"I am afraid he was vague. He thought the fireworks had not been on long, but first he said ten minutes and then twenty. He, too, noticed that Mr. Franklin looked very dishevelled."

"I'll have a talk to him. And now I think I must go and have a word with Miss Wiggins."

Daria put out a restraining hand.

"Just a moment, Inspector. Hadn't I better come, too? She's very nervous, and I can't think what she'll say when she sees the police."

Travers agreed and found that Daria was right. Miss Amelia, who had been regretting her confidences, nearly had a stroke when the purpose of the Inspector's visit was revealed.

"What *will* Honoria say? She has always warned me about letting my tongue run away with me."

Daria held her hand and patted it, and Travers used kindness and tact to extract the story. But though punctuated with bashful interludes it was exactly the same as she had told Daria.

"You won't let Honoria know I told you," wept poor Miss Amelia.

Daria walked with Travers to the gate.

"You're tremendously keen about this," he said studying her.

"Keener than about anything in the world," said Daria. "I have got to know who did it if it takes years."

CHAPTER XIII

"WON'T you join me?" said Ida Pelham-Reeve and she smiled upon Major Wrey.

She had just had a lesson with the professional at the Golf Club, and was about to order herself tea in a secluded corner of the Club House, and Major Wrey had come in to the room without seeing her.

His face brightened as he responded gratefully to the smile. He had been worried about the Holroyds' reactions to the recent enquiries and was afraid that it might cast a shadow over their friendship. This would have distressed him in any case but if it involved Ida he would think it disastrous. So when he saw her looking unusually handsome and waving a friendly greeting he became happier than he had been for some time.

"I should love to," he said warmly and rang for the waiter and ordered tea.

"We have seen nothing of you lately," said Ida in a tone of mild reproach.

"I wasn't sure——" Major Wrey found himself stammering—"It seemed rather difficult——"

"Only of your deputy," she continued, "and we could have dispensed with him."

"I know." Poor Major Wrey looked rueful. "I hated to think you were being bothered, but what could one do?"

"We could hardly believe it when he said you'd sent him," said Ida.

"But you must see that it was my duty. Private friendships can't weigh in a matter like that."

"I should have thought that my poor aunt and Leonard had been through enough."

"My dear girl, don't look at me as if I was a Spanish Inquisitor! You can't think I enjoyed sending Travers. And the dear Holroyds did blunder a bit when they suppressed that quarrel."

"It was foolish," conceded Ida, "but they were very sensitive about all that business with Gideon Franklin and I don't wonder."

"It may have been natural but it was very ill-advised. It was having concealed the quarrel that made it look suspicious, and when we were told about it we couldn't ignore it." He leant forward and said earnestly:—"Ida, don't look so worried. The Holroyds are my friends, too, and I'm as certain as you are that they had nothing to do with the murder, but I'm bound to investigate when I get information."

"I suppose the information came from Daria Lane," said Ida, and her lips tightened.

Major Wrey shook his head at her.

"I can hardly discuss that. In fact it is quite out of order that we should be talking this over. Now let's think of something pleasant. Tell me what you have been doing since I saw you last."

"I will in a moment but first you must answer one question. Do you think you will have to harry them any more? Do spare them as much as you can. My aunt is self-controlled but you don't know how she suffers."

"You are wonderfully devoted to them."

"But, of course. They have been my life. Everything that concerns them matters."

"Leonard's affairs as well as Mrs. Holroyds?" asked Major Wrey jealously.

"Naturally," she said calmly. "We were brought up together, and we were all happy until Leonard's marriage. When that girl came in to their lives everything changed. Money's overrated, I sometimes think."

"Well that's over now, and I promise you that they shall have as little trouble as I can help. But I can't disregard my duty even to please you, and Lord knows I'd do a lot for that," and Major Wrey laid a hand on hers. She did not withdraw it. She smiled on him as she said:—

"You are one of my best friends, and I know I can count on you."

Major Wrey was diffident where Ida was concerned, but it seemed a propitious moment to say more. The proposal that had been in his mind for some months was about to become a fact when an interruption occurred. Gideon Franklin came in with a Captain Yates with whom he had been playing golf, and as they had to pass close to the table where Ida and Major Wrey sat they stopped to greet them. While they were talking the door opened and the hall porter said—"Mr. Franklin is in here, Madam," and ushered in a lady.

Captain Yates moved away, as Gideon hurried forward followed by Ida's amused and inquisitive glance. Gideon's visitor filled the eye, for she was fair and fat and was dressed in pink. She wore a quantity of bracelets and rings, and Ida decided that she was five and forty. Snatches of conversation informed her that the lady had been asked to tea, and meant to drive Gideon home in her new Rolls Royce, on which she wanted his opinion.

They selected a table at the other end of the room and he leant towards her talking confidentially whilst Ida watched with a cynical smile. It was the same attitude that she had seen when he came to the Abbey on many occasions in the last year.

"Who is she? Do you know?"

"A Mrs. Hoskins. She took Welby Manor a few months ago."

"She gives the impression of riches," said Ida.

"Quite rightly. She is the widow of a newspaper proprietor. He owned the *Midland Mail,* and when he died he left it to her with all his other fortune. It has a big circulation."

"Well, well!" said Ida reflectively, "and how long has our friend known her?"

Major Wrey said he hadn't an idea.

"He must have a way with him," said Ida. "I wonder where his charm lies. However, I'm never likely to know as he won't exercise it on me. I've no money."

She laughed and got up.

"Must you go? It's so seldom that I get you to myself," pleaded Major Wrey, feeling that he had lost an opportunity.

But Ida, who preferred their friendship to remain as it was and had been well aware of his intentions, said that she was already late, and that her aunt expected her. He saw her off in the green Hispano that had been Merle's, and received a gay invitation to look them up soon as she drove away.

Ida seemed deep in thought, and her brows were drawn together in a frown. She had chosen to return by the side roads and presently came down the twisting lane by Jasmine Cottage, and saw the owner engrossed in tying a hollyhock to a stick. Ida applied the brake sharply, and Daria who was close by the gate heard the car stop and turned round. Her eyes fell on the familiar green car, and she flushed with a variety of emotions. Ida sat still, and studied her with a queer hostile expression. Daria put her hands on the top of the little gate and looked back at her.

"So it is you who have been stirring up the police," said Ida in a low furious voice. "What the hell are you doing it for?"

The clash was so sudden that for a moment Daria did not answer the challenge.

"Are you trying to deny it?" said Ida. "Well, I don't blame you for that. It isn't very pretty—to stop in people's houses, and then to spy on them and sneak about it."

"But I don't wish to deny it," said Daria quietly. "I *am* trying to find out who murdered Merle and when I heard about that quarrel I wrote to the police. I am going to get every bit of information that I can, and when I've got it I shall use it."

"There is nothing to use. All you can do is to stir up a muck heap—the muck heap that was of your friend's making."

At this reference to Merle Daria's temper flamed.

"How dare you speak of her like that!"

"I'm describing her as she was—a little vulgarian who came into a decent family and shamed it."

"It is the family who ought to be ashamed. She was tricked into the marriage when she was nineteen and not given a fair deal. She never had a proper home, and no friends but me. She supported her mother-in-law and you as well as her husband, and though you are all living on her money you haven't the decency to stop abusing her."

"No friends but you," said Ida with a disagreeable laugh. "Perhaps you are right. Gideon Franklin had got fairly sick of her by all accounts. Anyhow he seems to have consoled himself quickly, and I don't blame him."

"You may think you are better bred than she was," said Daria, "but I can't imagine Merle wreaking her spite on a dead woman. If she made mistakes the whole lot of you were to blame. If you had been kind at the start you could have done what you liked with her. She might even have given you a car!" Her glance dwelt on the Hispano. "But," she continued, "Leonard married her for her money, his mother interfered, and you sponged."

"Sponged!" Ida had grown white to the lips.

"Can you think of any other word for it?" said Daria whose rage was now primitive. "She detested you, and you knew it, but you stayed and stayed."

"You are insolent!"

"Possibly. But truthful."

"Then you intend to go on mischief-making and spying?"

"I intend to find out all I can. What is more it strikes me as curious that you are all anxious not to know what really happened."

"We do know."

"You may but I don't," said Daria, "so I'll go on till I'm satisfied."

For a moment Ida sat still staring in front of her, and Daria, whose anger had begun to subside, spoke more gently.

"You are devoted to the Holroyds. You take their side. Can't you see that I'm the same about Merle? I asked Mrs. Holroyd that question but she wouldn't answer. But you are young and ought to understand."

Ida did not reply. She did not even turn her head as she let in the clutch and the big car slid gently down the little incline. In another moment she had gone round the corner and was out of sight.

Daria sat down on the bench for her knees were shaking. What an unexpected scene, and what beastly things she had said! She had never suspected that it was in her to be so violent. Neither would she have believed it of Ida who as a rule was almost statuesque in her composure. It showed the condition of their nerves, a reflex from the dreadful events of a month ago, and was the result of brooding on horrors. She felt tired and miserably depressed. She made enemies and earned the disapproval of everyone. Was it wise to set herself against everybody's advice, or should she take the easier road and try to learn to forget? She turned towards the cottage that her friend had bought and furnished for her and as she went up the path her mind formed a vivid picture of Merle on the afternoon when she stood on the doorstep waiting to make her gift. She had looked gay and beautiful and full of vitality as she smiled her welcome. Twenty-one, foully murdered, and no one cared! The recollection supplied Daria with her answer.

• • • • •

It was whilst going down a few steps on the pier at Eastbourne that Miss Honoria Wiggins had the misfortune to fall heavily and turn her ankle. She was carried to her friend Mrs. Granby's house where she was staying, and put to bed. It was found that she had broken a small bone, and from here she sent a firm message to Miss Amelia to say that she was on no account to come. Mrs. Granby did not possess a second spare room, and it would be an unnecessary expense if Miss Amelia went into lodgings. Besides, added Miss Honoria unkindly, she would only be a nuisance if she kept fluttering in and out.

Miss Amelia came over in great distress to tell Daria, and was invited to come and stay for a week so as to take her mind off this agitating event. Miss Amelia accepted but she was still fussed. It seemed that Miss Honoria had promised to superintend the decorations at a big whist drive which was being given in order to raise money for repairs in the Church tower. She was always to be relied upon in village organisation and would be terribly missed, moreover she was exceedingly jealous if anyone else did her work. It seemed that though absent she was determined to retain control, and confused Miss Amelia by closely written pages of instructions which reduced her to the verge of tears. Daria studied the letter and took it to Mrs. Denham who was always ready to help. She read it, laughed, and said she would get all the ladies of the Committee together for a work party, and Daria must come too. She went off to make arrangements on the telephone, and presently returned.

"We have settled to have it in the barn to-morrow afternoon. That is the best plan as then we can measure the length of the wreaths on the spot. It is always a boring job, and however much trouble one takes the result is always horrid. I wish to goodness we had a better room. It is so inconvenient right out in the field with only a cart track up to it."

"I only went there once, and that was for the inquest," said Daria with a shiver at the recollection.

"Then you saw how unsuitable it is. Merle was very keen on giving us a new one."

"Perhaps Leonard will build one."

"Not he. He may have his wife's money, but he hasn't her disposition. Perhaps that's unfair of me since he never had enough in the past, and one can't expect everyone to be quixotically generous as she was."

"You are one of the only people who realized that about her," said Daria gratefully.

She was getting up to go but Mrs. Denham stopped her.

"Mrs. Holroyd came this morning. She says you and Ida had a quarrel."

"So we did."

"My dear, need you?"

"Ida said hateful things about Merle, and I was pretty offensive about all of them."

"Oh this dreadful business!" sighed Mrs. Denham.

"What did Mrs. Holroyd complain of?" said Daria trying to be patient.

"She says that horrible things are being said about them, and I'm afraid she thinks you are responsible."

Daria's face looked weary as she waited to hear more.

"It seems," continued Mrs. Denham, "that Harridge has been behaving tiresomely. She thinks you put him up to it. I told her it wasn't true, but she has got it firmly into her head."

"Harridge!" Daria was genuinely surprised. "What on earth has he been doing?"

"He talked in a foolish way at the Four Feathers. He was there two nights ago and seems to have hinted at something he knew. What he wouldn't say, but next day his daughter Ellen had a row with him about it, and he abused the Holroyds, and said you were the only lady he'd care to work for, and some day he was going to get even with the Abbey people."

"He has never said a word to me. What can he know? He was on the other side of the river during the fireworks."

"My dear, I don't suppose there was anything. He has a spite against Leonard, and there has been more friction lately. Something about an allotment. Leonard owns the ground, and wants to build a cottage just where Harridge had his plot. He has given him another quite as good, but Harridge isn't satisfied, so he talks a lot of nonsense."

"I will speak to him, and find out what it is all about."

"Yes, do, my dear. It is such a pity, and only makes mischief."

Daria questioned Susan that evening.

"Don't take any notice of father, Miss," she answered flushed with annoyance. "He just talks silly when he's put out and people have been standing him drinks. It means nothing. Ellen is fearfully upset. She fair went for him about it, asked if he wanted to lose her a good place, and he said she had no right to take a situation where people treated her father as they had. And Ellen said he was nothing but a disgrace to respectable folk, and couldn't keep a job. It's a worry the way those two scrap."

"I must speak to him about it."

Susan showed distress.

"Please don't, Miss, if you don't mind. It would only make him worse. Father's like that."

"But Susan I can't let it be unless I know what it is he hints. I wish you'd tell me."

"Only that he knows something more than he told at the inquest," said Susan reluctantly.

"What does he mean? Won't he tell you?"

"No, Miss, nor anyone else. He's got one of his obstinate fits. Unfortunately Robinson heard of it and went to see him, and you know how he feels about the police. After that all he'd say was that it had been a joke, and he knew nothing because there was nothing to know."

"But when he talked at the Four Feathers what was it that he implied? Had it anything to do with the quarrel?"

"Oh no, Miss. He just talked nonsense about something he had found in the punt."

"In the punt! Of course," said Daria reflectively, "he was the one who made the discovery."

"Now Miss, don't you get thinking there's anything in it. I don't believe he found a thing, except what he told us, the Regatta programme, the tea basket and cushions. He told me he'd been pulling their legs just to see what they'd say."

"I should feel much more certain of that if I had a talk with him."

"Well, Miss, if you must, you must, but if you take my advice you'll wait a few days. Father's that grumpy that you'd get nothing out of him, and he'd deny it flat. Maybe he'll be better tempered in a week's time if there's anything to tell, which I don't believe."

Daria always disliked delay, but Susan was a sensible girl and she understood her difficult family, so she decided to wait before seeing what she could do to wheedle Harridge.

CHAPTER XIV

IT was a hot afternoon and the ladies of the Committee sat at a long table making garlands and flowers of coloured paper so as to soften the austerities of their parish hall for the coming whist drive. This much abused place was part of a two-storied barn, of which the top had been converted into a room and the lower part was kept by Jenkins the farmer for his own use. It was constructed chiefly of timber and had some fine beams, but unfortunately the old lady who gave the floor and staircase had lined the walls with pitch pine. It had been impossible to find enough money to light or heat it satisfactorily, and it was either draughty or stuffy, and it was badly proportioned, as the end had been partitioned off to make a smaller room where refreshments could be prepared. For all these reasons the inhabitants of Wissingham disliked their hall, and said so loudly especially in muddy weather when they had to approach it by a muddy cart track.

But Miss Honoria Wiggins, who belonged to the pitch pine period, would never concede that the effect was unpleasing. The alterations had been made during the time her father was vicar, and with his approval, and that sufficed, and she considered that paper wreaths accompanied by Union Jacks made a decoration that was appropriate and tasteful. So she sketched a plan indicating where to hang the flowers and flags respectively, and looked to her neighbours to carry it out, and Daria as she snipped and cut looked about her, and thought what an odd collection had got together, and wondered what was going on in their minds.

Mrs. Holroyd sat at the end of the table. She wore the deep black she had assumed since Merle's death. Her face looked strained, and she had aged in the last weeks. Undoubtedly she found it objectionable to sit in the same room with Daria, but she had included her in a civil bow when she came in. Then in the royal fashion that she assumed she had signed to Mrs. Denham to come next to her, and invited the vicar's wife to occupy the seat on her other side. Mrs. Edwardes, the doctor's wife, Miss Amelia Wiggins and two other neighbours snipped and measured. Amongst the others sat Ida. Her strong fingers moved rapidly twisting the garlands into place. She was far more skilful than the rest, and her wreath double the length. Her face was bent over her work. It looked so calm as almost to be devoid of expression. It seemed strange to think that the last time Daria had seen it it had been convulsed with rage. She had taken no notice of Daria as she came into the room. But, with the exception of Mrs. Denham and Miss Amelia, Daria knew that she was an unpopular figure in that gathering. Mrs. Holroyd's fiat had gone forth, and she was undisputed ruler in Wissingham.

It had been an effort to come to this place which she associated with the inquest, and brought back the subject that was never far from her thoughts. That morning she had been to Ridgenorth, and had gone to see Inspector Travers, for she wanted his opinion about Harridge's outburst at the Four Feathers. Travers received her kindly, but the Chief Constable had been at him for lack of tact in his enquiries, and he feared Daria's zeal might have to be curbed. So he told her that he thought Susan's advice to leave the old man alone till he had had time to calm was wise. Since Robinson had made his report he did not take Harridge's hints seriously.

"He seems a vain sort of man, Miss Lane, and always has a grievance. I'm inclined to think all that talk was just a bid to attract attention. You will remember that when he was asked at the inquest if he had found anything besides what he shewed us he denied it emphatically. The daughter's right. He feels spiteful, and has taken that way of showing it."

Daria asked if the Inspector had learnt anything more that bore on the case, but he answered evasively and she went out feeling as if they had careered down a road, and found it a cul-de-sac. But the morning had not been wasted, for when she met Miss Amelia by arrangement outside the local library she heard that that lady's flair for news had brought in a fresh harvest.

Miss Amelia had come to Ridgenorth to buy a hat, and presently had a cream bun and a cup of coffee at the Chinz Tea Rooms, a treat without which her shopping was never complete. There she had met Mrs. Leith, an old friend. The two ladies had joined forces, and during their morning coffee Mrs. Leith began to tell Miss Amelia about Mrs. Hoskins who had recently taken her sister's house for three months. The sister, Mrs. Debenham had not wished to let, but it seemed that this Mrs. Hoskins had set her mind on the place, and although Welby Manor was very old-fashioned had offered a colossal rent which in these hard times could not be refused.

"How lucky for Myrtle Debenham," said Miss Amelia.

"Yes. The woman seems made of money. She has put in the telephone and a new bath, and installed an electric refrigerator and a super wireless."

"I should have thought Highfield Towers would have suited her. It has got all those things."

"It wouldn't," chuckled Mrs. Leith. "It had one disadvantage."

"What's that?" asked Miss Amelia, scenting something exciting.

"It's not close to Gideon Franklin."

Miss Amelia settled down joyfully to hear details. It seemed, according to local gossip, that Gideon had met the lady in London during the winter, and from the first moment she had felt his attraction. This had been powerful enough to make her pursue him to the country, where she had arrived a fortnight ago. Since then, continued Mrs. Leith, she had been in and out of his house morning, noon and night. If he went to town Mrs. Hoskins chose the same day and drove him up and down in one of her big cars. Three she had, and two chauffeurs. One wondered if it would end in an engagement. And indeed why not, since Gideon was not well off, and the lady seemed more than willing.

"Certainly why not?" agreed Miss Amelia, but she felt a little doubtful because if it had been Mr. Franklin she had heard in that conversation behind the bushes then surely he and poor Merle . . . but she reminded herself that Merle was a married woman so she was probably mistaken, at least she hoped so, and this seemed to prove it.

She poured all this out to Daria during their return journey, and Daria thought about it as she worked. It seemed important because it seemed to put Gideon among the suspects. Until then she had not liked to dwell on him because she was bitterly prejudiced. She was so sure that Merle's lover did not experience regret at her death. More probably relief. She had always thought he had as much opportunity as anyone to slip back and do the murder. The period between the time of the quarrel and his saying good night to Mrs. Denham would have been ample if he had hidden himself and watched the Holroyds go and had then joined Merle.

But the will had been a point in his favour, for by killing Merle he would have done away with his chance of getting her money since it was not signed. But, thought Daria, supposing he realized that Merle would tear it up if he did not proclaim himself as her lover? Gideon liked money, but mainly as a help to his career and that would be non-existent if she had had her way. Now it appeared that there had been an alternative,—a lady who was not only rich but the possession of whose money meant no sacrifice since she was free to marry.

Merle had said she would never let him go, and Gideon would know this was no idle threat. She had that streak of recklessness that had given the Holroyds trouble. If roused she had been indifferent to exposure. If this intimacy with Mrs. Hoskins had been growing and his former affair had become a weariness, Gideon might have felt that the blaring forth of the truth would end his chances and that he would never be secure while Merle lived. Daria thought that her attention had been too diffused, and that from now on she would concentrate on Gideon until she felt satisfied in her own mind of his guilt or innocence.

But as her thought revolved she felt puzzled by the Holroyds' attitude. They had every reason to loathe Gideon, so if they suspected him why should they be opposed to enquiries? Daria, like Travers, believed that Mrs. Holroyd knew more than she had told. It might be simply the dislike of being involved in further publicity,—just a desire to close a door on an unpleasant episode, and let justice take care of itself. She glanced towards the end of the table where Mrs. Holroyd seemed engrossed in what she was doing. No one would think that any act of violence had ever come near her life. Daria sighed, and was recalled from the problem by Mrs. Denham's voice rising plaintively above the gentle murmur of conversation.

"We shan't finish the wreaths to-day, much less hang them. What's to be done?"

"The whist drive is on Thursday, so that only gives us to-morrow," said Mrs. Edwardes, "but I'm afraid I can't manage to come again."

Neither it appeared could the other ladies. Mrs. Holroyd said with truth that she had passed the age for hanging wreaths, three of the others were going to a garden fête, the two village women who had been included on the Committee had their week's shopping to do in Ridgenorth as it was the cheap day.

"Oh dear, oh dear!" moaned Miss Amelia, and looked round appealingly. "It's dreadful! I can't manage it alone. Ida, won't you help us?"

"I have engagements all day I'm afraid," said Ida crisply.

"Can't Jenkins hang the things up if there is someone here to direct him?" said Mrs. Holroyd. "He is usually very obliging."

"No. Jenkins has to go to Munchester to-morrow to see his wife. It is visiting day at the hospital."

Poor Miss Amelia looked as if she was going to cry, and Daria who had planned a day's sketching came to the rescue.

THE PUNT MURDER 117

"I'll come," she said.

"Oh, my dear, how sweet of you! I shall be grateful."

"We'll lunch early and get here by two," said Daria.

Mrs. Holroyd rose and the others followed her example and were putting the completed wreaths on one side when Leonard came in. He had been over to see a neighbour and said the car was waiting for his mother.

" I brought Giles so he can drive you. I have had no exercise so I'll walk. What are you doing, Ida?"

"I'd like to walk too," said Ida.

Mrs. Holroyd offered a lift to Mrs. Denham, Miss Amelia, and Mrs. White and moved away. Mrs. Denham lingered to thank Daria.

"I feel very bad about not coming to help, but I have a cousin arriving for the day. Don't forget that you and Miss Amelia are dining with me tomorrow night. I have had a line from Martin who says he'll manage to get down."

"Of course we won't forget. We are both looking forward to it."

"Are you coming?" said Mrs. Holroyd who was standing in the doorway.

"Lock the door when you go out and leave the key on the window sill under that loose brick," said Mrs. Denham, and all the others went out and Daria was left alone to put some finishing touches to the work and tidy up.

It was nearly half an hour before she had done, and on the way home she decided to call in at a farm on the Holroyds' land that supplied her with eggs and butter. At the farmhouse she was told that Mrs. March was in the dairy and went across the yard to look for her. Failing to find her she looked into several of the large outhouses which were empty and went towards a barn which was used as a shelter for the carts. The door was ajar and as she came in out of the brilliant sunshine she could see nothing. Then as her eyes grew accustomed to the dimness she saw two people were sitting on the shaft of a cart and realized that she had intruded on a love idyll. They were in each other's arms, and in their preoccupation had not noticed her entrance. In her haste to go Daria stumbled over a piece of wood, and the man jumped up. It was Leonard Holroyd, and the girl who remained seated was Ida.

They looked at each other, anger on their faces, disgust on hers, then Daria went out without a word. Half-way across the yard she met Mrs. March hurrying to meet her. She gave her order and went off quickly in an instinctive desire to get as far as possible from what she had seen. All pretence of affection between Merle and Leonard had ceased, so perhaps it was unreasonable to feel as she did, but she had been dead such a short time, and he had been her husband and had benefited by her fortune. Good taste if nothing else should have imposed an interval before he started to make love to another woman. But as she walked a different idea came to her. Was this business between himself and Ida new? Small incidents that she had scarcely noticed at the time came back to her, Leonard's expression as he looked at Ida across the dinner table, their partnership in games, evenings when they had walked in the garden discussing the colour schemes of the flower beds. She remembered a day when she had come into the picture gallery, and they had moved apart and looked confused, and she thought of the hot afternoon when Leonard had rushed off in his car to save Ida the discomfort of a train journey. Unimportant things when taken separately, but taken together they confirmed what she had already seen.

She had an evening alone as Miss Amelia was dining at the Vicarage, and early next afternoon she and the old lady set off for the barn to finish the work of decoration. Daria got the steps so as to hang the wreaths, and then joined Miss Amelia who was working at the long table.

"You have lived here a long time," she said, "I expect you know every mortal thing that has ever happened in Wissingham."

"Well, I'm not unobservant," said Miss Amelia sedately, "though I daresay I should hear more if Honoria wasn't so strict about gossip. I do think that rule of hers cuts one off from a lot of pleasure. It is so nice to discuss one's neighbours."

"Do break it now. I want to know a lot of things that happened before I came here. Especially about the Holroyds."

"What can I tell you? I have known them all my life. Why I remember Mr. and Mrs. Holroyd when they first married. I thought them such a handsome pair. But he died two years later. It was very difficult for her to keep the place going, and we admired her so much. She denied herself in every way to save it for Leonard. For some years she lived in a corner of the house and didn't even have a carriage. And she was young and good looking and might have married again, but she felt the place and family had been left in her charge by her husband, and sacrificed her life to it."

"I see. That makes it easier to understand her point of view, also why she did not get on with Merle."

"I often thought that if Merle had had a son it would have drawn them together," said Miss Amelia, whose mind worked sentimentally.

Daria, who recollected Merle's ideas, thought otherwise. She could imagine bitter disputes over the upbringing and education of the heir to Wissingham Abbey.

"Was there any talk about Leonard and Ida? Did people ever think they might marry?"

"Oh yes, dear, we all did," said Miss Amelia placidly. "Naturally that was before he fell in love with your friend, but he and Ida were inseparable. The summer and winter before he married we expected an announcement any day. But we must have been wrong and they felt more like brother and sister, which was natural as the Abbey had been like a home to her."

"Do you think the fact that she had no money had anything to do with it."

"It may have. I know Mrs. Holroyd sent her away that spring, and she made Leonard come up with her and stop with relations in London, and that is how he met Merle who was being chaperoned by Mrs. Holroyd's cousin."

"I wonder if Ida minded."

"I don't know, but she used to be much gayer, and after that she changed. She seemed to get so hard."

"If that's so I wonder that she cared to come back to the house."

Miss Amelia sighed.

"She was a great help to her aunt, and perhaps she couldn't keep away. Not that that isn't a wicked thought of mine, for Leonard was married, and of course there could be no question of anything between them."

Daria got on the ladder and began to hang her festoons of paper.

"Is that how Miss Honoria wanted it done?"

"Yes, just like that. How clever you are, dear."

They worked for a few minutes in silence, then Miss Amelia said reflectively.

"The Chief Constable seems to think a lot of Ida. Have you noticed that?"

Daria said she had. She had been inclined to think that something might come of it eventually, but yesterday had shown her that the feeling was solely on his side. She wondered if Leonard and Ida would marry. With Merle's fortune at his disposal he could do as he chose.

"Major Wrey is a good bit older, but Ida is a serious-minded girl," continued Miss Amelia. She took up another wreath. "This is the last," she said joyously. "Everything will be finished in another two hours thanks to you. I'm so grateful."

Daria went off to drape the flags on the platform at the end of the hall according to the plan that Miss Honoria had drawn out for their guidance. She thought it ugly and was bored. Her only consolation was that it would have, been an unpleasant day for sketching, sultry and with a strong wind. She went into the small room at the back to sort the wreaths that had been stored there after the work party, and remained there about twenty minutes. When she returned to the hall she noticed that the door at the end was shut and supposed Miss Amelia had felt the draught from the staircase.

"It seems very airless," she said. "Do you mind if I open another window?"

"Do my dear."

Daria struggled with a cord. The windows were placed high up in the slope of the roof, and could only be opened in this way. Like in churches, thought Daria crossly, wrestling vainly as the window stuck. She gave it up and went to put away some of the things in the room behind. As she came back Miss Amelia called to her.

"Daria, don't you smell burning?"

"Yes, that's funny!" said Daria sniffing. "Jenkins must have made a bonfire in the yard, though I don't remember noticing it when we came in."

"Very careless of him as he was going out. I mean in this dry weather one oughtn't to leave a fire, especially with so much wood about."

Daria came down the hall. The bonfire must be a big one for she could see smoke drifting past one of the windows.

"I'll have a look outside," she said, and went to the door and turned the handle.

She pulled and rattled it without result, then bent and examined the keyhole. The door was locked on the outside, and she could see the key.

"But that's impossible! We left it open when we came in and I put the key back under the brick on the window sill."

"Are you sure?"

"Certain."

"I remember that I heard a slight noise, but I had my back to it and didn't turn." Miss Amelia had got up and joined her. "But I don't understand," she added in puzzled tones, "anyone who came up the stairs would have seen me."

"We must get out," said Daria quickly, for by now a crackling sound was audible, and the smoke was beginning to creep under the door.

She put a ladder against one of the windows and climbed up.

"Do be careful, dear," said Miss Amelia who had not yet grasped the significance of what was happening. "You might fall."

Daria could see enough to terrify her. A pile of wood that leant against the wall below was a sheet of flame, and she realized from the fierceness of the heat that was beginning to reach them that the staircase was already burning. Thus even if they were able to force the door their way of escape was cut off. And it was the only entrance. It flashed across Daria's mind that she had heard this was one of the many reasons why Wissingham wanted a new hall, but though a second staircase was necessary no-one wished to spend money if the place was to be given up eventually. She tried to keep from panic which is the easiest thing to give way to when faced by death from fire. Their chances seemed slight. The timbers were old and dry, the walls were pitch pine, Jenkins and his wife were away, she in hospital, he visiting her. There remained the hope that someone might see the blaze, but there was a thick clump of trees between them and the farm, and when she arrived she had noticed the labourers were working in a field on the other side of the hill. They were trapped.

Daria ran down the room into the small one beyond where there was a window. This had been put in to give more light and was on an ordinary level from the floor. Unfortunately it was on the side of the building that was burning. The direction of the wind drove the flames along that wall of the barn and had left the other side untouched. The window was shut and hard to open. Daria lost some moments wrestling with the bolt and the sash which had stuck, but at last she managed to lift it, and craned out. Nearly six feet below was a ledge, beyond that a long drop to the ground. It seemed impossible to think of lowering Miss Amelia, but it had to be attempted. She began a frantic search in the cupboards. At the back of a lot of rubbish she found a short cord, which in itself would be useless. She tore down the flags and started tearing them in strips and knotting them together.

Miss Amelia joined her, but one glance showed Daria that she could not be expected to help. The poor little lady had realized the truth, and her terror was pitiable. Daria told her to wave a flag from the window, but it was more to prevent her from collapsing than from any hope of being seen. The glare and heat increased, part of the floor of the room behind them was now on fire. Daria felt that soon they would be overcome by the fumes, and went on knotting with feverish haste. Stray thoughts came into her mind. Of Martin, and how Mrs. Denham expected them to dinner,—dear Martin to whom she had never been really kind because of the quest that engrossed her. And now she would never succeed in it, and never know if she had been right.

She tied the last knot and jumped up choking with the smoke. She pushed the heavy table against the window, and tied the improvised rope to a leg, and began to fasten the other end round Miss Amelia's waist. At its fullest extent it would still be short of the ground.

"I'm going to lower you, and when you get to the end of the rope you must cut the cord and drop. It is only a little way really. Then you must get away as far as you can from the building."

But Miss Amelia moaned and closed her eyes.

"I can't do it,—I can't!"

"You've just got to," said Daria.

"No, I'm old and useless. You go."

"Don't be silly." Daria tested the rope. "Now let me hoist you on the table. Shut your eyes, and trust me to lower you."

"I can't,—I can't! I never could stand heights."

Daria had a moment of despair. She doubted if she had the force to compel her, and if she still refused they must both die. For she could not leave her, and life suddenly became of immense value, full of happiness and promise, a thought she had not had since Merle's death.

"I shan't go and you'll kill us both if you don't try. Pull yourself together," she said, and shook the old lady.

Whether Miss Amelia had the moral force to respond she never knew for a faint sound reached her above the roar of the flames. It was a voice. She leaned out of the window and saw the figure of a man running across the field and waved. He gave a reassuring wave, but disappeared round the other side of the building. With a rush of thankfulness but no surprise Daria realized that it was Martin. In a few moments he came back dragging a short ladder which he propped against the wall.

The sight of him and the prospect of rescue had given Daria force. She lifted and pushed Miss Amelia on to the table, and propelled the almost fainting figure off the window sill. To lower her gently was a frightful strain, and Daria wondered if the flags would give way. Martin who was on the top of the ladder caught Miss Amelia and guided her feet on to the rungs. But she was as inanimate as a dummy and he was

THE PUNT MURDER

obliged to carry her most of the way and this made the progress slow. At the bottom he had to stop and undo the knots round her waist as she had dropped the knife.

In the room above the roaring had grown louder, and the flames were licking their way along the rafters. The time seemed endless before Martin shouted to Daria to pull up the rope. As he began to climb up the ladder he was aware of distant shouts and knew that others had seen what was happening, but it seemed doubtful if they would be in time. Daria was almost suffocating but made a supreme effort to tie the rope round her and climb on to the sill. The walls were hot, and burning fragments were falling. It was a matter of seconds. She was barely conscious when Martin drew her on to the ladder, but at the moment he grasped her there was a crash above as the wall between the two rooms fell and the rope that held her was burnt through by the licking flames. Still supporting her, Martin half slithered and half fell in the descent, but several of the labourers had reached the scene and dragged them into safety. Daria, whose arm was burnt and who was suffering from shock fainted, and Martin who did not know the extent of her injuries hung over her in an agony of mind. A few minutes later the local fire-engine appeared as a man who had seen the blaze had rushed to the village to give the alarm.

The rapidity with which crowds materialize has often been remarked. The inhabitants of Wissingham were soon grouped in the field with their old and young. Leonard Holroyd strolled up with a gun on his arm. Daria when she opened her eyes was vaguely surprised to see such a lot of people in a place where only twenty minutes ago she had looked despairingly on empty fields. There, too, was Gideon Franklin who said he had been driving by and had seen the smoke.

The doctor was ministering to Miss Amelia and had brought up his car to take her and Daria away. Martin bent over Daria.

"Darling, you're safe! My God, when I think of it!"

"I'm all right now." Daria smiled though she was white with pain. "Come in and see me later, Martin, dear."

Mrs. Denham now appeared. She had heard the news in the village. She was always to the fore when there was trouble and took forcible possession of both Miss Amelia and Daria. She thought they would need more nursing than Susan could give and she put them to bed in her own house. Some time later Martin was allowed to go in and see Daria who had asked for him. She lay back against the pillows, and though she was still pale and shaky she looked happy. He kissed her unbandaged hand, and held it in both of his.

"My dearest," he said softly.

"Martin, it was wonderful of you to come. How was it? Did you catch an earlier train?"

"I had an overwhelming longing to see you," said Martin soberly. "I often have it, but this time I gave way to it. I thought I might get an hour with you at the cottage before you dressed, and could bring you to dinner in my car. When I got there Susan said that you and Miss Amelia were in the barn, and she was sure you'd like help with the decorations so I came along."

Daria looked at him. Something in her expression gave him courage to bend over and kiss her.

"I do love you, Daria."

"I'm glad," said Daria, and Martin went downstairs looking radiant.

CHAPTER XV

AFTER dinner Martin got permission to look in and say good night. Daria who was now less dazed had a puckered forehead.

"I have been thinking things over," she said. "I can't understand how it happened."

"Try not to think about it at all, darling. You are safe, that's all that matters."

"But I can't help thinking. How did that door get locked?"

"What door?" said Martin, who had not heard anything of the story.

"The only door there was. Merle always said that was dangerous in case of fire. They discussed it at dinner one night at Wissingham when she said she was going to build a new hall. Merle said she hated going to village entertainments because it gave her a claustrophobia feeling. Mrs. Holroyd said she let her imagination run away with her. She always opposed what Merle said, but she turned out to be right."

"Still," said Martin, "I don't see what you mean about the door. You came in by it."

"And left it open."

"I suppose it slammed with the wind. There was a regular gale."

"No, it didn't. It closed quietly. Miss Amelia who was sitting with her back to it thought she heard a slight noise. When we smelt smoke I went to the door because I wanted to look into the yard, and it was locked."

"It must have jammed."

"I don't think so. It was an easy door to open. Also the key was in the lock."

"Wouldn't it have been there anyhow?"

"No. After we went in I took the key out and put it on the shelf under the loose brick where Jenkins kept it. I don't know why, but I just did."

"But anyone who came upstairs would have seen you were inside," objected Martin.

"Yes, that's what we said."

She was looking very tired and strained, and he got up.

"Well, don't bother your head about it, darling. We'll find the explanation."

Martin met his mother on the landing. She had just been in to Miss Amelia's room to give a sedative prescribed by Doctor Edwardes. The old lady had escaped without burns but her nerves were much upset. It seemed, said Mrs. Denham, that she too was puzzling over the mystery of the locked door.

After a moment's thought Martin went to the telephone and called up Inspector Travers. The constable on duty said the Inspector was in his own house, but could be fetched, and after a short pause Martin heard his voice.

Martin asked if he knew about the fire.

"I heard a few minutes ago,—the village hall, wasn't it?"

"Yes. Miss Lane and Miss Wiggins were inside, and might have lost their lives. They think they were locked in. This may be explainable but——"

"I'll come over at once," said the Inspector.

Martin went to meet him. The firemen had done their duty well and the flames were extinguished, but two men had been left on duty to watch the smouldering remains. The night was overcast and the wind had dropped.

"It is too dark to see anything," said Travers, "and in any case the place is too hot to examine. It looks as if we were going to get rain, and if so it will help to cool it. I'll be over early."

He told the men to keep everyone away till he came back in the morning.

"And after that I'd like a talk with Miss Lane, that's to say if she is up to it, and if you'll take my advice you'll get some rest yourself," he added. "You look about done in."

The rain he had prophesied started within half-an-hour, and it poured all night. Travers was delayed by a case of burglary and arrived later than he had intended. As he approached across the fields the results of the fire were clearly visible. The left side of the building had been completely destroyed, but the right wall was almost intact on account of the strong wind that had driven the flames the opposite way. As he got nearer he saw that the front and most of the staircase had been burnt away, but a bit of the landing and the three top stairs remained. So did the door which was on the extreme right close to the undamaged wall. But as he bumped over the rough ground the Inspector saw something that made him exclaim in annoyance. Jenkins and two other men were engaged in hoisting a ladder against the part that was still standing and Leonard Holroyd stood beside them.

Richardson, one of the men who had been left to guard the place, came towards him.

"What the devil do they think they're doing? I gave orders that nothing was to be touched."

"The Squire's orders, sir," said Richardson. "He owns this land."

Leonard turned at the sound of their voices,, and Travers came up to him.

"Having a look round, sir? It seems a bit dangerous. The place must be properly gutted."

"Good morning, Inspector. Yes, this is a bad business. It is my property, and it is lucky it is insured. I want to see the extent of the damage, but I fear the whole wall will have to come down."

"It looks like it," said the Inspector. "Has the Insurance agent come?"

"Not yet, but he should be down any time now. He comes from London."

"I see." Travers tested the ladder. "Those boards feel fairly secure."

"That's what I thought. It was lucky that the rain came when it did. It has cooled things down."

"Have you any idea how the place caught fire? "

"None. Of course, everything was bone dry, and there was a lot of wood lying about. A stray match might have done it."

Travers turned to Jenkins.

"You had not been burning rubbish?"

"No," said Jenkins, "nothing at all."

He went on to say that he had not been near the barn since the day before the fire, and before he took the train for Munchester had been down in the fields with his men.

"A tramp might have come along, lit his pipe, and thrown the match near the woodstack."

"Even so it's queer," mused the Inspector, "because the ladies didn't see any smoke when they came in and they had to pass it." He laid hold of the ladder, "I'll go up and have a look," he said.

Leonard did not seem pleased. It was clear that he thought Travers' visit unnecessary, but as he had begun to mount the rungs there was nothing to be done. There was always the possibility that the boards of the landing would give. Leonard looked as if this mishap would cause him no sorrow.

"I don't think that's safe," he called.

Travers was quite sure he was right, but he persisted, giving thanks meanwhile that he was lightly built. It might be risky but he meant to forestall other people's investigations. He reached the top of the ladder, and stepped with extreme caution on to the boards. His objective was the door. He moved towards it, bent and examined it. The key was in the keyhole and the door was locked. He remained beside it for nearly five minutes.

"You seem to be taking your time up there?" called Leonard impatiently.

"I'll soon be done," said Travers amiably as he looked about.

He had withdrawn the key, putting it away with the utmost care, then having decided that there was nothing else to find he went gingerly towards the ladder and regained the ground.

"The match needn't have been dropped by a tramp," said Leonard. "Miss Lane smokes."

"Quite so, sir," said Travers, and started round the outside of the building.

Jenkins came up to say the Insurance agent had just come and Leonard went to meet him. Travers poked about among the debris, but found chiefly charred wood, still smouldering. But presently he reached part of the barn that was underneath the right side of the parish room and found it untouched. In this Jenkins kept a certain amount of lumber, and also used it for a garage for his Ford car. Travers made a careful survey. He found three tins of petrol, two of them empty. He prowled round the remains of the wood pile, pocketed a match, and a small piece of newspaper, and further on a fragment of cotton waste which he smelt several times. After a time he was joined by the Insurance agent, a round-faced, breezy young man. In the distance Leonard could be seen taking a short cut home across the fields.

Travers called Jenkins and asked him if the petrol tins had been full or empty.

"Full," said Jenkins promptly. "I got in this supply on Monday and left them there. I meant to use the old bus yesterday when I went to the hospital, but didn't because I'd got a flat tyre, and hadn't time to see to it."

"Do you think this belonged to you?" said Travers, and pulled out the cotton waste.

Jenkins said he had some like that, and he used it for polishing the car. He kept it in a box in the corner of the shed. They went to the box and found it empty.

"What's your opinion?" said the Insurance agent confidentially as they made another tour of the ruin. "Personally I don't like the look of it. I know it was dry and there was a wind, but why did it burn so quickly? It looks as if the fire had started close to the outer door by that pile of wood, and you say two ladies were inside. If the place was smouldering they would have noticed it when they came in. Though of course if one of them had dropped a lighted match there would have been a terrible draught up those stairs with the wind that way."

Travers' answer was non-committal. He did not mention the locked door, and thought he would go and see Daria and get her account before returning to have another look round. She might have things to tell that might help him.

Mrs. Denham admitted the Inspector with reluctance. Daria was her patient, she was inclined to be feverish, and must not be excited. But she had to give way, and Travers was shewn up to Daria's bedside. She could not tell him much. She and Miss Amelia had walked to the barn after lunch. They had started later than had been intended, as at the last moment they had decided to take tea in a basket as they meant to stay till everything was finished. They got there between half-past two and a quarter to three. They had seen no one except the labourers in the field beyond the hill. They settled down to work and about three quarters of an hour later Daria found the door shut, but had not heard it close. She was positive that she had not left the key in the lock. She described the events of the fire.

"Did you smoke going across the fields or as you went in?"

"I do smoke, but I didn't take my cigarettes that afternoon."

The Inspector said he would step in and have a word with Miss Amelia.

Miss Amelia was flustered at receiving a man who was not a doctor in her bedroom, but when she had got over this she was anxious to talk. Her account was punctuated with exclamations and confused, but Travers got the impression that she enjoyed giving it. And he was right, for the new experience of being in the centre of the picture instead of an unimportant detail in the corner had rather gone to Miss Amelia's head. But from the wealth of detail Travers gleaned these facts. She had sat at the end of the table near the door and was absorbed in her task of joining the wreaths together. The wind outside had made a good deal of noise rattling the loose plaster in that old building. On thinking it over she had had the impression that the stairs had creaked, and once she thought she heard a footstep. She remembered this because it had made her wonder if one of the other ladies on the Committee had managed to come along after all. It was a little later that she had heard that click. She now supposed it was the key being turned.

Travers asked if by chance she had smoked a cigarette.

"So many ladies do," he said apologetically in answer to Miss Amelia's look of horror.

"Indeed, no. I may be old-fashioned, but it is a habit I dislike. I can assure you, Inspector, that I have never done such a thing in all my life. My dear Father. . . ."

Travers returned to Daria.

"Who knew that you would be at the barn that afternoon?" he asked.

"Crowds of people. It had been mentioned the day before to the whole work party. Mrs. Edwardes, Mrs. Holroyd, Ida, Mrs. White and Mrs. Denham, also Mrs. Brown and Mrs. Sykes from the village. Leonard Holroyd came in and probably heard it, and Jenkins knew and left us the key to get in. Susan Harridge got our tea ready."

"And any of those might have spoken of it casually to others," commented the Inspector.

He went off thoughtfully and returned to the scene of the fire to examine the lay of the land. The only house from where the conflagration would have been visible was the farm, and the Jenkins' were both away. The field was approached by a lane, but anyone could have come down the path through the wood without being seen. The field had been trampled by people who had come to see the fire. There were marks of several cars as well as the fire engine.

Travers went to see the labourers who had been working in the fields that afternoon. They had seen no one. Martin's shouts had been their first news of the fire, and then one of them had rushed off on his bicycle to give the alarm, and the others had run towards the barn. But one added that Squire had been out after rabbits. Possibly he might have come on somebody.

"I'll ask him," said Travers.

"Whoever did it," he mused as he rode back to Ridgenorth, "must have had a good reason for removing those two. And it was well planned. With the petrol at hand and the newspapers it wouldn't take long to light. If it hadn't been for the wind it might have passed as an accident. No one could have calculated on its driving the flames as it did right away from the door. But it was a bad break to leave the key in the lock. It looks as if our friend had lost his head."

When he got to his office he took the scrap of paper from his pocket book.

"Find out where this comes from, Wills," he said, "what newspaper and what date. You may get what you want at the public reading room."

He gave a list of names of people whose movements interested him, with instructions to check their doings throughout the day of the fire, mentioning in particular those who had come into prominence on the evening of Merle's death. By the following morning his subordinate had discovered that the fragment of newspaper had been torn from a copy of *The Times* five days old. This might or might not be of help. Enquiries at the village shop showed that in Wissingham, a Conservative district, *The Times* was supplied to practically all the gentry, whilst the poorer people took other papers, but, thought Travers, because you burn an old newspaper does not mean that it is necessarily the one you read.

For the next two days the Inspector was hard at work, and was far from pleased with the result. He went in to see the Chief Constable who had just returned from a visit in Dorsetshire and had not heard what had happened. He was listened to with considerable irritation.

"Really, Inspector, you mustn't let your imagination run away with you. A barn gets burnt after a spell of dry weather and you see a would be murderer lurking behind every bush."

"I'm sorry, sir," said the Inspector stiffly.

"No, no. You are quite right, but do you really think there is any connection between this and the punt murder?"

"I do sir. I think someone would find it convenient if Miss Lane was out of the way."

"I can't think why. I am sure if she had anything to tell us she would have done so long ago. Don't you agree?"

"Yes, I do."

"Then how can she be a danger? People don't attempt murder without some reason," said Major Wrey testily.

Travers produced a list.

"If you'd have a glance down this sir," he said.

Major Wrey took it.

"Gideon Franklin," he read. "He came into Wissingham during the afternoon, and left his car in the village, and went to call on Henry, the secretary of the Conservative Association. It seems incredible that our respected Member should burn down a barn. However, if he was with Henry he would have been nearly a mile away."

"He wasn't with Henry. Henry was playing in a cricket match at Yewden. Mr. Franklin called at the house and found him out."

"What did he do next?"

"He says he went for a stroll, but no one saw him between three and four o'clock when he turned up at the fire."

"H'm," said Major Wrey, and glanced at the next name on the list. "Mr. Holroyd was walking in the fields with his gun," he read. "Well, that is just what he does most afternoons if he is not playing tennis or golf."

"Quite so, sir. He also appeared on the scene shortly after the fire engine got there."

"Mrs. Holroyd. She seems an unlikely person to suspect, but what did she do? Went on foot to visit some of the cottages. One was half a mile from the barn, and she called there about half-past two. I feel quite glad I have an alibi myself."

The Inspector's face remained impassive.

"What about the ladies of the Committee?"

Travers had not forgotten them. He read the names from another list. Mrs. Denham had had her cousin to lunch and the two ladies had spent the afternoon on the lawn, Mrs. Edwardes, Mrs. White and Miss Crawford were at the garden fête twenty miles away, Mrs. Brown and Mrs. Sykes were in Ridgenorth shopping, and Miss Pelham-Reeve had taken the car and driven to Munchester.

"You seem to have left out Martin Denham," said the Chief Constable sarcastically.

"No, sir. I checked his statement. He arrived by the 3.5, and went home. He got there at 3.20 and walked to Miss Lane's house which he reached soon after half-past. Susan Harridge directed him to the barn. It was already blazing when he came in sight of it."

"What's your theory?"

"That someone knew those two were there and crept up and locked the door, then poured petrol on the wood and set it alight and trusted to the wind to spread it quickly. There's a terrible draught up those stairs."

"But it's horrible! Who could?"

"That's what we've got to find out," said Travers, "but it seems like the Regatta evening all over again. Everyone of them flitting about, and there's no way to check their movements."

Major Wrey drummed on the table with a penknife.

"First murder, then incendiarism and attempted murder," he groaned, "for that is what it appears. You tried the door yourself?"

"I did. It was undoubtedly locked on the outside. At first when I heard of it I thought it might have jammed but there was no question of that. I went up again to give a second examination."

"Any finger-prints?"

"None anywhere. I tested the key, the door itself, and the box where Jenkins kept the cotton waste."

"You say you found a match. What sort?"

"An unusual one, particularly large. I think they go by the name of Club matches."

"That may help. We must find out who uses that kind. Did you check Jenkins' movements?"

"Yes. He took the 1.15 to Munchester, got to the hospital at two, stopped with his wife till four, had tea with his sister and came back on the 6.5."

"That seems to dispose of him. Good Lord, how I wish the case was cleared up! I wonder if we had better call in Scotland Yard. I have half a mind to."

"Let me have another day or two sir," pleaded Travers. "We have hardly got going yet."

Travers, who had been making more enquiries in Wissingham, called at the Grange that evening, and asked if Mrs. Denham would see him. Though a little tired of police visits she received him with amiability, gave him a good account of the two invalids and asked if he wished to see them.

"No, thank you. I think I've heard all that these ladies can tell me, but I should like to know how long they will be with you."

"Miss Amelia's sister is nearly well and will return shortly. She will stay with me till then. Miss Lane is so much better that she talks of going back to her cottage on Tuesday."

This news did not seem to satisfy Travers.

"I wonder if you could see your way to keep her for a bit," he said.

Mrs. Denham looked surprised.

"Certainly I could, and I should be pleased as I am very fond of her. But why?"

"I think she's safer here, right in the village."

Mrs. Denham smiled. She thought the Inspector unnecessarily fussy, but of course that constant association with crime might tend to make one take a sensational point of view.

"I'll try to persuade her," she said.

"Thank you, ma'am, and if she goes back to the cottage I'd be grateful if you would drop me a line."

"Very mysterious," she mused when he was gone, but she did as she was asked and made Daria promise to stay on.

* * * * *

The following Wednesday, a week after the fire, Mary Brooke, a cousin of the Holroyds, was married to Sir Edgar Merriot at St. Margaret's, Westminster. Mrs. Holroyd, Leonard and Ida, who were strong on family observances went to town to attend the wedding. In their absence the Wissingham Abbey household relaxed. Burton had a day off, and the footman took himself to Ridgenorth to the cinema, and the maids amused themselves in different ways.

Inspector Travers, who had made a stealthy approach across the park, let himself in by a small gate which led him to the end of the shrubbery where he paused to reconnoitre. The old house seemed to slumber in the sunshine. The gardeners were at work the other side and the lawns were deserted. He crossed the rose garden and came to the west wing where there was a side door. It was unlocked and he went in. This part of the house was reserved for Leonard's own use, and contained the study, the business room and the gun-room.

Travers went into the study and stood looking about him. Leonard kept it as it had been in his father's time. It was essentially masculine with big leather arm-chairs, sporting prints, a huge desk, a padded seat round the fire, and the book-shelf was full of volumes devoted to shooting and fishing.

Travers' eye wandered. He went to the desk, and searched the drawers, he moved about and examined various objects. Presently he came to the mantelpiece. An enlarged photograph of Leonard's favourite retriever stood propped against the wall by the clock. Behind it was a match box, made of brass and with a lid. He opened it and took out one of the matches which he placed in his pocket. He seemed to find nothing more to engage his attention in the study and went into the passage. He had only gone a few paces when he heard a sound behind him. Somebody was coming across the hall, a woman, for he could hear the high heels on the polished boards. There was no cover, and in a moment he must be seen.

Travers opened the door nearest to him, and found himself in a large cupboard, almost the size of a small room, fitted with shelves on either side. There was no key and he stooped and looked through the keyhole and saw Ellen Harridge, who was the last person in the house whom he wished to find him. She walked past. Some garden baskets hung on a rack by the door. She took one, then returned down the passage, and presently the sound of her footsteps died away.

The coast seemed clear, but the Inspector did not seize the opportunity to slip out. He opened the door a little way to admit some light, and took stock of his surroundings. Leonard kept this cupboard for all sorts of odds and ends, and Travers saw things that interested him.

CHAPTER XVI

DARIA lay in a deck chair heaped with cushions in Mrs. Denham's garden. She was soothed by the sunshine and the sight of the river flowing past the lawn. It was now a week since the fire, and she was nearly well, and at that moment she was happier than she had been for months, because Martin, who had been away working on a brief, was due to arrive in a few minutes. As she reflected on incidents since they met she decided that she must have been in love with him from the first, but Merle's affairs had been paramount and distracted her mind. Since the murder it had seemed bordering on disloyalty to let love enter her life, and she had lived in such a state of tense emotion that she would not yield to Martin's pleadings. But during the awful moments while she knotted the flags whilst the flames roared and death seemed almost certain she had bitterly regretted that happiness she had thrust aside and might never know, and when she saw him running across the field to their rescue all doubts as to her real feelings dissolved and she knew she loved him.

To-day he would press for a definite answer. She had had a letter from him telling her so, and she was willing to give it. But this did not mean that she would abandon her search for Merle's murderer. Martin must not ask that of her.

Daria's nerves had been badly shaken by her experience. For several nights after the fire she had not been able to sleep without a sedative. Horrible dreams had come to her. Always a locked door and someone waiting just outside, a danger from which she could not flee. She would awake crying and wet with perspiration, only to toss from side to side, her mind a prey to all the powers of darkness. Who had locked that door? It must be somebody who bore a grudge, somebody on whom she had declared open war. Merle's murderer. But which of them was it? As she lay there and heard the hours strike she felt like a person drifting about in a fog. Vague shapes formed and dissolved, and her thoughts dwelt alternately on the people she had formerly suspected. Gideon had been near. She had seen him when she opened her eyes after her faint. But his presence in a large crowd proved nothing, and she knew she could not think of him without prejudice. Leonard Holroyd had also been oh the spot. Was it either of them? She couldn't tell. She would turn on the light and read for the rest of the night, and showed such a white face in the morning that Mrs. Denham became worried, for fear that she would have a breakdown.

Daria was a sensible girl so she took herself in hand, and realized the importance of having some interest to distract her. Three years ago she had made friends with a London publisher, who sometimes gave her commissions for book covers. She wrote and asked him for work. He had sent her a novel and told her she could take her time as it was not to be published till late in the autumn. She read the book in bed, got an idea that pleased her, and did a design in black and white. The colour could wait until she was able to use the studio. It had interested her, and had the right effect on her mind, and she now got her normal sleep.

Further up the lawn near the house sat Miss Amelia. She had been chatting with Mrs. Denham, who had just gone indoors to the telephone. Miss Amelia, who was now well, enjoyed being spoilt by her hostess and treated as a semi-invalid. On her knee lay a letter that had come by the evening post. She felt a strong disinclination to open it, for sad as it may seem she did not welcome communications in her sister's handwriting. Miss Honoria was in a belligerent mood. She had had letters from Mrs. Denham and others telling her of the fire. She had been genuinely horrified at the risk her sister had run, and with her this took the form of being cross.

"You are not fit to be trusted," she wrote. "Reading between the lines I cannot but realize that if it had not been for Daria Lane the ladies of the Committee would have made a point of coming to help." It did not seem clear to Miss Amelia how this fact would have extinguished the flames, but she turned over the page and continued. "The truth is you have become far too intimate with this young woman. No one knows anything about her except that she was a friend of poor Merle's, and that is hardly a recommendation. I can't think why you stayed in her house. Mrs. Holroyd says she is a terrible mischief-maker, and seems to believe that in some will that was not signed she expected to get more money, and she vents her spite on the Holroyds. I am glad that at the end of the week I shall be back to look after things," concluded Miss Honoria ominously.

Miss Amelia knew that she would not be glad, and the discovery gave her quite a shock. She perceived that during the past fortnight life had been freer, and, except for the horror of the fire, far pleasanter. She could say things that came into her head without having to wonder if Honoria would scold. She made mild jokes, and people laughed. She took pains with her dress, and Mrs. Denham and Daria encouraged her harmless vanity. She was a pretty old lady with soft skin and lovely white hair. They told her so, and she bloomed under their appreciation. She sat on that peaceful lawn and arrived at a decision. It came so suddenly that she felt dazed. In the future she would refuse to be bossed and told whom she was to know, and what she was to say. Though late in life the desire for self-expression, so well understood by the younger generation, awoke in Miss Amelia. Taking up the writing pad that lay on her knee she wrote her reply before she had time to feel frightened and repent.

"My dear Honoria,

"I am glad your ankle is better. It must have been very trying for you to he long in bed, and perhaps that was what made you write to me so crossly.

"You are quite mistaken about Daria. She is a sweet girl. She and Mrs. Denham are the two people I like best in the village, and I don't care what Mrs. Holroyd says and won't let it influence me. She was unkind to Merle, and would naturally dislike those who were fond of her. I am sorry to write like this, but I hope in the future you will criticize my friends as little as I have yours in the past.

"Your affectionate sister,
"Amelia."

Miss Amelia hastily addressed the envelope for this manifesto. Would she dare to send it? The thought of Miss Honoria's biting comments made her catch her breath. While she considered this, Lang, Mrs. Denham's parlourmaid, came out to look for Daria and she handed it to her and watched her go down the lawn. Miss Amelia wondered why she was wanted. She *did* like to know every detail that concerned her neighbours. A fault, but an engrossing interest.

Daria came up and paused.

"Susan's here, and wants to see me. I hope there's nothing wrong."

She went up to her room and got the book cover and ran down to see Susan in Mrs. Denham's sitting-room, and in answer to her enquiries said she was practically well.

"I'm pleased to hear it, Miss. I've been very worried about you."

"Thank you, Susan. I feel rather a fraud staying on here, but Mrs. Denham is very kind and seems to want me to. So before I forget it will you take this parcel and put it in the top drawer in the studio. I shan't need it till I get back."

"Then, Miss, if you've settled to stop on I wonder if you'd mind my going to my sister's for a night or two. I don't like sleeping by myself in the cottage."

"By yourself! But I understood your father was with you."

Susan looked troubled.

"Father's not very well, and he's with my sister."

"I'm sorry he's ill. What's the matter with him?"

Embarrassment displayed itself in Susan's manner.

"I'm afraid he's been foolish again. Oh, I know you are bound to hear, but they got treating him at the pub. Father isn't one to get drunk," she said fiercely, "but he's no head. A pint with him goes further than a quart with others, and then when he was going down the lane he slipped and fell into a ditch."

"Did he hurt himself badly?"

"Oh, no. He's just shook up, and they took him to my sister, as it's near, and Doctor Edwardes says keep him quiet for a few days and then he'll be all right." She looked anxiously at Daria. "Only my sister is angry and so's my brother-in-law, who works for Mr. Holroyd, and they quarrel with him all the time, and I thought I'd better go and look after him."

"What has Mr. Holroyd got to do with it? Has your father been talking again?"

Susan nodded.

"I'm afraid so, Miss. He is still that bitter, and lets his tongue run away. I thought they might complain to you."

"You had better tell me what he said."

"A lot of rubbish about getting even with the family at the Abbey."

"Well, he has said that before," said Daria with her eyes on the clock for Martin was due to arrive at any moment. "Anything else?"

"He said there was something that only you and he knew, and that others would give their heads to hear about," said Susan reluctantly.

"It's too idiotic! What can he mean? I wish you had let me question him when he talked before. I wanted to, but you asked me to wait."

"I know, Miss," said Susan humbly.

"Is it something he thinks he heard, or something he found?"

"He says that he found it, and that you have it."

"But he must be mad! I have nothing whatever. It is very wrong of him to talk like that, Susan. It makes dreadful mischief. I feel very angry."

"I'm so sorry, Miss, and after you've been so kind to us," said Susan tearfully.

There were sounds of a car outside. Daria knew it must be Martin.

"I must send you away now, but please tell him to be careful what he says. I'll come and see him either to-morrow or the next day. It is terribly annoying."

Susan's worried face made her feel she had spoken sharply and she added— "Never mind. It isn't your fault anyway."

Martin stood in the doorway, and Susan left. He came across, his eyes eager and questioning.

"Did you get my letter?"

Daria nodded. He was quite near to her, and Harridge's indiscretions and all other tiresome things faded from the world. She put her hands on his shoulders and his arms went round her.

"And you will, darling?"

"Yes, Martin. I think I knew before you went away."

"And you wouldn't tell me? Hateful of you, Daria."

He bent and kissed her, drawing her arms closer round his neck.

"It seems too good to be true," he said. "I loved you from the first moment I set eyes on you that day at the station, and I've been so uncertain about you. You seemed so detached as if I couldn't reach you."

"I couldn't help it. First I wasn't sure myself, and then I was so miserable that I felt frozen."

"And the fire thawed you! I am almost inclined to bless it," laughed Martin.

Daria agreed. She had felt the loneliness of being at odds with her friends, and now she had one of the greatest blessings life can offer, someone with whom she could share her thoughts. She leant against Martin and knew that he was the person that she loved best, and that she would not change.

After a little while Martin went to look for Mrs. Denham to tell her. She was undoubtedly pleased. She had gone through the usual agitations of mothers about her future daughter-in-law, but she thought Martin had made a wise choice.

"It is what I have been hoping for," she said. "I have grown very fond of Daria, and I'm the more glad as she will have something pleasant to occupy her mind. That dreadful affair has been a sort of obsession, but now I trust she'll leave it in the proper hands."

"She is more likely to now that Travers has got going again. Has he been in lately? "

"Not for several days. At first I think he and Daria and Miss Amelia had an idea that someone set the barn on fire. Which seems to be absurd, because who would? But, of course, dear, Daria has been very wrought up, and who can wonder after such an experience. Personally I'm inclined to agree with Mrs. Holroyd. Daria says she did not smoke, but she may have forgotten, and one knows how easy it is to set things alight in that dry weather."

"I rather wonder Travers hasn't looked in all the same."

"I expect he found there was nothing in it after all," said Mrs. Denham contentedly. "I can't say I miss his visits. It unsettles the servants to have the police constantly calling. Last time he came he seemed worried for fear Daria should go back to Jasmine Cottage. Of course I said she could stop here as long as she liked."

"Thank you, darling. I'm sure he's right until we know more, and I shall feel happier if she is safe with you."

They spent a joyful evening celebrating the engagement. Mrs. Denham got out champagne. Miss Amelia was told, and her romantic heart was stirred. She watched Daria and Martin stroll into the garden, and observed that they would make a handsome couple.

Martin had to go away next morning. He was intensely happy, and delighted because his mother seemed fond of Daria. Mrs. Denham might discount the idea of danger, but when she heard of Harridge's mishap and Susan's absence she said there could be no question of Daria going back to the cottage and remaining there alone. Harridge's behaviour was a subject of comment throughout the village. Most people thought it outrageous. Susan's account of it had by no means done justice to the gaiety of the evening that had preceded his fall. It was fortunate that his friends had been close behind to pick him up and convey him to the house of his married daughter. But it was understood that he did not mean to stay there longer than he could help. Anne Green, the daughter, was an ardent Chapel-goer with stern views and preached to him constantly. She was reinforced by Ellen who came from the Abbey, and drawing up a chair to his bedside, questioned him closely and disagreeably about what he had said at the Four Feathers. Goaded by her manner he had said more than he intended, and Ellen had gone away deep in thought.

"He is really a tiresome old man," said Mrs. Denham to Daria. "I wish you had never employed him. His abuse of the Holroyds is getting to be a nuisance. I daresay Leonard was inconsiderate about the allotment, but foolish talk does no one any good. I hope you'll tell him so."

"I'll go and see him to-morrow," said Daria.

It was impossible to go sooner as Mrs. Denham was taking her to a big bazaar in aid of the League of Mercy. This was to be held that afternoon in the grounds belonging to Lady Williams, the widow of a former Lord Mayor. A Serene Highness was to open it, and most of the influential people of the neighbourhood would be there. Mrs. Denham told Daria to put on her prettiest frock. She intended to introduce her as her prospective daughter-in-law and thought this big party a good opportunity. Daria felt shy, but excitement had given her a colour, and she was looking her best in a dress that Merle had given her for a birthday present. It seemed a pity, thought Mrs. Denham, that Martin was not there to see her.

The hostess, a large amiable lady, was having the day of her life. When she came the neighbourhood had accepted her grudgingly for she was vulgar, but she had established herself through large subscriptions to local charities, and after an uphill progress had attained her goal. She stood in the midst of county ladies to receive the Princess, and Mrs. Holroyd, who had been one of the most stubborn, was near her. The sun shone, the band played, the stalls were full of desirable objects. The Princess did her job, the Bishop said a few words, Mr. Gideon Franklin said some more. Lady Williams sat between the Princess and the local Marchioness and beamed.

When this part ended the important people left the platform and began to circulate in the wake of the Princess who was making a conscientious tour of the stalls. Mrs. Denham and Daria remained on the outskirts, and Daria watched Gideon with the fascination of dislike. He was walking with a plump, smartly-dressed woman whom she had not seen before. Gideon was attentive. He touched his companion's arm and led her over to some of his friends who were selling at one of the stalls. Important constituents, thought Daria cynically, as Mrs. Hoskins took a case stuffed with notes from her bag. She looked pleased with herself and the world in general, and seemed in a mood to spend freely.

Presently the Princess and a chosen few went to have their tea in a small tent, and others, less distinguished, crowded into a large marquee. Everything had been beautifully done at Lady Williams' expense. Mrs. Denham was soon among a group of friends and began to tell them about the engagement. Everybody was kind and said nice things, and they had tea at a table of pleasant people, and Daria enjoyed it, but when they had finished her contentment got a jar. Mrs. Holroyd and Ida came up, and Mrs. Holroyd stopped to speak to Mrs. Denham and ignored Daria who was close to her. But Mrs. Denham would not allow this. It was time, she decided, that the Wissingham Abbey people, who were among her oldest friends, should get over their prejudices. When Daria became Martin's wife they could not treat her as non-existent.

"You won't have heard our news," she said. "Daria and Martin are going to be married."

The pause that followed was expressive.

"No, I had not heard," said Mrs. Holroyd icily, and added with unpleasant emphasis—"I think *Miss Lane* is very much to be congratulated."

"So is Martin," said Mrs. Denham who was obviously annoyed at the tone.

Mrs. Holroyd moved on and began to talk to Colonel and Mrs. Delahaye, and Ida's glance gave no room for doubt as to what her thoughts might be.

"Oh Mrs. Denham, why did you tell them?"

"Because it is time to end this nonsense," said Mrs. Denham, and for once she spoke sharply.

Lady Williams came up like a ship in full sail. She had been seeing the Princess off, and was radiant because she was graciously thanked and told that her arrangements had been wonderful. Someone mentioned Daria's engagement, and she was interested for she liked anything to do with a wedding. She said she wished that Martin could have been there, and told Mrs. Denham that he was going to have a lovely bride. She stood fair and square in the gangway, blocking Mrs. Holroyd and Ida who wanted to escape.

"Mine seems to be a lucky party! Yours is not the only engagement I've heard of to-day."

"What's the other, Lady Williams?" asked someone.

"You'll never guess." Lady Williams paused to commune with herself. Should she be discreet or should she not? After all everybody was bound to hear before long, and she did enjoy being the first with a piece of news. Her eyes wandered round the tent, focused, and she beckoned.

"Mr. Franklin," she called a little loudly for she was excited. "Mr. Franklin! May! Do come here."

Gideon and Mrs. Hoskins heard and turned. They moved forward.

"I do hope you won't think I've been naughty and given away a secret," said Lady Williams archly, "but I'd be so proud if you'd tell them at my party." She looked round to see who was within earshot. "Mrs. Holroyd, now I know that you and Gideon are old friends," she added with a vague recollection that she had been told that he used to be a frequent visitor at the Abbey.

Mrs. Hoskins smiled reassuringly. She had known Lady Williams for years. The announcement might be premature, but she did not really mind. It was Gideon who was furious, and his face was unusually flushed. For him it was a detestable moment. The look on the faces of both Mrs. Holroyd and Ida was not flattering to his self-esteem, and Daria's glance expressed disgust that she did not attempt to hide. How many weeks was it since he and Merle——? For decency's sake he had meant to postpone making the news public till they went back to London, but May, of course, had babbled to her friend. But the thing was out and there was no help for it.

"Mrs. Hoskins and I," he began hesitatingly, and Mrs. Hoskins linked her arm in his with a jolly laugh.

"I believe he's shy! I'll forgive him as it's his first venture." She beamed on them. "We didn't mean to tell people yet, but Alice *can't* keep a secret, can you, dear?"

The effect on the group was various. A certain number crowded forward to shake hands and offer their good wishes, and Mrs. Holroyd and Ida took the opportunity to fade away. Lady Williams saw them disappearing, and called after them, but they did not seem to hear.

"How odd! They can't have understood," she said with a puzzled stare, then she turned back to Daria and brightened.

"Anyhow you will have a fellow feeling for Mrs. Hoskins and Mr. Franklin, Miss Lane, being as you might say in the same boat."

Daria looked steadily at Gideon.

"I wish Mr. Franklin all the happiness he deserves," she said.

"Rather a strange girl after all," reflected Lady Williams. "She said that queerly, and I don't know what ails Gideon Franklin. He seems thoroughly uncomfortable. I hope May isn't making a mistake."

These incidents spoilt the rest of the party for Daria. She went away seething with rage because Gideon seemed to slither through difficulties as easily as a cobra through grass. As slimy and treacherous, she thought, and possibly as dangerous. Also she felt ruffled by Mrs. Holroyd's open snub, though she owned that she could not have expected anything different. She even felt impatient with Mrs. Denham who refused to recognise the sincerity of their mutual dislike, and whose judgement was obscured by her charity. Mrs. Denham was sure that in time they would all understand one another better, and that Mrs. Holroyd would realise that if Daria had been over zealous it was on account of her great friendship and would forgive it. Because in spite of differences Mrs. Holroyd must have loved Merle just as she herself meant to love Martin's wife. With relations as well as neighbours one simply set oneself to get over difficulties of outlook. And the Holroyds were such nice people.

They left early as Mrs. Denham had to dine out, and when they got back Daria found a letter from the publisher asking if she could let him see her unfinished drawing. If he approved it she could have it back by return, but the date of publication was to be earlier than he had supposed.

"Isn't that tiresome," said Daria to Miss Amelia as they had their coffee. "It ought to go by the early post and it is in the studio at home. As Susan's not sleeping there I can't telephone to her to bring it."

"Then what will you do?"

"I'll run over and fetch it. It won't take me long."

"Must you do it to-night? I think there may be a storm. It has clouded over."

"I'll take a coat," said Daria.

"I'd come with you only I see so badly in the dark," fussed Miss Amelia. "Ought you to go alone?"

"Why, of course," laughed Daria. "What do you think this is? A den of gangsters!"

Daria took a short cut across the field to her cottage. It had grown very dark by the time she reached it, and she regretted that she had not borrowed a torch. She decided to return by the lane as it was difficult to find the footpath. The studio was at the back of the cottage and she let herself in that way. Susan had put the drawing where she had been told, and it struck Daria that it would save time if she packed it straight away. She scribbled a note, and got out brown paper and cardboard and was looking for some string when she heard a noise. It sounded as if somebody was moving in the house. The idea came to her that Susan must have come back. She listened, heard nothing and went on packing her drawing, and decided that it had been imagination when a sharp cracking noise broke the stillness. It came from her sitting-room.

Daria jumped up, went across the passage and turned the handle of the door. The reading lamp on her writing desk was alight, and a dark figure bent over a drawer which was usually locked. It had been forced open and this accounted for the sound she had heard.

Daria had gone in quickly without any thought of caution. Instantly, before she could grasp its significance the lamp was extinguished, and the figure groped its way towards the window which was wide open and vanished over the sill. Before she had time to reflect Daria followed. The window sill was only a few feet from the ground. She was out of it in a moment and ran across the orchard towards the gate that opened into the wood. The shadowy figure went through, so did Daria. The path was narrow and rough, the bushes closed in on her. It was pitch dark. Daria paused. The sound of the footsteps had stopped.

Daria called—"Who's there?" and as no one answered repeated this. Her voice was tremulous for somebody stood very near to her in that dark thicket. Anger and curiosity had made her rash, and she realised that she was alone with something furtive and evil. She had a vision of Merle's face as she had seen it distorted after death, and terror descended on her without warning. As in a nightmare her feet seemed to have lost the power of movement, and she was too paralysed to turn and run.

Then she heard the faint crackle of a breaking twig, and the acute sense of hearing that fear develops told her that this person was moving not away but just a little nearer.

Daria said a desperate prayer, and her nerves steadied, and at the same moment there came to her ears a new and comforting sound. It was the good crunching noise of someone walking down the lane to the accompaniment of cheerful whistling. "Trees." That was the tune. It was one that Daria had detested when Jack Mills, the young man Harridge had got in to help dig had whistled it hour after hour. Now she thought it the loveliest melody ever composed. Her voice returned to her and the use of her limbs.

"Jack!" she screamed,—"Jack Mills!" and she started to run.

Even as she did so she was aware that the rustling behind had given place to something less cautious but now going away into the wood and not following her.

Jack Mills jumped over a stile from the lane and hurried towards her.

"Who's that?" he called, then as she ran up panting—"Why it's Miss Lane," he exclaimed.

"Yes . . . yes." Daria's voice came in gasps, "somebody broke into the cottage, and I followed, and then I got frightened."

"Which way did he go, Miss?"

"Into the wood."

"Shall I go and see?"

"No." Daria felt that nothing would induce her to be left. "Come back with me and let us see what's happened in the cottage."

They climbed in through the window and turned up the light. Here were plenty of traces of the intruder. The drawer of the writing table had been forced with a chisel and all the papers had been turned on to the floor. In a search for what reflected the puzzled owner? She possessed so little of value. But the burglary, if it was one, must be reported. When she had telephoned to the police station and got through to Robinson she started to make a tour of the room to see if anything was missing. To her surprise two one pound notes had been tossed aside and lay on the top of the papers. They had been in the locked drawer. Further examination of the cottage showed that the bedrooms had been visited, but as far as she could see nothing had been taken. She was still puzzling about it when Robinson arrived, and a short time after Inspector Travers came chugging up on his motor bicycle. Robinson had carried out his instruction to inform the Inspector at once if anything unusual occurred.

It was evident that Travers suspected that this was more than an ordinary burglary. Daria was asked what she had touched and moved and was urged to describe the figure she had seen. But it was difficult to do this. The opening of the door and extinction of the light had been almost simultaneous. She had got the impression of someone in a loose dark coat bending over the table, but could not even say if it had been a man or a woman. She described her experience in the wood, her fright, and her impression that the person crept towards her instead of retreating. Travers gave her story close attention. He asked Jack Mills if he had seen a car in the lane, or had heard one drive away, but there had been nothing of the kind. Travers then made Daria accompany him and Robinson to the wood, and show him where she had been standing. He went in further and flashed his torch up and down in the darkness, but saw nothing more than a scared rabbit, and decided that whoever had been there had gone home.

He sent Daria back to Mrs. Denham's in charge of Robinson, and returned to the cottage to continue his search. So seriously did he regard Daria's burglar that he passed the night on her sofa in the sitting-room.

CHAPTER XVII

THE Inspector was up early. As soon as it was light he made a thorough examination for traces of the intruder, but when he returned to the cottage to brew himself some tea he had to own that his search had met with no results. It had been dry for about a week and there were no footmarks, and though he looked diligently in the hope of finding some shreds off the intruder's coat among the brambles he got nothing at all. Nor were there any finger-marks on the chisel, the writing table, or on any of the objects that had been turned over.

Travers was feeling glum when Robinson came to relieve him about eight o'clock. He told him to remain in the cottage and rode off to breakfast at the Four Feathers. After ordering tea and eggs and bacon he summoned Curtis the landlord to sit with him while he ate. To him he put some questions.

"Harridge," said Curtis thoughtfully. "Yes, he was a bit troublesome a few nights ago. They'd stood him drinks. No, he wasn't drunk," he added hastily, "that I shouldn't have allowed, but he's a crotchety temper, and he's set against the gentry at the Abbey."

"How did that show?" asked Travers.

But Curtis did not wish to commit himself. He hadn't rightly listened, he said. All he remembered was some nonsense about something he'd found and hadn't mentioned. One of the others had asked him what he'd done with it.

"What did he say?"

"That it was in a safe place and no one but himself and Miss Lane could guess where that was."

"Who was there when he said this?"

Curtis had to think a bit. Finally he said Jones, Harman, old Grigg, and Thomas were there. He didn't believe there were any more.

Travers reflected.

"Isn't young Thomas engaged to one of his daughters?"

"To Ellen, the one who works at the Abbey. A stuck-up piece of goods. Susan is far the best."

There was nothing more to be learnt from him. Travers considered his next move, then set off for Mrs. Denham's where he asked for Daria. Directly she came in she wanted to know if he had made any discovery.

"No, but as you have probably heard Harridge has been saying that he had found something in connection with Mrs. Holroyd's death, and has hidden it. It is possible that this may account for what happened last night."

"I have been thinking that, too. A burglar would have taken the money."

"So I've come to ask you to come back with me to the cottage. You are the person who will know if anything is missing, or if anything strange has been put in your house."

Daria said she would come at once. When they reached Jasmine Cottage they went through each room thoroughly, as well as any hiding places they could think of. They searched the kitchen and the bedrooms occupied by Susan and Harridge, but at the end of the time Daria owned that she was baffled.

"Everything has been turned over, but as far as I can see nothing has been taken or added to."

"Thank you, Miss Lane, and now I'll get along and have a word with our friend Harridge."

"I had intended going to see him myself this morning." Daria hesitated. "I suppose you wouldn't let me have a go at him first. I can't help thinking that I might do more with him than you could because of his complex about the police. I believe if he has kept anything back it is from an absurd idea that he might give you all trouble."

"You think he might tell you?"

"He might. Susan says he is attached to me."

Travers reflected.

"Well, have a try. I'll be grateful if you will. I have to go into Ridgenorth as I'm expecting a telephone call, and it's possible that I may have to run up to London either this afternoon or tomorrow morning. But I'll try and get you at Mrs. Denham's to hear if you've had any luck."

But when Daria reached Mrs. Green's cottage she drew blank. Harridge it seemed was better in body, but considerably worse in spirit. He and his son-in-law George had had words with the result that he had got up and taken himself off, refusing to say where he was going, but they expected he would be back to sleep. Daria left word that she would come again the following morning and hoped Harridge would stay in and see her.

When she got back to lunch Mrs. Denham thought she looked very white, and she owned that she had not slept and had a headache.

"The best thing you can do is to take an aspirin and see if you can get a nap this afternoon. Go and lie down and I'll send up your tea to your room."

Daria was not sorry to obey. There had been too short a time between the experience of the night before and the fire, and her nerves had not recovered as completely as she supposed. But as soon as she got on her bed she went fast asleep and was still dreaming when the housemaid came in with the tray. Her dreams had been of Merle, and as she opened her eyes she had the illusion that she was still at Wissingham Abbey with her friend. For the figure of the maid was connected with Merle, and her drowsy brain saw nothing curious in this as it fitted in with her dream. Then as she became more awake she sat up and stared.

"Cecilia," she said. "What on earth are you doing here?"

"I'm here temporary, Miss, while Mrs. Denham's housemaid has her holiday."

"I didn't know you'd left the Abbey."

"Oh yes, miss, a month after my lady died."

Daria was now fully roused. Cecilia had originally been one of the housemaids at the Abbey, and had waited on Merle, who had found her so efficient that she had not troubled to get a personal maid. Cecilia had been devoted to her. Daria remembered that there had been constant friction between her and Ellen.

"Then you are doing temporary work?"

"Just for the summer, Miss. After that I want a place in Sussex near where my mother lives."

"I expect you missed Mrs. Holroyd," said Daria gently.

"More than I can say," said Cecilia and her eyes filled. "She was so kind to me, and when mother was ill she paid all the expenses. There weren't many people as good as her whatever they may say."

"I like to think you were fond of her," said Daria.

"Anyone would be who saw her as I did," said Cecilia. "But, Miss, if you'll excuse my saying so, she never had a chance with that stuck up crowd. That Ellen was always carrying tales. Beastly things she said even when the poor lady lay dead in the house. I told her what I thought of her sneaking ways, and I'm glad I spoke my mind. But she went straight to Mrs. Holroyd to complain, and I got my notice."

"I detest Ellen," said Daria.

"Yes, Miss, but none of them were fair. They say my mistress had a temper, and perhaps she had, but it takes more than one to make a quarrel, and I've heard things said to her that wouldn't sound too well if they came out. And that's what I told Ellen."

"Who by? I'd like to know, Cecilia."

"That Miss Ida was always sneering, and Mrs. Holroyd, but it wasn't only them. Her own husband was worst of all."

"How do you know?" asked Daria.

"Because I was there, Miss. Do you remember the evening before the Regatta? My Mrs. Holroyd had been to London. Dashed off she did, and when she came back she seemed upset. And Mr. Holroyd had been away that day, too, but he didn't get home till after dinner was over."

"I remember it well," said Daria, and had a vision of Merle in her orange teagown, her cheeks flushed, and her eyes darting defiance at her mother-in-law as they sat over dessert. "Please go on, Cecilia."

"My mistress went up to her room before he came in. I think she talked to you for a bit in her sitting-room. I was down at my supper, and she didn't ring as usual for me to help her undress. But after you'd gone to your room she did ring, and said she had a headache and would like me to brush her hair. While I was doing it she seemed very down, and never spoke, and looked as if she had been crying. After a while she told me to turn on the water as a hot bath always soothed her. I left the door open between her and the bathroom while I got it ready and then I found I'd run short of bath-salts, and went out by the passage door to fetch them. When I got back I found that Mr. Holroyd had come into the bedroom, and they were going for each other hammer and tongs. 'Do you think it's wise to try me too far?' he said in a nasty voice, and she gave a queer sort of laugh and said—'I expect you think you would be better off if I was dead!' And he answered very quick—'My God! we should all be!' Then, Miss, I put down the jar I was carrying, and I suppose it made a noise, and my mistress said much lower—'Do you know Cecilia is in there,—or don't you care who hears you?' He said something I didn't catch, and went out. But that doesn't seem the way for a gentleman to speak, and if I hear things against my mistress, I tell them that there's another side to it."

"There's one more thing, Cecilia, that's always puzzled me. That evening you speak of there was someone listening while I was talking to Mrs. Leonard Holroyd. We were on the window seat, and the window was open. Could it have been Ellen?"

Cecilia thought for a moment.

"I shouldn't think so. Ellen did listen, but she would have been at supper the same as me. More likely old Mrs. Holroyd or Miss Ida. Either would tell the other if it was anything against my mistress. Banded against her they were. More shame to them."

Daria decided to tell Travers of this conversation immediately. She rang up, heard that he was not in, and left a message to explain her failure to see Harridge. She then wrote out an account of her talk with Cecilia which she posted to him to Ridgenorth.

Later in the evening she was called to the telephone to speak to Martin.

"Darling, are you all right?" said an anxious voice.

"Perfectly. Why?"

"The Inspector has been in to see me and told me about the burglary."

"The Inspector! What was he doing? I know he said he might have to go to London, but I shouldn't think it was just to pay calls."

"He didn't tell me his business, only that he had to come to town. He dropped in at my chambers. How is it that you didn't write and tell me yourself?"

"I wrote this evening, but there wasn't much to tell. Nothing had been taken."

"Travers doesn't make as light of it as you. Do you know, Daria, I think I'd be happier if you went away from Wissingham for a bit."

"Nonsense, my dear boy. Don't be absurd!"

"I'm not absurd, but I am rather angry with you. What made you go trapesing off alone in the dark?"

"I had to go to the cottage to get a drawing."

"Damn the drawing!"

"Hush, my dear! You mustn't use language down the telephone. The young lady at the exchange might complain."

"Daria, promise me you won't do that sort of thing again. It worries me. I wish to goodness I was down there to look after you."

"So do I, but for the pleasure of your company, quoth she prettily, and not because I'm scared. Still I'll own it was rather beastly."

"Look here," said Martin, "there's a chance of my getting down before the end of the week. If I do I could reach you about four. Let's take tea on the downs if it is fine? "

"I'd adore that."

"And prepare yourself to be thoroughly scolded. Darling, you don't know. . . ."

The conversation continued for another six minutes.

"Did the Inspector say when he would be back? " asked Daria just before they rang off.

"I think he was going straight to the station."

"I do wonder what he wanted in London," said Daria.

"Possibly to get his hair cut," said Martin flippantly.

CHAPTER XVIII

IDA came into the garden. She had been playing in a tennis tournament and still carried her racquet. Mrs. Holroyd, who was sitting in the shade under a group of lime trees, looked up from her work.

"Well, my dear, did you win?"

Ida sat down on a pile of cushions.

"Nothing like it. I played vilely. Leonard is to blame. He ought to have entered."

"Isn't Captain Strong any good?"

"Yes. It was my own fault. I couldn't hit a ball." She fidgeted. "It's all nonsense. Why should Leonard live like a hermit? It is bad for him."

"I think he is right. It is too soon for him to be going to tennis tournaments."

"Brooding won't do any good," said Ida, "and conventional mourning has gone out. Besides why should he? It isn't as if he had ever cared for her."

"There are decencies to be observed even in these days, and I don't suppose he feels in a mood for meeting people. It is impossible to get the thing out of one's mind."

"Isn't that morbid?"

"It might be if the thing had ended, but it goes on and on. Unfortunately the police seem more active than ever."

"Damn them!" muttered Ida.

Mrs. Holroyd took up her work.

"It was inevitable," she said. "One can see that they think that the person who set fire to the barn also killed Merle. Whoever it was shewed great lack of judgment, because in spite of all those enquiries there was no evidence to convict anyone, and Shadwell could still have done it. But the fire has cleared him and shewn the police that Daria Lane was justified in what she said."

"Daria!" said Ida. "Don't you loathe her, Aunt Octavia?"

Mrs. Holroyd's lips tightened as she bent over her work.

"She has certainly done her best to make things unpleasant for us."

"Why couldn't she let it alone?" said Ida passionately.

"She is the only person who can tell you that. It is unlucky that the affair of the barn followed by the burglary has played into her hands and set the whole village chattering. No wonder Leonard can't forget."

They sat in silence for a minute, then Mrs. Holroyd continued—

"Leonard got an invitation to-day from Count Hoyos. I don't think you knew him, but he and Leonard were at Oxford together, and he stayed with us here two and a half years ago when you were away. He asks Leonard to stop with him in Austria for a fortnight's fishing on the Danube. I have urged him to accept."

"To go soon?" said Ida in a voice of dismay.

"At the end of the week," said Mrs. Holroyd, "and I hope he will remain for some time. He would like Prague and Roumania. It would be a good thing if he left Wissingham for several months."

Ida looked up.

"Why?" she asked belligerently.

"For several reasons. I should have thought they were obvious," said Mrs. Holroyd.

"Do you mean on account of me, Aunt Octavia?"

"That among other things," said Mrs. Holroyd calmly. "You haven't been very discreet."

"What makes you talk like that? It isn't as if you didn't know how it is between Leonard and me,—how it has always been."

"I know how you felt," said Mrs. Holroyd.

"Well—and now there is no longer any obstacle what can you have against it?"

Ida had risen and stood looking down at her aunt, her face white with emotion.

Mrs. Holroyd matched her silks carefully without speaking.

"You came between us before. Didn't you do enough harm then?" said Ida in a shaking voice.

"I am inclined to agree that I made a mistake," said her aunt. "As I look back on my life I realize that I have made many, all unfortunately important. Perhaps one of them was giving you a home. My dear," she went on, "you mustn't think I'm not fond of you. You have been like a daughter to me, and when I say that I mean it, but coming here didn't bring you happiness."

"It did till you made Leonard marry Merle," said Ida fiercely.

"I was wrong to let you come back after the marriage."

"You were wrong in ever letting it happen."

Mrs. Holroyd did not deny it.

"I suppose I have always been inclined to interfere too much in other people's lives," she said reflectively, "but at the time I was desperate.

Without Merle, Wissingham would have had to go, and with it all I had worked for for twenty-six years. Love is not the only thing, Ida. I'll own I sacrificed you for what I thought was the best. I believed that Wissingham and Leonard mattered most. I still do. I hoped that Leonard would grow to care for Merle. She was in love with him, and lots of people thought her beautiful. But I miscalculated. He disliked her even on the honeymoon. He is fastidious, and she jarred, and he did not even admire her looks."

"And you grew to hate her. Why don't you say it outright?"

"Certainly I hated her. I expected she would adapt herself and try to learn our ways, but she refused to have children and insulted us on every possible occasion."

Her frankness startled Ida. The lack of emotion in Mrs. Holroyd's face and voice gave her words a special and peculiar emphasis.

"What did you feel about her death?"

"What you did. I am not a hypocrite," said Mrs. Holroyd.

"So I was sacrificed for a failure," said Ida bitterly.

Her aunt looked at the house.

"Except that we still have Wissingham," she said.

"And now you have other schemes for Leonard," said Ida. "You own you want to manage people's lives and fail, but it seems to teach you nothing. I wonder what is in your mind. Has this Count Hoyos a sister?"

"Not that I know of."

"Aunt Octavia, you cheated me once. You shan't again. So I'll tell you. Leonard has asked me to marry him as soon as we can do it without scandal."

Mrs. Holroyd sat quite still.

"I see," she said. "Well, Ida, I will be quite truthful with you. Get two things into your head. First that after what has happened I am not going to urge Leonard to marry anyone, and second that I shall try to prevent his marrying you."

"Tell me why."

The two women looked at one another.

"You can probably guess," said her aunt, and getting up she went towards the house.

After she was left alone Ida stood for a few moments in deep thought, then her face became contorted, and tears poured down it. Presently she moved slowly in the direction of the side door of the house known to Inspector Travers, and went to Leonard's study. He was at his writing table and looked up as the door opened. She came in, shutting it carefully. When he saw her expression he got up with an exclamation. She came close to him and he put his arms round her.

"What has happened, Ida? Darling, tell me! Why, you're trembling!"

She clung to him speechlessly.

"My dear, what has frightened you?" he said stroking her hair.

"Your mother." Her voice came in gasping sobs. "She means to separate us. Leonard . . . Leonard, say she can't!"

"Of course she can't."

"But she will. She's strong and ruthless, and she did it before."

"The conditions were different, as you well know."

"It doesn't matter. She'll prevent us marrying. She says so."

"Darling, don't be silly. How can she? It isn't in her power."

"She is different from other women. She always gets her way."

"I don't know what's the matter with you," said Leonard, "but I suppose it's natural. These horrors have got on your nerves. But why fix on poor mother as an enemy? I thought you were devoted to her."

"I can't explain," said Ida, and wept without restraint, choking sobs that alarmed Leonard who in all the years he had known her had never seen her lose control. He continued to soothe, but ceased to question till the paroxysm died down. At last the storm spent itself and she raised her head.

"Leonard, are you sure you love me? Absolutely? I have to know."

"Of course," he said tenderly. "Haven't I always?"

"Then if you do will you prove it?"

"If I can."

"Marry me at once, and don't let Aunt Octavia know."

・ ・ ・ ・ ・

Inspector Travers was obliged to return to London next day. He had spoken to Daria before starting, and heard that she intended to go to the Greens' cottage, and see if Harridge had returned. She promised to ring him up that evening to tell him the result. The Inspector set off on his motor bicycle, completed his business after some delay, and felt he had earned his lunch. He was in a cheerful mood for the pieces of his puzzle seemed as if they were falling into place. He rehearsed the story to himself as he walked and tested its probabilities, and hoped that no new and disconcerting bit of evidence would bob up at the last minute to upset it. For he had known that to happen, and the effect on a hardworking official in search of further promotion was shattering.

The Inspector had a mind that found pleasure in platitudes, and in the course of the day the saying that it is a small world occurred to him more than once. First he ran into Major Wrey walking up St. James's Street. The Chief Constable was up for a meeting, and stopped to have a word.

"Hullo, Inspector, are you here on business?"

"Yes, sir, and I hope to-morrow to put the whole matter before you."

"Any progress?"

"I trust you will think so, sir. Things have begun to move at last."

The two men walked to the corner of the street, and stopped for a moment to talk, then Major Wrey went to his club. But he was in a gloomy mood and found he had no appetite, and presently he went to the writing room where he spent a considerable time composing and destroying letters. In the end he read what he had written and addressed it to Miss Ida Pelham-Reeve. It was a proposal of marriage.

. . . . .

The Inspector who had no club walked on and got some lunch at Lyons' and then went to fetch his motor bicycle which he had left at a small garage belonging to a friend. He thought of the conversation he had had with his Chief. Though Major Wrey had uttered words of praise the fact that he viewed the result without enthusiasm did not escape Travers. It was unfortunate but it could not be helped. He walked on briskly and it was at this moment that he again had reason to notice the smallness of the world. A woman was going in the same direction some yards ahead and her figure seemed familiar. She wore a neat coat and skirt and a small hat. He was not absolutely certain about her for he could not see her face, and she had gone up some steps and entered a doorway before he could get nearer. He strolled up and examined the brass plate on the door. It was a Registrar's office and his interest was immediately aroused, because if he had not been mistaken it was curious that she should be there. He hung about for a quarter of an hour. A few people passed but no one came out. He looked at his watch and wondered if he should go on waiting for he had a lot to do when he got back. But while he hesitated he saw two people come out of the door, and felt glad that he had stopped. Ida Pelham-Reeve stood on the steps, and her hand rested on the arm of Leonard Holroyd. As they walked away she smiled up at him, and it was clear that they were far too absorbed in one another to notice the loiterer on the opposite side of the road. At the corner they hailed a taxi and drove off. Travers returned and went into the building. He knocked at a door, was told to come in, and entered a room like, but less pleasant than, a station waiting room. A forbidding female sat at a large table making entries in a book. The walls were decorated with warnings to people who might make false declarations. A grim place.

The female looked up over her glasses.

"I can take you now," she said. "I presume you are Mr. Openshaw. Where's the bride?"

"That isn't why I've come," said Travers hastily. "But I have just seen two people I know leave this place. Mr. Holroyd and Miss Pelham-Reeve."

"What of it?" said the woman, and the smile she turned on for happy couples faded.

"I want to know what they were doing here," said Travers. "This is my card," and he drew up a chair and sat down.

• • • • •

When Daria set off for the Greens' cottage she had been prepared to hear that Harridge had not returned and she was right. After his quarrel with his family he had gone to Munchester where he intended to quarter himself for a few days on a cousin. But reports that he had been making himself unpopular had preceded him, and the cousin who had always disliked him showed no inclination to extend hospitality. But Harridge felt it would be ignominious to return at once after the words that had passed between himself and the Greens. He ignored the pointed remarks of his unwilling host, and his determination triumphed. Yet it was not a pleasant visit. He spent his money at the cinema and various public-houses, but in spite of these distractions he did not enjoy himself. He had no friends in Munchester and he was lonely. The cousin was sulky and took no pains to make him comfortable, also he was haunted by the thought that Daria's garden to which he gave devoted labour, must now be full of weeds. Then Susan would be worried, and she was a good girl, and not down on her old father like the rest of them. So he suddenly announced his intention of going home, a decision that he nearly retracted when he saw his cousin's pleasure. But the thought of the weeds prevailed, and he set off that afternoon and reached the Greens. He had a cold reception from Anne and George, and even Susan was silently reproachful. But he was alternately furious and nattered to hear that the police had been trying to find him. They had been balked because he had been given a lift by a passing van that ran between London and the sea, and his extreme dislike for the cousin had made Susan rule out that destination as impossible.

Susan went to tell Daria of his return, and promised to keep him at home next morning, and Daria telephoned the news to the Inspector.

When she reached the cottage Daria found Harridge sitting alone in the parlour, looking and feeling disgruntled. His conscience was far from clear, and he evidently wondered what she was going to say. But Daria was on a diplomatic mission, and she successfully disguised her conviction that he was a tiresome old man. She had called in at Jasmine Cottage on her way where she had found Robinson still on guard, and had picked Harridge a bunch of flowers of his own cultivating. She gave him these, and made delicate enquiries as to his recovery to which sheepish answers were returned. He brightened considerably when he was asked if he could return to work tomorrow, and so by degrees they reached the subject that had brought her there.

"I expect you know I had a horrid fright the other night?"

"Yes, Miss, and I was sorry to hear it."

"Someone got into the cottage and broke open my writing table."

"A tramp, I shouldn't wonder," said Harridge.

"I don't think so. No, this person was looking for something definite."

Harridge did not speak, and a look of cunning came over his face.

"Harridge," said Daria, "I want your help. Have you any idea what the thing could be?"

"How should I know?" growled Harridge.

"I hoped you did," said Daria boldly, "because of something you are reported to have said in the Four Feathers." She glanced at his sulky face and added—"Please don't keep anything back from me. It is really important."

He turned his head away and avoided her eyes.

"As things are I'm afraid to go back to my own house," continued Daria. "It puts me at a hopeless disadvantage if I don't know what this person is looking for. Can't you see that?"

Again silence.

"Harridge, what have I done that you won't help me?"

"Nothing, Miss, and I'd like to—only——"

"Only what?"

"It's those police nosing round." His obstinate look deepened. "What I said at the Four Feathers was foolishness. Sometimes I get talking like that. It didn't mean nothing."

"Somebody thought it did."

"I'm sorry," muttered Harridge, "but they ought to have seen I meant it as a joke. Whatever happens people put the blame on me. Even my own daughters. You'd hardly believe it if I told you how they went on at me."

"Not Susan."

"Oh no, but Ellen and the Greens. It's because they think their precious Abbey people might hear. And Mr. Holroyd's a bad man. He's hard. He took away my allotment, and I'd put a year's work into it. Who's going to pay me for that?"

"But that isn't my fault, is it Harridge? I've always been a friend to you."

"Yes, Miss, and I know it. Don't think I'm not grateful. You've been kind to me and to Susan, too. No one could want a better lady to serve."

"Then don't you see that it isn't Mr. Holroyd or the police you are hurting. It's me."

Harridge moved uneasily.

"I shouldn't like to feel that, Miss."

"Then tell me the truth. Did you find something or did you not?"

"I did find something in the punt," said Harridge reluctantly, "but I made a lot of it just to get folks rattled. I don't suppose it was of any importance."

"And where is it?"

"In a safe place," said Harridge with a cunning smile.

"Hidden in my cottage?"

He made no answer, and Daria felt exasperated.

"Harridge, that isn't fair," she said angrily. "What's more it can't go on. How can I live in a place where I may not even be safe? Do you want me to shut the cottage and go away?"

"You wouldn't do that, Miss!"

Harridge was aghast. Into his slow brain had crept the thought that if he lost this job it would be his last. Not only was his garden as dear to him as a child, but it would mean dependence on Anne and George. Daria waited. She knew speech would do no further good.

Presently he gave a gulp.

"I'll not tell you what it is, because I've said I wouldn't do that for anyone, but I'll say where I hid it, and then you can see for yourself." He leaned forward, his eyes on Daria's. "You know that box of yours made of shiny yellow wood?"

"My grandmother's workbox? In the sitting-room on a little table by the door?"

"That's it. Well, look in that, Miss, and see what you make of it. Nothing that could matter. I found it in the punt that morning and slipped it into my pocket. I don't know why,—a sort of idea it might be useful. When that policeman asked me I forgot. I did truly, I was so flustered. Then later they badgered me and I made up my mind to say nothing, and I didn't, for why should I help people who had never been anything but hard on me? What's more they would never have heard a word about it if I hadn't had a drop too much, and I suppose I was worked up about the allotment."

"But I don't understand," said the puzzled Daria. "We opened that workbox only two days ago. There was nothing in it but what you'd expect, needles and silks and oddments."

"This is different," said Harridge with a grin, and Daria could get no more out of him.

She started back and went into the post office to telephone to Travers on her way, and told him what Harridge had said.

"What would you like me to do? Look myself or wait for you?"

"I'd better come," said Travers. "I'll just have time before I meet a train at twelve o'clock. If you walk to the house I'll be there almost as soon as you are."

The Inspector must have gone considerably beyond the speed limit as he came through the various villages, for Daria found him getting off his cycle when she arrived. They went into her sitting-room and put the workbox between them on a table. It was square, and made of inlaid satinwood. Daria raised the lid. It was lined with blue watered silk, faded in places. Round the sides was a narrow shelf divided into compartments that held cotton reels, silks and odds and ends. The well in the middle held rolls of ribbon and balls of wool, an old ivory needle case, another with a screw top, an emery cushion shaped like a boot, a funny collection connected with the past industry of the owners. Daria and the Inspector took these objects out one by one and examined them carefully. Both were puzzled.

"It looks as if Harridge had been having a joke," said Travers, fishing a set of pearl buttons out of one of the little receptacles.

"If he has I shall give him notice," said Daria wrathfully.

The compartments at the corners of the shelf had velvet covers. Delia took them out and discovered more buttons and a roll of ribbon of an old design. Travers glanced at the clock. It seemed as if there was nothing more to find. Daria began to replace the various objects. She felt disappointed and indignant. As she fitted the little lids that belonged to the corners she found that one would not go in and turned it over, and saw that the lining underneath was either slit or worn with age. She passed her fingers over it and found that a flat piece of cardboard had been slipped between the lining and the wood. She shook it and the thing fell out. Both of them pored over it curiously. It was the return half of a railway ticket from Heygate to Wissingham, numbered and stamped with the date. July the seventh.

Daria sat staring at it, and Travers looked at her enquiringly.

"Now that's odd!" she said slowly.

CHAPTER XIX

THE Inspector arrived at Ridgenorth Station in time to meet the London train. From it descended a small man with a shaggy grey moustache. Travers greeted him, and they walked to the town hall at the top of the High Street. The Bench was sitting, and Leonard Holroyd was the Chief Magistrate. The two men found places halfway up the hall. A case of petty theft was being tried, and when judgment had been given and the next case came up, they slipped out. Their next visit was to the office where the Chief Constable was waiting for them in his private room. Travers ushered in the visitor.

"This is Mr. Evans, sir."

Major Wrey shook hands.

"We are grateful to you for coming so quickly," he said. "I understand you only got back from abroad the night before last."

"Yes. I've been in the Balkans for two months wandering about collecting material for a book. Inspector Travers came to see me yesterday. He says he had been trying to get in touch with me before, but when I go off like that I leave no address. He told me you would like me to come down."

"Please tell Major Wrey exactly what you saw on the 9th of July, Mr. Evans."

The little man cleared his throat, and spoke in slow precise tones.

"As you know I occupy the flat below Mr. Franklin's, and as I was going abroad next day I had stayed in to pack. During the morning I went into the main hall to give directions to Hales, our porter, and while I was talking to him a young woman came in. She was exceptionally good looking, small, fair and beautifully dressed, but what made me notice her particularly was the fact that she seemed agitated. She came up to Hales and asked him if Mr. Franklin was at home, and when she heard he was asked him to take her up. She apologized to me because I hadn't finished my business, but she was obviously in a hurry and I said I could wait. When Hales came back I enquired if he had ever seen her before. He hesitated, looked a bit strange, then said he had. She had been there several times. 'Though perhaps I shouldn't say so, sir, as I'm not supposed to talk about what goes on in the building.'"

"And then, Mr. Evans?"

"Well, as I stood talking I faced the door into the street, and my attention was attracted by a man who was standing still and staring up at the flats. It made me curious, and when I got back to my own rooms I took a look from behind the curtains and saw he was still there. I went on with my packing, but every now and then I went to the window, and though I did this at intervals for over an hour he was always watching. Sometimes he walked up and down, and occasionally he stood under a portico belonging to Goodman, the house agents. I took good note of him, in fact I got my opera glasses, and there's no question but it is the same. I picked him out directly the Inspector took me to the town hall. The lady didn't come out for a long time, and when she did she got into a big green car that she had left by the curb. I'm sure she didn't see the man for as soon as she appeared he walked into the house agents', and two minutes after she had driven off he came out and hailed a taxi."

Mr. Evans was thanked for his information. Travers took him to the door and returned to his chief.

Major Wrey was sitting in front of his desk, and his attitude showed that he was depressed.

"It is certainly another piece of evidence to add to the rest," he said.

"Will you let me go through the facts, sir?"

"Yes, that will be best. Sit down, and run through the case as you've worked it out till now."

Travers obeyed.

"I think, sir, we've got to go back to two years ago when Mrs. Holroyd, senior, persuaded her son to go up to London to meet the lady who became his wife. Everyone knows that things were in a bad way financially at the Abbey, and anyhow the thing was soon fixed up, and the marriage took place quickly. Mrs. Leonard never got on well with the family, but about a year later Mr. Franklin turned up, and I think there is no doubt that they became lovers. The lady went to his flat on several occasions, and before Miss Lane's cottage was ready she spent afternoons there with him alone. As far as I can make out Mr. Holroyd had no suspicions until she asked him to give her a divorce. This he refused, and she then threatened to leave him and take her money with her. There had been no marriage settlement, and she decided to alter her will, and fixed the Monday after the Regatta for the date of signing it. Mr. Ryman affirms that Mrs. Leonard Holroyd repeated her directions for the new will when she rang him up, and Miss Lane says it was easy to intercept telephone conversations owing to extensions to various rooms. Except for a few legacies she had left everything to Mr. Franklin, and cut her husband out. A talk between herself and Miss Lane in which she expressed herself very freely about the Holroyds was also overheard by someone in the garden just below the room in which they were talking.

"Now it appears that most of the Abbey expenses were paid by Mrs. Leonard Holroyd, so if she cleared out the place would have to be sold. This supplies one motive, and the discovery of her infidelity is another. After a quarrel Mr. Holroyd followed her to London and saw her go in and out of Mr. Franklin's flat. That evening Cecilia, the maid, heard them having another scene. Mrs. Holroyd said, 'I expect you think you'd be better off if I was dead,' and he answered—'My God! we should all be!'

"The following evening he came across his wife and Mr. Franklin at Mrs. Denham's party, and knocked Mr. Franklin down, and we must not forget that he made a false statement on this point."

"That applies equally to Mrs. Holroyd and Mr. Franklin," said Major Wrey.

"They have given their reasons for that."

"So has he,—but never mind, Inspector. Go on."

"After that they *say* they went back to the lawn and that Mr. Holroyd stood somewhere behind till everyone went into the house. But for a period of half-an-hour no one seems to have seen him. This gave him ample time to return to the boathouse, strangle his wife and put the body in the Aitkens' punt.

"Everything as we know pointed to Shadwell having done it to get the pearls. Then they were found by Miss Lane, who also got Miss Amelia Wiggins' story, and a few days later Harridge began to talk. This was followed by the affair of the barn. There is no question that it was done deliberately, and as I believe with the intention of getting rid of Miss Lane, either from revenge or else because some piece of evidence was in existence and in her possession. She would tell the police."

"Surely he would expect her to do so immediately."

"Yes, but his daughter Ellen found out that though it was in Jasmine Cottage he had not actually shewn it to Miss Lane. It was after this conversation between Harridge and his daughter that the attempted burglary took place."

The Inspector paused, but Major Wrey did not speak.

"Now as you know sir, all the village came to look at the fire. Mr. Franklin and Mr. Holroyd had both been seen within a short distance of the barn during the afternoon. I went into this, but found that Mr. Franklin would have been two miles away during the period that the ladies were working in the hall, and I cannot believe that the fire had been started before they arrived or they would have seen it when they came in. Mr. Holroyd, however, had been wandering about the estate most of the day. He set off in the morning in his small car, taking a packet of sandwiches for his lunch, *The Times,* also his gun. So it seemed natural that he should catch sight of the smoke, and come to the scene of the fire. But when I got to the place next morning I found him already there, and a ladder had been placed in readiness so that he could mount to the part of the landing that had not been burnt. I went up first, and it was then that I realized that petrol and newspapers had been used. I picked up half a match, and a scrap of newspaper."

"*The Times,*" said Major Wrey, "but the piece was torn from a number several days old."

"Yes, I'm coming to that," said Travers. "When I found the match I realized it was one of a large kind known as Club matches, and not often used in private houses. First I concentrated on Mr. Franklin. I made friends with his butler, and in the course of conversation I showed it to him and asked if he knew where I could get that size. He said they never had that sort. Then I chose a day when the Wissingham Abbey people were off to London for a wedding and dropped in and had a look round. On the mantelpiece in Mr. Holroyd's study I found a box of these matches and in a cupboard a pile of old newspapers. Since then I have learnt that it is a fad of Mr. Holroyd's to keep back numbers of *The Times* for the past fortnight. It was the housemaid's duty to put them in that cupboard, and to clear them after they had accumulated.

"I wanted to be certain that Mr. Holroyd had spied on his wife and Mr. Franklin, so I went to London and saw the porter at the block of flats who told me that the day before he went away Mr. Evans had noticed a man watching in the street, but as you know I could not get the full proof till to-day."

"Anything else?" asked the Chief Constable wearily.

"Yes. I find that on the night of the attempted burglary Mr. Holroyd went straight to his study after dinner. This was not unusual as he often wrote his letters at this time, and afterwards he occasionally took a stroll in the garden before going to bed. He did so that evening for the footman saw him outside when he went to his supper. But no one saw him come in. It is the custom at the Abbey to leave a tray of drinks in the hall, and Burton had orders not to shut the study window on warm nights as his master liked to write with it open, and closed it himself when he went to bed. Miss Lane's cottage is only three quarters of a mile away if you take the short cut through the park. Everyone knew that she and the maid were away, and the cottage should have been unoccupied. He could not have anticipated her return to fetch the drawing."

"Have you discovered what this mysterious thing was for which the burglar was supposed to be looking?"

"Yes, sir. Miss Lane tackled Harridge, and as a result we found this."

The Inspector brought out the railway ticket and laid it in front of Major Wrey, who frowned.

"I am afraid I don't see the connection."

"Neither did we, sir, at first. Then Miss Lane remembered. Three days before the murder Miss Pelham-Reeve went to Heygate with the Girl Guides, and took a return ticket. Mr. Holroyd had been in London and when he came back at tea time he asked where she was, and his mother told him, and said she would not be back till late as the trains did not fit. He set off in his car, met her at Heygate just as she was getting in to the train, and drove her home. He must, I imagine, have taken her return ticket from her, and probably put it into his pocket, and forgot it. On the evening of the murder he knew enough to wipe the side of the punt to destroy finger marks, and possibly pulled it out with his handkerchief. That is only a guess, of course, but it fits in."

"And now," said the Chief Constable sadly, "you are asking for a warrant."

"I am, sir, and quickly, for there is no time to lose. I hear that Mr. Holroyd intends to leave the country immediately. He says he is going to the Danube for fishing, but that's a blind. Three days ago he applied for a double passport."

"A double passport! Whatever for?"

"For himself and his wife. He and Miss Pelham-Reeve were married in London yesterday, and that, sir, might supply us with yet another motive if it was needed," concluded Travers, absorbed with his case, and not noticing the expression on the Chief Constable's face. "From all accounts he was always sweet on the lady, and there was only one thing that stood between them and that was his wife."

CHAPTER XX

MAJOR WREY'S heart was sore as he drove slowly down the long avenue to the Abbey. He felt stunned as if he could not grasp the two calamities that had befallen him, first in having to issue a warrant for the arrest of his friend, and then the loss of Ida. Ida who had been in every plan he made for the future, and whom he hoped to marry.

He cast his thoughts back and remembered sundry twinges of jealousy when she had gone about so much with Leonard that year before he married Merle. Later, when Ida returned to the Abbey, he had grown to believe that their constant companionship was due to the fact that they were favourite cousins, and made good partners in games. But now in the light of his new knowledge he saw that there must have been more in it even in Merle's lifetime. He had snapped at Travers who was ready to give him details of their intimacy. He didn't want to hear. Facts were enough. Leonard had married Ida secretly within a few weeks of his wife's death, and she was preparing to go abroad with him at once. On the very day of her wedding he had written his own proposal. Half scornfully he thought of his anxiety that morning as he looked for her answer among his letters, and when it was not there how he had hoped that she would ring up and ask him to come to her. Well, that dream was over, and he supposed he would get over it in time, but for the moment it had taken the pleasure out of life.

But poor child, he reflected, how could she? There must have been some depth of passion he had never suspected to make her act so precipitately, and in a way that threw such a new light on her disposition. She who seemed so well poised, so conventional in her outlook. Of course she did not know what Leonard had done, but even so—— The lack of good taste and feeling astonished him in one to whom he had attributed both to a large degree. And now her husband would stand in the dock, and she would share the publicity that she had shrunk from.

And Leonard, too. With the knowledge of his guilt it had been a ghastly piece of selfishness to involve a woman in his life. Yet in spite of his indignation Major Wrey could not forget their long friendship. But Leonard Holroyd, the murderer, was never his friend. This man was a stranger and had no connection with the pleasant host, the good son and landowner, the conscientious magistrate that he had known. Though he had no choice but to issue the warrant he still could not bring himself to believe the evidence. Surely, even now, something would turn up to disprove it.

He drove up to the door and got out. As he stood on the step he recalled the many happy times when he had come here as a welcome guest never foreseeing this dreadful day when he would arrive to take over his friend's papers, and break the appalling news to Mrs. Holroyd.

Burton came in answer to his ring. He had been thirty years in service at the Abbey. Major Wrey fancied that the last two months with its horrors had aged him. And they were not over; the worst was to come.

He followed Burton into the picture gallery where Mrs. Holroyd sat at her embroidery frame. She was in her favourite chair under the great Van Dyck. It struck Major Wrey how she fitted her surroundings, her fine profile bent over the work that she held in those strong yet delicate hands. The beauty and dignity of the place was her lot. She represented what he most admired, continuity and tradition. In spite of the tragedy and worries she retained her composure. The stormy, vulgar little daughter-in-law might never have existed. She had been an unhappy episode in the history of the old house, and had gone from it like a puff of smoke.

What was Mrs. Holroyd's attitude towards Leonard's new marriage? With her rigid notions of what was suitable he could not believe that she had approved, and she had certainly not been present. It was all part of the enigma that seemed to have changed the expected into something unreal.

Mrs. Holroyd raised her head.

"Oh, Major Wrey, what a pleasure!" she said as she got up and held out her hand, for he was one of the people whom she really liked.

"I'm afraid I'm bringing you bad news," said the Chief Constable sadly, "but I thought you would rather hear it from me."

She flinched at his words, but her voice was as steady as usual as she said:

"Bad news! Then please tell me quickly."

"Leonard has been arrested."

"Leonard! Oh, impossible! What for?"

"He is accused of murdering his wife."

"He did not," said Mrs. Holroyd firmly. "There has been some extraordinary mistake. He was with me. I swear it."

"I hope he will be able to prove that." A pause, then Major Wrey added,—"You will of course get into communication with your lawyers without delay."

Mrs. Holroyd did not answer. For the time she seemed almost to have forgotten his existence, and he did not know what to say or do. He could not go because he had still to tell her that the police were on their way to take possession of Leonard's papers and search the house for evidence, and he knew how much this would be resented. It was a relief when she returned to the present from the absorption of her thoughts.

"I thought you were our friend," she said reproachfully.

"And so I am." He spoke impulsively. "I've never minded anything so much in my life, and I'd have given all I had to stop it, but how can I when the ghastly thing is my job?"

"You can't," said Mrs. Holroyd, "and it was good of you to come and tell me yourself. Now please sit down and excuse me if I don't talk. I want to think this out."

She went back to her chair, and Major Wrey sat a little way off feeling wretched. The grandfather clock seemed to tick louder than he had ever heard it, he thought irritably. Mrs. Holroyd was very still. It was a relief when the door opened and Burton came in.

"Inspector Travers is here, ma'am," he said.

"Please ask him to come up." Mrs. Holroyd turned to Major Wrey. "What is it he wants?"

"I am afraid he has to——"

"I understand. To search Leonard's things. Isn't that what people do? Well, it is waste of time, but, of course, he must do his duty." She turned. "Oh, good afternoon, Inspector. The Chief Constable has explained why you are here."

Travers made an awkward bow, and looked at Major Wrey.

"I do not think many of my son's things are locked," said Mrs. Holroyd, "but if so I am sure you have means to open them. Burton will show you his rooms."

"Thank you, madam. I'll be as quick as I can."

"And you will no doubt wish to talk to the servants," Mrs. Holroyd went on, "if you have not done so enough already."

"Thank you madam," said Travers again, "but I think I would rather have a word with your daughter-in-law before I speak to the other people in the house."

Mrs. Holroyd's face took on a blank expression, and she leant forward as if she had not heard properly.

"Whom did you say?"

"Your daughter-in-law," repeated Travers.

"I don't understand what you mean. My daughter-in-law is dead."

Then they had kept it secret even from her, thought Major Wrey, and this was another blow that must be dealt by him to his old friend.

"Leonard and Ida were married in London yesterday at a Registrar's Office," he said baldly.

Mrs. Holroyd's hands tightened on the chair till the knuckles stood out. This was a calamity for which she was not prepared. Her face shewed anger and dismay, then as if she could not bear the others to witness her emotion she covered her eyes with her hand. Nearly a minute passed before she looked up.

"I did not know," she said simply. "Please tell me how you do."

As Travers explained Major Wrey admired her self-control which she had completely recovered. A wonderful woman, he thought, indomitable, who could stand up in spite of the shattering end to all her hopes. When the Inspector had finished she got up.

"I will go and tell Ida about Leonard's arrest," she said to Major Wrey, "that is if I can find her as she was going to do some errands for me in the village. It would be kind if you would let the news come from me. This need not delay the Inspector if he wants to begin his search. May I do this?"

Secretly Travers did not approve. To him the case was everything, and the human element did not trouble him, but he could do nothing in the face of his chief who immediately gave permission.

Major Wrey went to open the door for Mrs. Holroyd.

"I may be a little time," she said pausing in the doorway. "It will be a shock for her."

"Of course," said Major Wrey sympathetically, and Travers went down to the hall where Robinson was waiting, and together they turned into the passage where Leonard's study was situated.

• • • • •

Mrs. Holroyd walked upstairs slowly but with a firm tread. She looked into a sitting-room where Ida usually wrote her letters, found it empty, and went on to her bedroom. She opened the door without knocking. Ida stood by a chest of drawers. Mrs. Holroyd glanced at the bed. Dresses, handkerchiefs and underclothes lay in neat heaps. At the sound of her aunt's entrance she turned and instinctively thrust back a pile of gloves that she had been sorting.

"You seem very busy," said Mrs. Holroyd quietly. "It almost looks as if you were packing."

Ida flushed.

"I was tidying my things," she said confusedly. "Did you want me, Aunt Octavia?"

Mrs. Holroyd sat down.

"Yes, I have several things to say to you."

If her intention was to break the news kindly as she had implied her manner held no trace of softness.

"Major Wrey is downstairs,".she continued.

"Oh!" Ida looked annoyed, also embarrassed. She thought of his letter to which she had not replied. Had he come in person for his answer? This was difficult. Should she put him off by asking for a week to consider, or, should she settle it at once by a definite refusal? Which was wisest? She looked up, and saw that her aunt was watching her intently.

"Need I see him to-day?" she said quickly. "I don't want to. He has written to ask me to marry him, and I——"

"Don't you know what to say?" asked Mrs. Holroyd.

"Yes. I must refuse, but I'd like to let him down gently."

"He is not a bad match," said Mrs. Holroyd, "and he is very fond of you."

"But I don't care for him. You know why. Please don't pretend, Aunt Octavia."

"I do not pretend, and I know why. So does he."

"What do you mean?"

"Major Wrey hasn't come about that. He realizes that there is now no question of it since you married Leonard yesterday in London."

Ida gasped. Her hands closed on the bed-rail as if she needed its support.

"How did you know?"

"He told me. Inspector Travers was in town, and saw you coming out of the Registrar's office."

"Well," said Ida recovering, "it's true. I told you what we meant to do, and you said you would prevent it. For once you haven't been able to get your way. When Leonard goes abroad I shall go with him."

"I think not."

"What do you mean? It is no longer in your power to stop me. We have the passport, and I am his wife."

"I can't stop you," said Mrs. Holroyd, "but the police can."

Ida's face was drained of all colour.

"Why do you say that?" she said hoarsely.

"Because they have just arrested Leonard for murder."

She got up quickly to catch Ida who tottered as if she was going to fall.

"It's impossible!" said Ida hysterically. "Leonard! Oh! no . . . no! Of course it isn't true. You are only saying it to frighten me."

"As if I should!" said Mrs. Holroyd contemptuously. "You silly girl! Go down and look for yourself. The police are searching his rooms at this moment."

Ida stared back at her wildly.

"But why should they suspect Leonard? It's incredible. Fools! What did they say?"

"Very little. Just the fact that he had been arrested. They don't have to tell you their reasons."

Ida made a great effort.

"People do get wrongfully arrested. One reads of it. The police will find out their mistake and let him go in a day or two."

"I shouldn't count on it," said Mrs. Holroyd. "Major Wrey would never have issued the warrant unless they had a good case. The man's genuinely upset." She removed her supporting hand. "Well Ida, it's up to you. I think you can tell a story that may satisfy them of Leonard's innocence. Am I not right?"

The two women looked at each other. Ida stood as still as a statue, then she said quite slowly.

"I love Leonard."

"I believe that," said Mrs. Holroyd, and surprisingly she leant forward and kissed her. "I should suggest," she went on "that you sit down here and now and write out certain facts. When you have finished I will take your statement to Major Wrey."

· · · · ·

The Chief Constable stood in the picture gallery waiting for Mrs. Holroyd's return. She had been a long time, and he felt the strain of watching for the door to open. When she came back would Ida be with her? He could not help shrinking from the meeting. Ida must have taken the news badly. Possibly she had broken down under the shock. It was a ghastly affair. He picked up a paper, and threw it down, for he could not concentrate on the news. He fidgeted about, stopping sometimes to glance from the window. What were they all doing? Travers and Robinson ferreting in Leonard's desk, no doubt, the servants whispering and wondering, and Mrs. Holroyd with Ida. It was more than three-quarters of an hour since she went up. He felt he must go outside for a breath of air. This long room with the cabinets and pictures and the *objets d'art* that he had admired seemed to him as horrible as a prison. As a prison, he repeated to himself, thinking of its owner. He heard a sound and turned, but it was only Travers.

"Finished, Inspector?"

"So far, sir. I left Robinson in charge. Have you seen either of the ladies?"

"No."

"They seem to be taking their time."

"It is hardly surprising," said the Chief Constable coldly. "One of them may be ill."

But as he spoke the door opened and Mrs. Holroyd came in alone. She looked white and walked slowly. "You told her?" said Major Wrey.

She bent her head.

"She took it badly, poor child. It is terrible for her!"

She sat down leaning her head against the back of the chair with her eyes closed.

"Would it be possible for me to see Miss Pelham-Reeve,—I mean Mrs. Holroyd?" asked Travers.

"In a few minutes." Mrs. Holroyd spoke faintly. She looked up at Major Wrey. "Would you mind ringing the bell. It's stupid but I feel rather queer."

The Chief Constable hurried to obey, and there ensued a few minutes' confusion. Burton came and was told to fetch brandy. He returned with it accompanied by Ellen who brought smelling salts. Mrs. Holroyd leant back without moving, and Major Wrey looked stricken. Travers waited awkwardly in the background, and as he did so he heard the sound of a motor car. Was it a caller arriving all unknowing in this scene of disaster? He listened and realized that it was not coming but going, and stepped to one of the windows. But these only looked on to the garden, and the drive was the other side of the house. He turned with a feeling of misgiving. Something did not ring true. What it was he couldn't say. Mrs. Holroyd had every reason to look and feel ill, but in spite of her attitude of collapse he got an impression of tenseness, of a brain working at top speed. It caused him to leave the sympathetic group surrounding the fainting lady and run downstairs. Burton was now in the hall clearing the letter box for the post.

"Who was it that went out in a car just this moment?" asked Travers.

Burton glanced up from what he was doing. His manner showed his resentment of the trouble that had come to the house he served, and his eyes were hostile.

"I couldn't say," he answered briefly.

"Didn't you notice it?"

"No," said Burton, "but I'm an old man and I don't hear as well as I did. Probably it was the fishmonger from Ridgenorth. He has a car."

Travers was dissatisfied. He went into the garden to take a short cut to the garage. The picture gallery windows looked out the way he was walking and as he glanced up at them the Chief Constable came to the window. He signalled and leant out.

"I want you up here, Travers. Mrs. Holroyd wishes to tell us something."

Before obeying Travers went to find Robinson who was still in Leonard's study.

"Find out if anyone has gone out in a car," he said, and then went upstairs.

In the picture gallery the scene had changed. Ellen had gone, and Major Wrey was seated besides Mrs. Holroyd who seemed to have recovered, and was upright in her chair. She spoke in her usual level tones.

"I have a statement to make, Inspector, which I should like you to hear. I can prove that my son did not murder his wife."

"If you can no one would be more glad of it than myself," said Major Wrey fervently.

"If you have anything to tell us, Mrs. Holroyd," said Travers, "why haven't we heard it before?"

"You will understand that better when I have explained," said Mrs. Holroyd, "but you must let me tell my story in my own way. I must go back to the Thursday before the Regatta which was the day that my son found out that his wife had been meeting Mr. Franklin secretly. As you already know there had been a violent quarrel during which she had asked him for a divorce. He refused. The next morning he followed her to London and saw her enter and leave her lover's flat. Late that evening there was another quarrel which was interrupted by her maid. As he came out of her room I called him into mine, and got him to tell me the whole story. It wasn't so new to me for I had known how things were going for some time," continued Mrs. Holroyd wearily, "and I had warned him after Ida had come upon the two at Jasmine Cottage. All the same I did my best to persuade him merely to get Merle to break the connection. I was uncertain how far the affair had gone, and we could not do without her money.

Not that I was banking on my dear daughter-in-law's virtue, but I believed that Gideon Franklin would put self-interest before love, and that a hint would be sufficient. From my own observation I had decided that it was she who was the pursuer, and he was willing to extricate himself from an awkward mess. If I was right he would not have welcomed her visit to his flat, and their interview might have opened Merle's eyes. So I urged Leonard to exercise patience and control himself. He promised to do his best, and on the day of the Regatta there was no clash till we got to Mrs. Denham's party. Unfortunately Merle realized that Gideon Franklin was trying to avoid her and went after him. To my horror Leonard followed. I dreaded a public quarrel, and told Ida who had been in my confidence all along. We went after them, but in the garden we met Colonel and Mrs. Delahaye who delayed us. Presently I managed to slip away whilst Ida remained with the others. At first I could not see any of them, but as I got near the shrubbery I knew I had not been quick enough to prevent a scene. I heard angry voices, and came up as Gideon fell. I begged him to go, which he was only too glad to do. He is not a fighter," said Mrs. Holroyd contemptuously.

"But we know all this," said Major Wrey.

"Up till then, but not what followed. Leonard, who was by then beyond my control, turned on his wife and called her what she really was. They wrangled for several minutes, and then she said—I remember her words distinctly—'You needn't talk. You are not above living on your wife, and keeping a mistress in your own house!' "

"What did she mean?" said Major Wrey.

"She meant Ida."

"Was it true?"

"No. I am sure of that. But Leonard and Ida had been in love with one another for years."

The matter of fact tone startled Major Wrey.

"You knew it and yet you threw them together!"

"It was a mistake, but after Leonard's marriage I thought it was all over. I did wrong, but my conduct is immaterial. What mattered was Leonard's reaction to Merle's accusation. He was absolutely furious. He told her to hold her tongue, and not speak of a woman whose shoes she wasn't fit to black. Then Merle said that was the end of everything. She would leave the Abbey next day and take her money. If Leonard brought a divorce she would defend it and cite him with Ida. And then she went into floods of tears, and I took Leonard's arm and led him away."

"You swear to that?"

"I do. What is more I walked with him as far as the lawn and as we went I made him promise not to go back."

"But how do you know he kept the promise?"

"Because I went back myself. The thought of what it would mean if Merle kept her word appalled me, and I saw there was no time to lose. Merle was hasty, and she would do something irrevocable if I didn't stop her. I meant to reason with her, even to try and soothe her, also to persuade her to go home for I did not want anyone to see her after her fit of crying. The racket of the fireworks was behind me, but the garden was quiet and seemed deserted. I walked towards the shrubbery."

"And then, Mrs. Holroyd?"

"When I reached the place where I had left Merle she was no longer there. I thought she had forestalled me and slipped off home. And then—" she paused, and spoke with an effort—"Ida came up the steps from the boathouse."

"Ida!"

"She seemed startled when she saw me. I said, 'Where's Merle, and what are you doing?' She said—'Merle's gone. She wouldn't stay after the row.' I said, 'How did you know there was a row?' She said, 'I was close by and heard it.' Then I asked which way Merle had gone because I thought it strange that I shouldn't have seen her at some point as I came back through the garden."

"One moment, Mrs. Holroyd, how long do you think it was between the time you left your daughter-in-law and got back to the boathouse?" asked Travers.

"Quite ten minutes. I had gone back with Leonard and stood discussing what had happened and arguing with him before he went on the lawn."

"And what did your niece say?"

"She told me that Merle went away immediately after we left by the upper path that leads toward the garage. I asked if she had spoken to her but she said no, so I said we had better return to the fireworks which we did. Mrs. Denham found me a seat, and Ida, I believe, sat on the bank."

"Please go on, Mrs. Holroyd."

"When we got home and Merle was not there I thought it was just what I had feared. She had rushed off to her lover's house. I didn't want to make enquiries because I hoped he would send her back. When she did not return I got worried, but until her body was found I did not suspect that anything had happened. Then Leonard and I agreed to say as little as possible so as to keep our private affairs out of the papers, and I sent a note to Mr. Franklin to ask him to do the same. There seemed to be a good explanation. That thief had been seen hanging about, and the pearls were missing."

"You believed that Shadwell had done the murder?"

"At first. It was much later that I began to realize that there might be another explanation."

"And that was?"

"Ida," said Mrs. Holroyd. "She had every motive. She hated Merle. She had overheard our conversation and the insult to herself, and she knew that if Merle lived her money was lost to Leonard. She strangled her, and put her in the punt, and I met her coming back. After the pearls were found I began to suspect, but I was not certain till after the incident of the barn."

"You think she did that!" exclaimed Major Wrey. "It is impossible!"

"Why?" said Mrs. Holroyd. "I believe her brain was no longer normal. Looking back on things I see that her nature seemed to change after Leonard married Merle."

"If there is any truth in your story it means that you have deliberately deceived the police," said Travers.

"Ida was dearer to me than anyone in the world but Leonard," said Mrs. Holroyd simply.

"Yet you bring this terrible accusation!" said Major Wrey. "No, the whole thing's incredible,— the barn as well as the murder."

"But she was frightened of Daria Lane," said Mrs. Holroyd. "She knew that she would never let the matter rest, also Ellen terrified her by saying that her father had a piece of evidence that might throw light on the whole subject."

The Chief Constable shook his head.

"I'm sorry, Mrs. Holroyd, but I don't believe a word of it. Your son matters more to you than anything, and he is in danger, so you are trying to put the guilt on someone else. Isn't that your opinion too, Inspector?"

"Let us ask Mrs. Leonard Holroyd to come and give her version, sir."

Mrs. Holroyd got up.

"I will go and fetch her."

"I would rather you sent for her."

"As you please. Will you ring for Burton?"

Travers did so and Burton appeared, and Mrs. Holroyd told him to find Ida.

"I think she's in her bedroom," she added.

While they waited Major Wrey stood by the window filled with passionate disbelief. He saw Ida young and smiling as she had been at her first ball. Ida as she was only a short time ago when they had tea at the Golf Club, the typical outdoor girl, interested in activities connected with the village. Healthy, capable, good-mannered. The ideal wife. This shocking accusation revolted him. No, it was Mrs. Holroyd whose brain was abnormal, not Ida's. He turned as Burton came in.

"Miss Ida is out, ma'am. She took the car."

Travers was watching Mrs. Holroyd narrowly. Her air of surprise was well done but he didn't believe in it. Unlike Major Wrey she had impressed him with a feeling that she was speaking the truth, yet he was puzzled by the notion that there was something behind.

Burton was holding out a salver.

"Miss Ida gave this letter to Ellen for you, ma'am, just before she went out."

"One moment, Mrs. Holroyd," said Travers. "What car did your niece take?"

Mrs. Holroyd looked questioningly at Burton who said it was the Hispano-Suisa.

When the butler had gone Major Wrey came forward.

"Mrs. Holroyd," he said. "I tell you frankly that I can't accept your account. I think I shall go now, but Travers had better wait and see Ida just to hear her story, though I don't believe it will make much difference."

She looked up at him calmly.

"Please wait," she said. "This may change your opinion, for I think the letter may have been meant for you to see."

She tore it open as she spoke, glanced down the page, then began to read it aloud.

"Dear Aunt Octavia,

"I am sending you this to give to the police. You have guessed that I killed Merle, but you do not know just how it happened. When the Delahayes left me I followed you. I saw Gideon go though he did not notice me, then I went nearer and heard what Merle said about Leonard and me and all the rest. After you went I stood and watched her, and thought of the harm she meant to do, also how she had destroyed my happiness and couldn't even value what she took. She had her back to me and leant against a tree, and she was sobbing noisily like an angry child and did not hear me come across the grass. The long ends of her scarf hung down behind. I think she gave a cry but it mingled with the sounds on the river, and I was quick. She was small, and I am strong, and I knew just what to do. I had clapped my hand over her mouth as I twisted the scarf. In a few minutes she ceased to struggle and her body sagged and slipped down in a heap at my feet. I bent over her to make sure. At first I couldn't believe that it had been so easy. I found I was shaking, and I couldn't think what I was doing. Then my mind cleared. I found her pearl necklace had broken and I had it in my hand. I knew I must get rid of it, and went a few yards down the bank and threw it into the water. The door of the boathouse was open, and inside I could see a punt with a cover. I carried her down the steps. It was more difficult than I expected though she was no bigger than a child. I had to drag her and I still hear the noise her shoes made as her feet bumped against the steps. I pushed the things that were under the cover on one side, and hoisted her into the back of the boat, and pulled the canvas over. Then I pulled out my handkerchief to wipe the marks off the side of the punt.

"As I came away I met you and that frightened me, but I thought you believed me when I told you that Merle had gone home. When we got to the lawn I sat in the dark and decided how I should behave if she was found that night, but those two days went by and my nerves had time to steady. I was asked very few questions, as everyone but you thought I had never been in that part of the garden. When Shadwell died it seemed as if everything would be all right. What had happened was like a dream. I couldn't feel sorry. Leonard had his money, and that vulgar little creature was gone. Even the police seemed satisfied.

"Then just as I began to be happy Daria Lane started to stir it up. At first I felt safe because Major Wrey didn't believe her, and Amelia Wiggins' account didn't worry me because she seems to have left before you and Leonard. What frightened me was Harridge's story. I couldn't think what he had found. Even now I don't know. I might have dropped a second handkerchief with my initials. It wasn't the one with which I wiped the boat, for I remember returning that to my pocket. I couldn't sleep for puzzling over it. If Daria had it she would tell the police. Then why didn't she? Night after night I lay and thought till I was nearly mad.

"It was at the work party that the idea came. If I could get rid of Daria everything would die down and be forgotten. It all fitted in. I heard Miss

Amelia and Daria arrange to come to the barn on the day Jenkins would be away. I laid my plans carefully. I rang up Mrs. Lestrange at the Deanery and proposed myself for tea, and I asked you if I could do any errands in Munchester. Leonard had gone out and I took some newspapers from his cupboard and a box of matches, and put a tin of petrol in the car. I backed down the side lane close to the barn. This was the one time I might have been seen for I had expected Daria and Miss Amelia to get there earlier and was climbing through the hedge as they came across the field. I allowed them time to get settled and followed. It was a shock to find they had left the door open but the wind was making a terrific noise as I crept up the stairs. Old Amelia was alone with her back to the door. I knew where Jenkins kept the key. As I turned it it made a click and I was afraid she would hear and get up, but nothing happened. I soaked the newspapers and poured the petrol over the stairs, and to make things sure I got the two tins Jenkins had left in the shed and used them for the woodstack. When I had set it all alight I went away as quickly as I could. No one was about, and I did not meet another car for over a mile after I had turned into the main road. I took your watch to be cleaned, and got the new Bradshaw at the stationers, and arrived at the Deanery in time for tea. I thought it wiser to return by the North road, and when I got back to the Abbey, Burton told me about the fire. To my horror he said the two ladies had been rescued. So my trouble had been for nothing. What was more I saw that I had made things worse by my attempt. Then Harridge talked again and I had to know what he had found. I slipped out after dinner and went to Jasmine Cottage. I thought the place was empty but Daria came in. She followed me and I would have killed her, but someone came.

"Later when you said I should never marry Leonard I saw you suspected me, but I knew you would never give me away if I was his wife, and I meant to snatch a little happiness. How could I tell it was to last only twenty-four hours?

"That Leonard should be accused was a thing I never imagined. He had nothing to do with it, and has no idea of the truth. He is all I ever cared for. He is still."

She had signed "Ida Holroyd" in a firm hand.

Mrs. Holroyd laid down the sheets and looked up, but Major Wrey seemed incapable of speech or action. It was the Inspector who jumped to his feet and went to the fireplace where he kept his finger on the bell, then ran to the door and shouted for Robinson.

Burton and Robinson appeared simultaneously.

"Has Miss Pelham-Reeve returned?"

"No," said Burton.

"Where's the telephone? Robinson, get on to the police stations. Find out which way the Hispano-Suisa went. Give them the number, and have it traced and detained. Hurry!"

He turned back and saw Mrs. Holroyd watching him, and burst out—"So that's why! You wanted to give her time to get away."

Without waiting for an answer that he did not expect the Inspector dashed out.

CHAPTER XXI

MARTIN arrived in good time that afternoon in his car and picked Daria up at the cottage. He had brought a tea basket and they drove to the downs about ten miles from Wissingham. As they went she told him about the railway ticket and of Leonard's arrest. She had heard this from Travers who had called in on his way to the Abbey. Martin was astounded.

"The police must have good reasons otherwise they wouldn't have arrested him, but I can't help thinking there is some mistake. It's so unlike what one knows of Leonard. He isn't violent and the only excuse for a crime like that is to say it was done in a fit of fury on account of Merle's affair with Gideon."

"That hardly applies to the business of the barn," said Daria.

"No. That looks as if his brain had given way, yet he never seemed neurotic. It's all ghastly and incomprehensible," sighed Martin.

He had never been a great friend of Leonard's but they had been on good terms, and even the pleasure of being with Daria was dimmed by the news.

They had been running up a rough track on to the downs. At the top was a small wood. They left the car beside it, and spread a rug where they could see the view. Martin put his arm round Daria, and they sat in silence for a time. Neither of them could forget what was happening at the Abbey, and though Daria seemed to have reached the end of her quest she was troubled.

"Come," said Martin presently, "it's no good brooding over something we can't help. Let us try and put it out of our minds and think of ourselves. I want to know how soon you will marry me?"

"You have been wonderfully patient," said Daria gratefully. "I know how much you have loathed my doings. So did I. I haven't really a taste for crime, but I *had* to know."

"And now?" said Martin again.

"And now I'll give you all the time you want," said Daria with her head on his shoulder.

"It is lovely to have the world to ourselves," said Martin presently looking over towards the sunny valley.

"Have we?" said Daria. "Listen! That sounds like a car. The world's over populated. Even here we can't get clear of trippers."

The wood hid the track from sight but a car was certainly approaching up the twists and turns of the long slope. A moment later it appeared round the edge of the trees about thirty yards from where they sat. With a sensation of dismay Daria recognised the Hispano-Suisa. Martin seemed to share her feeling for he scrambled to his feet.

At the sight of them Ida had stopped. She understood the significance of the scene she had disturbed, and contrasted it with her own ruin. As her face froze into a mask of hate her hand went to the gear lever. In a moment the car shot forward, sweeping straight on to them, and guided by the hands of a maniac. Martin jerked Daria to her feet, and dragged her back with only a couple of feet to spare. As the car thundered past them Ida swung the steering wheel to the right, nearly upsetting on the uneven ground.

It was fortunate for them that the wood was only a few yards away. Martin jumped the little ditch with Daria. She stumbled but he pulled her through the undergrowth as they heard the mud-guard hit a tree behind them. The car stopped.

"Let's get further into the wood," said Martin, and they ran to take cover behind a big tree trunk. Ida was now between them and their own car.

"Is she coming?" said Daria shakily. The attack had been so sudden, and the glare of Ida's eyes was something she would never forget. "She's mad! She must be. It is because of Leonard. She thinks I'm responsible."

When the car stopped Ida sat motionless, and seemed to be considering what to do next. She peered into the wood, saw them, and decided to follow. She tried to open the door, using both hands, but without success as the force of the impact had jammed the panel. With a mad laugh she slid along the seat to the other door when a sound made her pause and listen. The others heard it too as they waited behind the trees. A motor bicycle was coming up the hill driven at tremendous speed. It conveyed a message to Ida's brain of such urgency that she forgot Martin and Daria. She returned to the driver's seat, backed and got the car round. It bumped forward over the rough grass, and gathered speed as the ground began to slope sharply over the shoulder of the down.

"Good God! Where is she going?" cried Martin in sudden horror and he and Daria ran forward towards the edge of the wood. "She is heading for the chalk pit, and won't be able to stop."

As he spoke the motor bicycle with Inspector Travers came round the corner. Below and only half way up the ascent was another car containing two policemen. Martin ran to tell the Inspector what he had seen. But the pursuit was a minute late. Ida had never intended to survive discovery and sitting in Merle's car she went at terrific speed over the edge of the big chalk pit, and crashed to death.

· · · · ·

The Chief Constable had not left the Abbey when the telephone message came through, and he went to tell Mrs. Holroyd. It was what she had expected from the moment when Burton had given her Ida's letter, and she received the news with the courage that never failed her. She sat still until she felt sure of her self-control, and then spoke quietly.

"Ida has done right," she said. "It was the best thing for all of us."

THE END

Printed in the United Kingdom
by Lightning Source UK Ltd.
132628UK00001B/76/A